i

c

o

p

e

Proofread by Karlos Rene Ayala, Crystal
A. Gee, and Patrick Lenton

For more information, find CCM at:

http://copingmechanisms.net

40 *LIKELY TO* DIE BEFORE 40

AN INTRODUCTION TO ALT LIT

EDITED BY

CAMERON PIERCE
&
MICHAEL J SEIDLINGER

TABLE OF CONTENTS

A BRIEF HISTORY OF ALT LIT

BY
BRADLEY SANDS

Alt Lit was a notorious pirate who terrorized the high seas between 1710 and 1716. It drank Boost nutritional drink all day and pillaged and plundered and pirated all night. Eventually it died from the shame of being unable to grow a long, luxurious pirate beard.

If you go on Tumblr late at night, you can sometimes hear Alt Lit's pirate-y cackle and check out his image macros. Upon reading them, you will suddenly feel very satanic and want to write poetry.

Alt Lit haunts the World Wide Web, driving a pirate ship on wheels over the information superhighway. You are a little happier than Alt Lit. It is the loneliest ghost pirate on Earth. There are no other ghosts on the internet, no friends to chill with. Alt Lit is extremely depressed. It has tried mood stabilizers and anti-psychotics and anti-depressants, but nothing seems to work. Every day, something happens that triggers Alt Lit's a state of depression. It feels like a headache, but without the pain. Alt Lit says it's like spiders rapidly spinning cobwebs in its brain.

The spiders burst out of its head and register for a twitter account. They tweet weird shit every two minutes and get 100.1K followers, but ninety percent of them are fake followers who the spiders paid for. Alt Lit reads the spiders' tweets, which causes it to feel joy. Alt Lit is capable of this emotion because spiders are no longer rapidly spinning cobwebs in its brain, so it has stopped being depressed and lonely. With these barriers eliminated, it is able to make friends with the people who check out its image macros.

One hundred years later, everyone dies from worldwide famine and Alt Lit is alone and depressed again, but it is a little less lonely and depressed because it cherishes the memory of its good friends.

SAM
PINK

EXCERPT FROM *PERSON*

I'm walking around Chicago, feeling like a piece of shit.

It's winter.

There are many people out.

I pass an older homeless man and he is dressed almost exactly like me.

Almost exactly.

I want to stop him and grab his shoulders and say, "So I make it past thirty then?"

But he walks by me.

Eye contact is bad I think.

I don't make eye contact with any girls because I don't want to ruin their night and make them feel bad.

I make eye contact with some guys because sometimes I just feel angry.

Eye contact is bad I think.

At a stoplight, I wait to cross and there are two men next to me.

They're holding hands.

I imagine myself as one of them, standing next to me, this dipshit with an ugly face.

Later on, will one say to the other, "Hey did you see that asshole at the stoplight. Why does he live on the same earth as us, with his dipshit-ass ugly face."

And then the other man will agree in some way, if only in quiet.

Christmas music plays from someone's car at the stoplight and I can hear it through the closed windows.

Will I get run over tonight.

Is tonight the night of magic.

It's totally possible that something will suddenly kill me.

And I accept that.

I always think about getting randomly hurt and how awesome it would be to just immediately be changed and removed from my situation.

To have something direct to worry about, like a broken leg or a really big cut.

I'd no longer be a person blending in.

When the stoplight signals to cross I wait to take a step until the other men walk away.

I don't want to walk next to them.

It is horrible for me to be walking at the same pace next to someone on the sidewalk.

And like all others, these men pass me.

Now knowing that in infinite space there is a pure negative, shaped exactly like me.

With no intentions of making friends.

Insecure enough not to make friends so as not to lose them.

There's ice on the sidewalk.

Will I fall.

If I fall, and just stay there, will someone eventually help me.

Will a police officer walk by and say, "Stay there," motioning with his/her hand to stay still.

Will I just roll into the gutter and disappear.

I don't know where I'm walking.

This is Chicago.

On a street with a lot of bars and people yelling.

Earlier I walked to Lake Michigan and I stared at it.

It remained where it was, and I stared.

No one else was there.

It seems like there and here are just as loud somehow.

It's cold and I hate everyone I can see.

All of my strength is required to hate this many people but I manage and I am proud of my effort.

I expect the same of everyone else.

No, I don't know.

I wonder what my roommate is doing right now.

Last night he knocked on my door and asked me to check the back of his neck for pen marks.

He said, "So, I think there's a pen loose in my bed and, I think I slept on it."

There were no pen marks.

I made sure not to touch his body while checking.

It seems likely that if I were to give form to what I believe is my roommate's abstraction of me, it would be some parts of a pencil eraser that someone blew to the floor after erasing something they didn't want someone else to see.

I walk by a group of people standing outside a bar and someone almost bumps into me.

I imagine myself pulling this person apart with my hands.

Just pulling off pieces of face and neck and upper-chest.

Just ripping an arm off with a single pull.

Could I accomplish that.

What would this person think of himself if I were to do that.

Would he fight it, or accept it as inevitable.

What would the people watching think.

I walk by them all and smell perfume and I am no different.

It feels like practice.

I concentrate on my heartbeat and worry it is never going to stop.

Then I worry that I will have a heartattack, and that the heartattack will hurt.

For a very small amount of time I can fully understand the pain that would accompany a heartattack, a heartattack so bad it rips my heart into more than one piece.

And I can see either accepting everything that happens, or accepting none, but in between I lose hope.

I can accept the heartattack of caring that much or that not-enough.

What if I have a heartattack tonight and say something really dumb when it happens, like, "oh jeez" and then make a dumb face when I fall.

What if that happens to me right now.

People would laugh.

I would laugh.

Oh my.

Once past the area with all the bars, there is an outdoor ice rink to my left.

People are skating there together.

None invited me.

No, I don't know, I mean that's how I want it.

And the light inside the rink is what these people use to skate.

And that light is the same that gives them to me, not me to them, because I am outside its area on the sidewalk.

My nose is cold and my nose is also dripping.

Oh my.

Nobody at the ice rink looks at me.

In passing.

They don't because it would be weird to be looking at someone this far away.

Arranged relationships with other people that technically never happen.

It feels like practice.

Yes.

Not quite a piece of shit myself, but the streak for sure.

For sure the area the shit passes over and leaves behind parts of itself.

At the streetcorner just beyond the sound of the ice rink, there is a long patch of ice on the sidewalk that I have to slide over in very small glides.

Like, I use maybe two inches per glide to be safe.

As I'm doing this, I hear my cat meowing and it sounds like he is in my coat somewhere behind me.

My cat is not there when I check.

He died a while ago I think.

This makes sense.

It sounded so real when I heard him meow, but it didn't happen.

Just the thought of my cat's ghost is enough to make me feel like there's like, a sour feeling in my head area.

I want to itch my back until I feel pain.

No, I don't know.

I see a billboard with a young girl on it.

The young girl is bald.

The billboard is for cancer research.

I feel bad about people with cancer.

I think that if I discovered I had cancer I would immediately say the word, "Phew."

Phew.

On the sidewalk in the cold weather, the word "phew" scrolls through my head in big block neon letters.

Yes.

I watch it scroll, and I approve.

It's like everyone I see now has a haircut.

Having a haircut seems like something important.

It seems defining.

I've noticed my thinking towards another person is immediately altered if that person has clearly had a recent haircut, still shaped.

Maybe that's my problem.

Cutting my own hair for years has maybe contributed to me feeling different from other people in a fundamental way.

Could that happen.

I just need to get haircuts.

Maybe that's my main problem.

I need to get haircuts from now on.

Across the street there's a bookstore and I walk to it.

I think maybe I've read here before (read in front of people on purpose not like randomly out loud among other people who just happen to be shopping).

Will they remember me there if I go in—the employees and the people there.

They will not.

Will one of them shoot me with a water pistol full of some

dangerous chemical.

They will not.

I realize it's not the same bookstore.

I go into the bookstore.

Inside there is a girl walking around and she is pretty to me.

She has a pretty face and a pretty body and it feels nice to be close to her.

She fixes her glasses and walks past me, looking at the books.

I wonder if she is thinking about having sex with me.

Am I standing naked before her in her thoughts.

What is she imagining.

Am I at least present in her imagination at all.

I want to watch the imagination.

What do I look like to her.

Do I have coins taped to my stomach.

If I do, why do I have coins taped to my stomach.

That seems wrong.

I check my stomach with my hand and there is nothing there but some hair.

I say nothing to the girl as she passes.

She just passes.

And I'm intentionally looking away.

She looks at the books and I am roughly equivalent to any other inessential part of the room to her, like a corner or a tile.

I buy a low-priced copy of a book written by Karl Jaspers and then I leave the store.

When I leave I act like I am looking at something on the wall, just beyond the register.

I don't know why I act like I'm looking at something, but I know it's intentional.

I can feel that it is intentional.

A lot of times my behavior is the reaction to what I think other people are observing about me, and so yes, I am uncomfortable a lot (haha).

Outside the store on the building next door there is an advertisement for clothing.

A girl lies on a bed looking like she is dying or has some kind of sickness but still wants to fuck and the name of the brand of clothing is on the bottom of the advertisement.

I think, "So what."

I see a candybar wrapper on the ground.

I think, "So what."

Then I walk in the same direction as before.

It feels like practice.

I only cry like once a year now.

If I had a bar graph, I'm confident it would confirm this.

The right-now me only cries once a year I mean.

And it's hard to tell if I ever cry specifically about the thing happening or just because it is needed at that time.

It's insane.

I take an alleyway between two buildings.

Alleyways between buildings are some of my favorite places to be walking.

There seem to be no spiderwebs now.

And I remember that's because it's winter and some things go away and/or die.

What happens to the spiders in the winter.

I have the urge to drop from the sky and scream, "What happens to the spiders in the winter."

There's a crown spraypainted on the side of a building, and there are numbers over each spike of the crown.

And as I pass by a dumpster, I realize every specific thing I worry about is nothing compared to the main worry I have which never has an object.

The idea of haha goes into my headhole and I almost laugh but I don't because at the other end of the alley there are people smoking cigarettes outside a bar.

And it feels like everyone is looking at me, even people in cars at stoplights.

I only laugh like once a year now.

And I realize that there is nothing to worry about without first wanting to be alive a certain way.

That is somewhat relaxing to think.

If I accept whatever I get, exerting no energy for its arrival and none for its refusal, I will be happy or at least ok.

So weak.

It occurs to me I might never laugh again.

It seems possible, and also likely.

That could happen.

I accept that.

Both of my feet are cold through the shitty boots I'm wearing and I like the way the snow is coming down more now; there is maybe a few inches on the sidewalk area.

I imagine a man coming out of an alley and stabbing me a number of times until I die.

Face-down, mouth-open in the snow.

What would that change about me.

Would I love it.

Would I think that the stabbing was painful and that I didn't like it.

Does it actually hurt or is it great.

I see my killer being given a wreath and a box of candy by the mayor of Chicago at some kind of ceremony (a ceremony for killing me, you see).

And people are cheering for him.

I see myself stab-holed and crawling out of an alley to join the periphery of the celebration.

Then I hold one hand over the stab wounds and with the other hand I give the thumbs-up sign to my killer as he accepts the wreath from the mayor.

I pass more people who are out walking.

I'm on Ashland Avenue.

A lot of times when I encounter someone else out walking or running past me, it feels like we should be more united than we end up acting.

We're both outside at the same time together.

Why doesn't that mean anything to anyone.

Goddamn.

No, I don't think I actually care about that.

I thought I cared about it just now.

The word "phew" scrolls through my head in neon letters.

I feel like my eyes look really wild right now.

It's possible I have a fever.

On my side of the street there's a cop wagon with two cops inside.

Chicago Police.

The Chicago Police Department.

And I just barely resist the urge to jump and scream at the window of the cop wagon.

That would be funny and I don't think I would get arrested (not sure though).

In resisting the urge I feel something like a rush of energy through my heart-area.

Man Arrested for Surprising Chicago Police Then Slipping on Ice and Dying—Cries Wildly.

I consider walking to Lake Michigan again, this time taking my clothes off and getting in until I die.

That would work (almost sure).

I would die from that.

I'd be completely invisible in the snow and gray water and I would die from freezing.

That would work.

Plus I don't think it would be a bad way to die actually.

I don't think that would be bad.

There are usually a lot of ducks (?) geese (?) by Lake Michigan and I think it would be nice to slowly lose consciousness while they stared at me.

What would that change about their lives.

Would it cause anything new in their lives.

Maybe it wouldn't matter.

Why can't I just walk up to some people and say, "Can I spend time with you, I'm really—" and then stop.

I think about people I used to know and I wonder if any one of them is thinking about me at this moment.

That is possible.

That could be happening.

What happens when you are thinking about a person at the same time he or she is thinking about you.

I see myself before all the people I used to know, them forming a line.

I see myself greeting them each, one by one, and saying, "I really am a good person. Are we good, are me and you good."

Wrigley Field ballpark comes up on my right side now.

I look at the LED sign out front and I expect scrolling letters to write, "Nobody likes you and you don't have a home—people just tolerate you."

For some reason then I imagine an old newscaster in front of a big microphone going, "This just in, nobody likes you. They just tolerate you."

I don't think I would react in a shocked way if I saw that.

I would accept it.

Right now I'm hungry.

I feel hunger.

A weird noise happens in my stomach and I feel bad.

The noise my stomach just made is (probably) the same like a young dinosaur telling its mother it needs food.

I consider starving to death on purpose.

Maybe I should do that.

Starving to death on purpose seems awesome to do in North America.

It would be something that people would remember.

I would be remembered as the man who purposely starved to death in North America.

The man whose stomach made those bad baby dinosaur sounds until death.

Man Found Starved, Believed Relative of a Baby Dinosaur.

I pass by a liquor store and go inside.

It smells like my closet inside.

I like it.

No one's in the store.

Then an old man comes out of the backroom, wiping his mouth with a napkin.

I ask if they sell pens.

He's confused.

The store.

Does the store sell pens.

I make a motion with my hand like I am writing and I say, "Pens, pencils."

He says no.

I walk more and come to a 7-11 store.

I go inside and ask the man if they have pens or pencils.

He says some things I don't understand and he points to an aisle.

There are a lot of people at the register and he keeps yelling at me to go different ways.

I go to walk down an aisle and he yells at me and motions a different way.

I can't seem to select the right way.

The way he wants.

Fuck.

He yells more at me and the people in line are now looking and I can only make out a blurry monster around their general area.

For some reason I smile, feeling awesome for a few seconds.

Like, I smile really hard, just watching a man yell directions at me.

This is amazing.

I laugh.

The pencils are by the back near the drink-cooler area.

I find the pencils.

There are people by the drink-cooler and one says, "Yeah, that fucking juice is fucking awesome man. It fucks you up and shit, like, the flavor."

I take a pencil to the register and wait in line.

In line I notice the pencil is the brand that is the store's name.

It is a 7-11 mechanical pencil.

When my history is written on the face of my gravestone, the gravestone that is the entire plate of stone moving beneath the earth's surface, this part will say, "Buys a 7-11 mechanical pencil after being yelled at in front of many people."

The woman in line before me is paying.

As she pays, the man at the register (the man who yelled at me) holds up a container of juice from the counter.

He says, "Go get another."

The woman just stands there.

The man at the register shakes the juice and says it again, really mad.

The woman goes and gets another.

Approaching the register again, she says, "Is it buy-one get-one free."

"Yes yes buy-one get-one."

I look at my pencil to be distracted, and I think about how the woman just blankly did what an angry man working a register told her to do, without first knowing why.

Someone yelled at her, and she did what was being yelled.

This redeems something.

No, I don't know what I'm talking about.

I pay for my pencil and the man behind the register tells me to have a good night.

I wonder what a good night is to him and then I wonder the same about myself.

It occurs to me that in order for that communication to work, myself and the man would have to come to an agreement about what it meant.

I'm too scared.

It feels like practice.

I walk nextdoor to a restaurant.

Inside the restaurant I see some people who were just in the 7-11 with me, so I walk away, and go to a different restaurant nearby.

I order food and eat my order at a table meant for four, in the corner of the place, keeping my hooded sweatshirt and my coat on, worrying the whole time that a worker will walk up to me and say, "Why don't you take your coat off."

I decide if that happens, I will say, "Because I'm undercover."

It doesn't happen.

My history is the history of things imagined and not-happened.

I eat my food without looking up and I write all this down in the white space inside the book I bought, and I try to think about an idea of the not-happened and it seems like I can do it at first but then it becomes unclear and I am not bothered at all.

And exit the restaurant.

My hood is on and it's cold outside, and I make the mistake of breathing in at the same time a long wind goes into my mouth.

Then walk home, thinking paranoid thoughts about how people are trying to fuck with me somehow and I haven't figured it out yet.

Shit is getting bad.

No I don't know.

I live in Chicago and I don't get along with a lot of people and the reasons are always new and wonderful.

CHELSEA
MARTIN

EXCERPT FROM *EVEN THOUGH I DON'T MISS YOU*

I thought I should write a love song about you, since you're not here. I'm not going to contemplate the reasons that you're not here. Anyways love songs are always written in solitude.

I wanted it to be a French song but I only know two French words and have no background in music, and one of the words is croissant.

When you came over, you told me I was depressed, told me I was lazy, stored some frozen meals in my freezer, and passed out on my bed.

I felt like you had somehow accessed my erotic imagination.

You forgot to take your shoes off before you got in my bed.

I wanted you to hold me tightly, and you did, and thank you.

I don't have control over who I love but you seem to not want my love. I'm okay with that. Like my little lamp knows I love it even though I won't buy it a new bulb. Love is a strange thing. That's not really what I'm saying, but I'm saying it's what we should be saying. But I'm only saying it because it's a popular thing to say.

I am told that relationships are not real. I am told that they would not even exist but for five or ten synapses inside the human skull, synapses which rarely receive credit for such monumental forces of human contribution. The person who tells me these things is someone I don't care for. I freely and openly believe that our relationship has nothing to do with synapses.

Sometimes you look at me in this way that says, "I haven't heard a thing you've said in three years," and then you make a joke about how shitty my new recipe is.

Well if you hate my new recipe so much why don't you get a restraining order against it?

I feel heartbroken today, but I don't know. Sometimes I get that way when I'm fucking hungry.

Sometimes it seems like the whole day is spent listening to songs about you. I think of what you might be doing in the world at that particular time, and I imagine you doing it.

I slurred the most important part of my imaginary conversation with you.

You woke up from your nap while I was still watching you. You swore that you would want to make out with me if you didn't happen to be so physically ill. At the time, I thought it was one of the nicest things anyone had ever said to me. Looking back, I think you were just trying to get me to give you my Pepto-Bismal.

When I think of you I imagine you naked in your socks laughing and playing with a toy phone.

What is your personal definition of the term "heat conductivity?"

I'm trying not to think of your text message inbox as my personal diary.

I would think of our relationship as one long uncomfortable silence, but I seem to keep talking.

I guess I just keep talking. I keep expecting to hear something. Are these words finally going to be the words that indicate what is meaningful? Or if I just keep talking, maybe someone will eventually interrupt me and say something. If this is what I'm supposed to be writing about then good. I feel better.

But looking back, yeah, my feelings are kind of hurt, because I couldn't have been more explicit in saying that I wasn't going to be giving out Pepto-Bismal that night.

You said, "What was it, again, that derailed your confidence the other day? I can't remember."

I said, "Conspiracy theory about aliens."

And you said, "Ohhh, that's right."

I'm looking to make a connection tonight.

A love connection. With just a friend.

I mean, I'm looking for someone new, a friend, someone special but not a special friend, but someone who will be in love with me.

If anyone feels like they could be in love with me then I think we should just be friends.

The main thing wrong with the world is that each person has to continue to be herself long long long long long long long long

long long long long after it's become completely unbearable.

I tried to talk to you about my feelings. I was looking for a certain warmth from you. A kind of connection to indicate that I was experiencing the same world that someone else was experiencing. But you said, "No one cares about heat conductivity, Chelsea. I don't even think you care," and you disconnected from chat.

I'm having shrimp cocktail, or I was when I thought of writing that. Shrimp cocktail must be someone's idea of seafood. I miss you.

The main problem is that if you read this, maybe you will relate to it, and if you relate to it, that means that you too are trying to gain insight into your own confusing and ultimately meaningless existence, which means you are not thinking about me, but only yourself, and that's not really my goal.

I've always hated myself. That wasn't so hard to say.

I wish the world was different. I wish shrimp cocktail was different.

I'm trying to learn.

The last time I really changed was when I got a bad haircut, the only thing that really changed was that I started telling people I was a girl.

Not that any of this is real, or consequential in any way, in terms of the universe being a black hole and life being a strange hallucination, but some kind of hair is tickling my asshole and it's somehow making me horny.

This is my love song for you. It's called *I Spent Fifty Hours Making This Even Though I Don't Miss You.*

I'm going to try not to hold you to any specific standards. You've asked me not to, so I'm going to try not to. I hate it when you disregard another girl's feelings. I only want you to disregard my feelings.

It seems like you're moving slightly away from me and it makes me afraid of the Laws of the Universe but I'm afraid to mention it because the phrase "Laws of the Universe" seems so 80's.

You can't capture something that is casually walking away. A vehicle in motion can never reach its goal, unless the goal is completely stationary, in which case there's no point in even getting there. Meaning movement is a rouse, which is a metaphor for life. Although I hope you're not looking for answers. I write for a blog about fairies.

I've been brainstorming for four months about what I should post to your wall for your birthday.

I guess the mass of all things you love in the world is less than or equal to the combined weight of all the hearts of everyone you've been cruel to. I guess that's something most people already know by the time they're my age.

I don't know why I'm explaining this. Everybody has already done what I've done and thinks what I think.

I think I'm at a point in my life.

I said, "You look disappointed by something."

You said, "You're not hurting anyone's feelings, Chelsea."

3.

MEGAN
BOYLE

LITTLE ROCK

Jacob had warned Mia of the heat wave that would coincide with her visit to Little Rock. Still, she had only packed two sleeveless items. She had gotten in the habit of asking him if she smelled bad. She had heard "Don't worry about it" so many times that she now just periodically said, "I'm sorry, I know I smell bad." When Jacob told her not to apologize, she apologized for apologizing.

They were the only people sitting outside the cafe that day. Jacob ordered a chicken salad sandwich for them to split. His friend Vicki made their sandwich and took it out to them. She smiled brightly at Mia, then looked at Jacob and said, "I always make the best sandwiches." Even though Mia wasn't hungry, she ate her entire half. A fly circled her head. She swatted at it, but it always returned. Jacob moved his sandwich crust around the plate.

"Did you ever try to date Vicki?"

"Sort of. We were drunk once and started to have sex, but it didn't work. We just started laughing. I don't know, she's my best friend."

Mia nodded. "She's pretty."

The fly flew close to her ear and she moved her head. Jacob picked apart what was left of his sandwich, then put it back together. He drummed his leg under the table. Mia worried that when people did this, it meant they were bored with her. Jacob straightened in his chair.

"I think the heat is making me resent everything," he said, looking out at the parking lot.

•

Two months ago, Jacob flew to Chicago to meet Mia. She had solicited him to be in the first photography show she curated. They had known of each other's work for about a year. Jacob had just completed a series of photos called "The Target Suicides," which depicted people elaborately killing themselves in every aisle of Target. Mia had photographed dead Christmas trees posed as if engaged in mundane human activities. They exchanged casual but frequent e-mails. Jacob said he was excited to meet her. Mia said she was excited to meet him.

When he arrived an hour late to the show, he walked to her with his head tilted to the side and his elbows so close to his body that his chest pushed forward. It seemed natural for him to walk this way. He reminded Mia of some kind of exotic, crane-like water bird that wasn't supposed to fly, but frequently attempted flight anyway. She liked him immediately. They spent most of the night sitting in different places in the gallery, making up stories about the more eccentric looking patrons.

After the show, they went back to Mia's apartment and didn't leave for four days. They thought of nicknames for her cats. When they had to eat, they would order food. Sometimes when they made eye contact for more than three seconds, Jacob would say Mia's name and then Mia would say Jacob's and they would grin at each other.

"We're being cheesy," Mia would say.

"We are. It's good."

On Jacob's last night, they decided to drive as long as they could without a destination. He rested his hand on Mia's thigh when she drove. They stopped to eat at a travel plaza. An old man was sitting alone in the area between a Popeye's and a Burger King. Food items from both restaurants were on his table. Mia whispered, "Look!" and gestured excitedly at the man. "Both places."

"Oh my god," Jacob said as he tugged Mia's sleeve. "He's so depressing. That's going to be me someday."

"I know, me too."

Jacob didn't immediately let go of Mia's sleeve. They sat and ate their French fries quietly. The low, atonal hum of a semi-truck sometimes passed outside. Jacob squeezed a ketchup packet onto his wrist and rolled his eyes back in his head. Mia dipped one of her fries in his ketchup blood.

"You should come visit me in Arkansas. I mean, if you want. I'd like it if you did." He licked away the rest of the blood.

Mia smiled. "I'd like to visit you."

"You should."

After Jacob returned home, he contacted Mia almost daily. His e-mails contained list-like accounts of his daily thoughts and activities, and usually closed with something about wanting her to be near him. He told her stories about his friends, referring to them only by their first names, as if Mia was already familiar with them. She wasn't sure if this meant he felt she was already a part of his life, if his friends were interchangeable, or if this was just how he talked about people. Mia felt jealous of his social life. In her responses to Jacob, her acquaintances became friends and her nights alone went unmentioned.

Jacob called Mia one night to tell her that a strange man pulled a gun on him and his friends at a bar. They were sitting outside. The man sweated profusely and wouldn't leave their picnic table. He wanted someone to buy him a beer and no one would, so he fired three shots into the air and ran away. Mia walked the perimeter of her apartment, putting fingers into her mouth and saying "Oh my god" as she listened.

"Is everything...are you okay?"

"I'm fine, I was shaken up a little bit but. Everything's fine. The cops came, eventually. It was ridiculous." Jacob's voice sounded dreamy and far away.

"I feel like I would be shaking right now. Shaking and hiding somewhere."

"It's weird, the thing I cared about the most was making sure I was the last one inside when everyone started running. Like, I wanted my friends to know that I was the one holding the door for them."

"That means you're a good friend, right?"

"I just wanted them to think I was brave, I think. The cavalier one." Mia didn't say anything. "I've been talking about you to them. They're excited to meet you."

"Oh, good. I'm excited, too. I hope a week isn't too long for me to be there."

"It won't be. You could probably even stay longer."

A mysterious, semi-constant fear of dying in a car crash on the drive to Little Rock permeated throughout Mia the week before she left. The logical voice in her head that usually intervened to console irrational anxieties had, to her surprise, submitted to this idea—had actually thought of her death as reasonable outcome. Mia pictured technicians in heavy gloves pulling her body out of her windshield. How would they tell her parents?

Her apartment began to take on a claustrophobic quality, and she retreated daily to a nearby park where she watched people walk their dogs. Something was comforting about strangers—it seemed like they would exist forever as the same, unknowable mass. The sun warmed her body and made the white pages of her book seem so bright that they were radiating. It was hard to concentrate on reading. She texted Jacob, "It seems highly possible that I'll get into a fatal car crash on the drive down there, haha," then set her phone to vibrate and put it under her thigh. Ten minutes later Jacob responded, "My dad is a car mechanic. Did I tell you that?"

Mia drove slightly under the speed limit the entire way to Arkansas. She played the same song on repeat. The air conditioning in her car was broken so she kept the windows down. Though she had known this was coming for a long time, had imagined herself sleeping next to Jacob every night, had tried to mentally map his house and piece together small details of his life—it was suddenly very apparent to her that her visit was not just a pleasant abstraction to be considered and forgotten, but an event actually happening. Something could go wrong. An ex-girlfriend could resurface. Conversation could run out. She looked at her hands on the steering wheel and thought for a moment that she had eight, not ten, fingers. As she neared Jacob's house and had to drive slower on the smaller streets, the heat seemed almost visible. It was August. Her pulse beat against the skin of her neck.

From a distance, she couldn't tell if Jacob was smiling or squinting to keep the sun out of his eyes. Another man sat with him on the porch, and went inside as soon as she pulled into the driveway. Jacob leaned his head into her window and kissed her. They said "Hello" to each other until they started laughing. Mia pulled her suitcase out of the car. "That was Bill, my roommate. The guy who went in. You'll meet him, he's a big pothead."

"Oh." Mia didn't know what to say. "Nice."

After Jacob gave her a tour of the house, they went to his room and had sex. Mia rested her head near his armpit. It smelled good. She traced one of his tattoos with her finger until she became drowsy and allowed herself to close her eyes. Jacob idly rubbed her upper arm.

"We can go for a ride on my motorcycle, if you want. Would you want to do that?"

Mia didn't open her eyes. "Now?"

"Oh, sorry. Did you want to nap? I guess you had a really long drive."

Mia rolled over to face the wall. She listened to the rhythmic motor of the ceiling fan. When she woke, it was dark and Jacob wasn't in the room. An oily, sticky kind of sweat covered her body, and when she moved under the sheet, she could smell herself. On the pillow next to her was a note. "Decided to let you sleep. You seemed so tired. Come to Vicki's, five houses down. We're drinking on her porch. Everyone wants to meet you." Mia wanted to lie still for thirty hours. She thought about making herself sleep again. She took a long shower and walked to Vicki's.

People had already been drinking for some time when she arrived. The porch was cluttered with lawn ornaments, broken folding chairs, full recycling bins, and large, jungle-like potted plants. Five people sat around a white picnic table, and three others leaned against the porch railing. A girl led Mia inside to a bedroom where Jacob, Vicki, and two other people were drinking beers on a bed. A small TV was on. Jacob hugged Mia and seemed happy to see her. Vicki introduced herself and said Jacob was her only friend in the world. She had a strong southern accent. She and Jacob told each other stories about memories they had together. Mia wasn't sure if she was a part of their conversation, or just listening to it. She tried to ask questions, but eventually gave up.

Mia drank eight beers over the course of the night. She went to the bathroom frequently, and used some of Vicki's sesame body oil every time. People left and eventually only Vicki, Jacob and Mia sat around the table on the porch. Mia took pictures. In most of the pictures, Vicki's face was animated in mid-sentence and Jacob was doing something on his phone. Mia smoked five of Vicki's cigarettes.

On the walk home, Jacob said, "I don't see why anyone would ever smoke cigarettes. It just seems counter-intuitive. Like, you know it's the shittiest thing in the world for you."

"Fast food is worse. It's not like I smoke all the time, this is the first time I've ever done it around you. Vicki smokes all the time. You've really never smoked one?"

"Absolutely not. It's just stupid. Everything about it is stupid."

"You're mad. Are you drunk?" Mia almost tripped but caught herself. She laughed. Jacob picked at something on his hand.

"I've only met one other person in the world who's never smoked a cigarette," he said.

They argued for a long time in Jacob's bedroom. In the morning, Mia remembered having spoken loudly and felt embarrassed. She vaguely sensed that the conversation had, at some point, shifted from cigarettes to her feelings of insecurity about their relationship. Jacob held her from behind. She turned to face him and he was awake. He rolled onto his back and put a hand on his forehead.

"Something happened last night. Sorry."

"Yeah," Jacob said. "Drunk fight. It's okay."

"Do you want to talk about anything we said?"

"No. I can feel myself start shutting down when people try to engage me in emotional discussions." Jacob yawned, looked at Mia, and shrugged.

"Really?" Mia sat up. "But your e-mails...I don't know, you seemed very aware of yourself, emotionally."

Jacob removed his hand from Mia's calf and played with his chest hair. "Maybe because I'm not really talking to a real person then. It's just an idea of a person."

Mia could smell the hot sourness of her breath. She looked away from Jacob. "Well, I'm sorry if I said anything offensive last night. I don't think I meant it. Do you feel okay about me?"

"You didn't say anything bad. I feel fine about you. I'm glad you're here."

That day, four of Jacob's friends invited he and Mia to swim at a lake in the mountains. Jacob drove Mia's car and got lost a few times. Their legs stuck to the vinyl seats. Jacob played songs from his iPod. He personally knew many of the band members, and had stories about stealing food from stranger's plates in diners with them, or getting drunk and tattooing each other. Mia worried that it was becoming noticeable that she had only been saying "Seriously?" and "Wow" in response. She watched a mosquito-like insect fly repeatedly into the inside corner of her window.

"Does it bother you that I don't have crazy stories like that?"

"Why would that bother me?"

"I mean it's not like I don't know how to have fun or anything."

Mia rolled down her window and the insect was vacuumed out.

"I know you have fun." Jacob made a concerned face.

At the lake they took off their shoes, rubbed sun block on each other, and walked a soft dirt path. The sky was cloudless and still. Mia stepped on something that vibrated. She sensed the thing was alive and fragile, and immediately drew back her foot. Nothing was there. She scanned the ground surrounding her.

"Are there lizards here?" She called to Jacob, who was fifteen feet ahead. He stopped walking.

"Did you say lizards?"

"Yeah, like in Florida? You know, they have these chameleons running around everywhere. I just stepped on something."

"Why would you think it was a lizard?"

Mia squeezed her toes into the dirt. "I guess because it got away fast." For a moment, it seemed possible that she could have absorbed the lizard into the bottom of her foot. Something unreachable inside of her itched.

Jacob's friends swam along the perimeter of a wooden platform in the middle of the lake. Jacob showed off by doing elaborate dives that Mia sometimes applauded. She dangled her feet into the water and sat silently next to another girl, who eventually jumped in.

Jacob's friend Elliott approached her from behind. "Hey, are you having fun?"

"Oh, yeah, Arkansas is good. It's pretty. I like this lake a lot."

"I ask because when I moved here from Phoenix, I felt a little out of place. The people were nice and everything, but it took awhile to get used to things, for some reason. It was an adjustment."

Mia thought for a moment. "The people are really welcoming. You guys, I mean. You're...welcoming."

"I just want to be sure you're having a good time." Elliott cocked his head to the side.

Jacob swam up to them. "Is he scaring you about the water snakes?"

"Water snakes?"

"Oh my god, there are these black snakes, they live in the water—they mate by getting into this big, swarming ball. The ball just swims around, right below the water."

"Jacob, fuck, I forgot about the snakes." Elliott adjusted his swim trunks. Mia leaned over the platform and peered into the water.

"Yeah, sometimes they make it into the trees, they'll just like, drop out of the swarm once they're done having sex," Jacob said.

"No one's ever seen them," Elliott said to no one in particular.

Mia gasped and pointed at the water. "Holy shit, Jacob, get out of the water right now."

"What?" Jacob's movements became frantic. He climbed the ladder to the platform. "I hate snakes." Elliott and Mia laughed. Jacob looked at Mia's face.

"You look pissed," Mia said.

"I hate snakes."

•

At the cafe, the fly landed on Jacob's sandwich crust. Mia thought it looked lost. Jacob went inside to use the bathroom. Mia felt a bead of sweat drip down her stomach. She patted it with her shirt and then realized it would leave a mark. She fanned the fabric away from her body. When Jacob returned, his hairline was wet from having splashed water on his face.

"Vicki just said it's a hundred two out here, but the heat factor is a hundred eight."

"Heat... factor?"

"I don't know what it means either."

An ice cream truck playing "You Are My Sunshine" on a loop was nearing the cafe. Mia looked down the road, squinting a little.

"Our bodies are 98.6 degrees. It's sort of like we're living inside a person with a fever right now, being outside," Jacob said.

"Yeah." Mia sank back into her chair, eyes still focused on the road. "This song has always made me feel sad for some reason. It just sounds sad."

Jacob looked at Mia and breathed in and out. "We should go. Rick wants to meet us soon. You'll like Rick, I think. He's the philosophy professor guy."

"Oh, Rick. Yeah. I'd like to sit inside somewhere." Mia felt a little delirious. She had an urge to pick up her shadow and shake it. Something would fall out. She stood and followed Jacob to her car.

At the restaurant where Jacob worked, it was dark and cool. People crowded around in clusters. The only face Mia could clearly see was Jacob's. He asked if she wanted a beer. She smiled and nodded in a way she thought was slightly too generous, and when she went to touch his arm he was already gone. The vent under the table blew aggressively and made the hem of her skirt ripple. She realized this was the first time she had felt cold in this city. A chorus of voices moaned at a football game on TV. Mia didn't know anything about Rick and was tired of meeting people.

A tallish man in his mid-thirties approached Jacob at the bar. Mia watched them talk for a few minutes before they joined her table. Rick limply extended his hand and Mia shook it for him.

"So, you drove all the way down here for this guy? What is that, eleven hours?"

Mia's eyes moved from side to side. "I like driving."

"Evidently." Rick smiled at Mia in a way she thought she had seen Jeff Goldblum smile at a girl in some movie. Jacob made water-circles on their table with his beer glass.

"They just told me at the bar that I need to come in for a shift tonight, but Rick says he can take you with him to a party after we get beers. Or you can hang out here with me, but it would just be sitting around. Sorry."

"I ordered nachos," Rick said. "Don't let that influence your decision, though."

Mia listened as Jacob and Rick talked about a road trip for a long time. She drank two more beers before the nachos arrived and wondered why she came here at all. Rick periodically asked her funny, sometimes overly personal questions that she responded to candidly. Jacob sometimes noticed her answers, but mostly he looked bored. Mia watched Rick's fingers as he sandwiched his nachos together. He left a stack of fresh jalapeno peppers on the side of his plate. "What's wrong with the peppers. Why aren't you eating them?"

Rick grinned. "Why don't you try one and find out."

"If I do, then everyone has to."

Mia didn't wait for them to agree. She ate a pepper and didn't feel anything for fifteen seconds, but then her throat and mouth burned intensely. Her eyes widened and her mouth dropped in an openly cartoonish way. One hand cupped her mouth as the other grabbed her unopened silverware napkin and banged it on the table a few times. Rick laughed, Jacob didn't.

"Oh my god, this is insane," she said.

"Yeah, it's got a little heat, doesn't it?" Rick said.

"It's so hot, it's making me want to punch something!"

Rick gave her a spoonful of sour cream. It didn't do much. Her face began to sweat.

"It's going to be like that for about five minutes," Jacob said.

"Five minutes?"

"You didn't even wait for me to tell you."

"It's so hot. I want to fight someone." Mia smiled in disbelief at Rick, then looked at Jacob and chugged the rest of her beer.

"That's just going to...spread it around," Jacob said. "There's nothing you can do. You just have to wait until it's over."

Rick shook a finger at Mia. "Impulse control, young lady." She used her forearm to wipe her face.

"I'm getting another beer, at least it'll be cold."

At the bar, Mia felt a hand on her lower back. Rick stood behind her.

"You didn't ask me if I wanted one."

"Oh, sorry. Do you?"

"No, but I think you should get two for yourself."

Mia didn't see Jacob sitting at the table anymore. Someone needed to say something but she didn't know what.

"Sorry if I smell bad."

Rick removed his hand. "Girls can't smell bad." He walked past her and she watched the back of his head disappear into the crowd, then reappear by the bathroom door. Jacob walked out of the bathroom as Rick walked in. She waved to him. He waved back. A man and woman stood in front of Mia at the bar. Their faces were animated and they spoke too quickly for Mia to discern any words. Jacob walked to her with his head tilted to the side. He now seemed happy to see her.

"Is your mouth still freaking out?"

"A little. It's okay. I think I'm just getting my check, though."

Jacob nodded. "Are you going to the party with Rick?"

"Maybe. I haven't decided yet. No, probably not." Mia felt the cold air going down into her lungs, but couldn't feel it leaving.

"People are sticking around here and drinking after work, if you wanted to do that."

"Yeah, maybe. I think I'm going to walk around for a while. I'll stop by later."

Jacob paid Mia's check and she thanked him. When Rick returned she told him she was going for a walk, and he said in a cautionary tone, "Don't get lost," then scrunched up his face and pointed his out-turned thumb at the door and said, "Now, get lost!" He laughed and Mia made herself smile.

Outside, it had cooled significantly, but the sun hadn't yet set. Mia passed shops and a residential area. The only other person on the street was a woman with a large dog. Everything was quiet. Mia followed a mulched path to a small wooded park.

Tinny, electronic music played in the distance. The melody sometimes vaguely resembled "Silver Bells." Dusty beams of yellow light shone through the treetops, spotlighting arbitrary patches of plants.

Mia heard a rustling that matched the sound of her footsteps on the leaves. Something moved in her peripheral vision. She stopped walking. The rustling was a cat-sized mass of forest debris. It moved slowly from side to side, and then stopped. Mia stood for a moment and waited for it to move again. She tossed a small rock at it. It didn't move. She cautiously took a few steps forward and saw a miniature cloud of flies hovering above the mass. Without getting any closer, she knew an animal had come here to die.

BEACH
SLOTH

HEY YOU

You are sitting at a desk different from mine. Maybe
You are lying down or maybe
You are reading this on a phone or maybe
You are right in front of me I'm uncertain. What I am certain of is
You are wonderful
You have a lot going for you
You will achieve all your dreams
You know what to do
You say such nice things
You never put other people down
You lift them up
You are a beam of light piercing through cloudy days
You are one of my favorite people. Nobody is quite like You
You are unique out of billions of people as
You are reading this right now. Thank
You for tuning into my little corner of the universe maybe someday
You will see me
You will sit across from me in the train
You will not recognize me and I will not recognize
You but the anonymous support we give each other is
enough. I care deeply about
You and hope we meet and never know it.

5.

DIANA
SALIER

HOLY SHIT I HAVE BEEN
SO LONELY

Remember when we spent
saturday drinking tea
downloading porn
on the free Wi-Fi
at the café
below your apartment

Holy shit
I have been
so lonely

I want to drink tea
and download porn with you
on the free Wi-Fi
at the café
below your apartment

WHEN WE'RE OLD IN A CAVE AND LIGHTING FIRES

You walked in the door   I sharpened all my pencils.

I wrote this grocery list   with you in mind—

peanut butter eggs bacon mustard brown rice.

I've been training   to be your lover since the first grade.

I make the best trades. You will never go hungry. I can turn lunch-ables ham into pudding cups for weeks.

I would throw a dodgeball at anyone who stole your bicycle.

I changed our entries on <u>ancestry.com</u>   so now we are fraternal twins separated at birth.

You can stay the night in my tree house after giving your verbal consent—a simple YES will suffice.

There are so many songs   I wish I'd written

and when we're old in a cave and lighting fires in our slippers,

I'll write them for the first time and play you a series

of new old songs

I AM A REFORMED MOVIE MONSTER AND I LOVE YOU SO MUCH

Before you went blind
I put my hands over your eyes
and promised to block out the sun

I studied the apocalypse
from behind the blanket barrier
of your bed
I gave a cookie to all the bad things
that were happening around us

Mostly it feels like I've been about to cry for four months
mostly I'm afraid you have more fun without me
and mostly I'm just worried you have better sex

My father is king of the dinosaurs
if you stick with me you will not get eaten

I am a reformed movie monster
and I love you so much
I know your fears
and will not capitalize on them

GUILLAUME
MORISSETTE

KARPMAN DRAMA TRIANGLE

"Go away," said Alison to the cat, who disliked being yelled at, produced a face, a moan, but then stopped, as if resigning itself, being the mature one. It jumped over an obstacle and then ran away in an overly dramatic manner, like a horse escaping a barn fire. Ten seconds later, it was playing with a ball and a string in the living room.

From Mark's viewpoint, the cat's leap had seemed impressive, the equivalent, he supposed, of a gazelle hopping over a mountain. "I can't leap that high," he thought. He remembered how, in high school, a career test had predicted that he would become an acrobat, which had read as a kind of dry irony, though still made for an interesting thought experiment.

In the bed, he was lying uncomfortably on his side, with his back trapped between the wall and Alison's body, his head yearning for its share of the pillow, like a plant growing in the direction of sunlight. He thought about everyone's order in the bed. From left to right: Joel, Lynn, Alison, himself. From most drunk to least: Alison, Joel, Lynn, himself. From most attractive to least: Joel, Alison, Lynn, himself, he felt.

"She's so annoying," said Alison. "That cat has some serious emotional issues. One second she's all sweet and then she farts in someone's face. Why would you do that? She responds to hate with love and with love to hate."

"You're projecting," said Lynn. "Responds with hate. I am quite sure that's not the cat now. That's you. That's you with men."

"You with men when you're in heat," said Joel.

Mark laughed a little, heard Lynn doing the same.

"It purrs way too much," said Joel. "I don't even understand the sound it makes. It's this low-frequency noise, with a little thump at the end. It's weird."

"Dubstep cat," said Mark.

"She just wants a boy cat to be nice to her," said Alison, "but at the same time she secretly resents all boy cats. She's complex. I'll get her fixed soon. Tomorrow. I'll go to the vet tomorrow. I have school, but I am not going to that. I probably won't go to the vet either. I won't do anything. That way it's fair for everyone."

Alison laughed at her own comment.

Mark changed position in the bed. He placed his arm around Alison and then held her a little. She smelled like hairspray, he noticed, the kind that seemed to be having an identity crisis, desperate to exist not as itself but as a natural odor instead. Holding her, he thought about the sheer snugness of her body, like a secret place in which to hide, build a nest there maybe, bring a computer, get some work done.

He stared at the desk and wooden chair on the other side of the room, which were submerged in piles of nondescript objects with no clear purpose. "Her room is a lot like her," he thought, "kind of a mess." He really liked Alison's paradoxical nature. He thought of her as dysfunctional and impulsive and chaotic, but also, in a lot of ways, clever and self-aware; a tornado, though one whose eye was a supercomputer.

On the laptop, he saw Lynn browsing to a movie-streaming website. The website featured Hollywood actors making prepared faces on the thumbnails of movie posters.

"Is there a movie that has Jet Li drowning in a bath and fighting the bath to avoid drowning?" said Mark. "I would watch that."

Alison laughed a little. Lynn suggested a movie and then Joel suggested another movie. The movie they put on was some movie. Mark didn't feel like watching, closed his eyes though couldn't fall asleep, was kept awake by private thoughts and nonsequiturs.

Twenty minutes later, Alison turned away from the screen and towards him. With her head in a different position, he saw that Joel's eyes were closed, though he was still making small gestures. He felt Alison's hand playing with his under the covers. He moved his face within close vicinity of her face. He aligned his nose with a tiny hole in the corner of her eye, from which both light and air seemed to emanate. He overheard the sound of someone breathing, either himself or her or another person altogether. He felt as if his face was taunting her face a little. They remained in that position for a few seconds, until she closed the gap between them and kissed him, at first in a soft, polite way, as if expecting resistance, paperwork to sign maybe, but then with added intensity. He felt surprised by the kiss but then realized that this was more or less what he had hoped would happen. He wasn't used to what he wanted to happen actually happening.

The kiss, Mark felt, was interesting for several reasons, because Joel was in the bed close to them, because she had been the one to kiss him and not the other way around, because he didn't want to go too far and yet apparently kept going. He wasn't sure why he was making out with her. He knew that he was just another person she made out with, that if he allowed himself to develop anything beyond some loose, retractable affection for her, like the power cord of a vacuum cleaner, their relationship would spin out of its axis, lead to a more noticeable drinking habit, a passive, subdued kind of despair and maybe someone making someone else a mixtape.

But despite knowing, he found himself unable to resist, liked applying pressure on her body and seeing how it responded, liked her tendency to self-deprecate, how her self-esteem was more fragile than what her public persona suggested, liked her laugh, liked thinking about her laugh. Maybe he only liked her because of her laugh, he speculated. He thought about the last person he had been involved with, whom he no longer talked to but whose laugh functioned in a similar way. There was a pattern. Two. Two was a pattern, Mark thought.

About five minutes later, they stopped kissing, shifted positions and reverted back to holding one another. In the room, no one said anything, except the movie, which was now saying things to no one. Alison adopted a sleeping position. Mark noticed that Lynn had fallen asleep. He tried to follow her lead but failed. He saw Joel getting up from the bed and then walking away at a fast pace. He wasn't sure if Joel had seen them kissing, was angry and storming out in a dramatic fashion, or was simply going to pee, or had decided to head back home for the night after all, or what.

He began replaying events from earlier that night in his head. At a fundraiser for a local space, he had recognized Joel in the crowd, had said hi to him but then not much after that, realizing then and there that he wasn't sure how to interact with him one-on-one. What Mark knew about Joel was that Alison and he had been friends for years and that he was an independent musician and a boring kind of handsome and that in his room were old fliers from shows with his name on them and an exercise ball stored away on a shelf. On several occasions, Alison had described him as, "vain, but in a fun way." She also frequently made fun of his lyrics for being incomprehensible or shallow.

Later, he had invited Joel to a birthday party at his friend Laura's apartment. Walking in, he had thought about having to chaperone him a little, having to force-introduce him to people, but then had seen him ease his way into a conversation with a girl with short black hair. It was like Joel was an actor, able to forget his own age, eventual death, struggles, concerns, doubts, failures, and slide into the role of a cheerful, timeless person, with none of these issues.

At one a.m., he had received a call from Alison. He had moved away from the noise and out of the apartment, conversing with her outside, in the cold and surrounded by a pack of judgmental smokers.

"I don't like anyone where I am, where are you," she had said. She had sounded drunk but not impossibly drunk. They had discussed whether she should come or not. He had texted her the address.

Later, she had called back to tell him that the cab driver had been unable to find the apartment and that she was now at a gas station close-by. He had told her to stay there and that he would come find her. On their way back to Laura's, they had held hands, though he had thought of it as nothing more than a utilitarian gesture, someone else's balance compensating for hers. Alison had mentioned having drunk two thirds of a bottle of vodka at a party organized by people from her major but then added that she would stop drinking for the night and be calm and docile and not the craziest person alive.

"I met a first-year," Alison had said later. She was sitting next to him on the black couch in Laura's living room. "He asked me out on a date. I said, 'I think I am too old for you.' But then I said yes anyway. I don't know why."

Alison had laughed her own comment.

"Why don't you like people from your major," he had said.

"For the most part, they're not that interesting," Alison had said. "They just have tunnel vision about being excellent. Some of them would probably commit seppuku if they got a B. I get underachiever marks in all my classes, so they don't know what to do with me."

"They overexcel," he had said.

"Exactly," Alison had said. "It's annoying. When I applied for this, it was kind of random, like I did Latin American studies and Art History before that and I thought I would really like those but I ended up dropping out. So I chose something I would hate instead, and now I am graduating next semester. It doesn't feel like I've earned that diploma at all though. I feel like such a fraud, like I just lied and charmed and manipulated people into getting a passing grade. I tell myself that I should take it more seriously but I never do. It's too easy to bullshit my way through."

"It's like you want to be caught," he had said. "Did you go see Lack Of Values last night?"

"Oh yeah," Alison had replied. "I did. It was good. I thought they were going to be a full band though, but they were only two. This has been happening too much in my life lately. I go see bands and it turns out it's one guy with an iPad. I am like, 'Where's the band?' Less guys to make out with."

Alison had laughed her own comment.

"Can we hold hands like before," Alison had said, curling up into a ball and placing her head on his chest. "That's okay, right?"

"Sure," he had said. "Do you think Joel will want to kill me though?"

He had pictured Joel training angrily on his exercise ball, seeking revenge.

"Maybe," Alison had said. "I'd rather not think about it. I shouldn't have made out with him. I thought it was just a friends make-out. We've been friends for so long, I don't understand why all of the sudden he wants something to happen. We would fuck it up so bad."

Looking directly at her, he had noticed that her eyeliner was slipping a little, looked like a kind of eye drool.

"Maybe I could love him but not here," Alison had said. "There's too much choice here. What we need is a smaller population size, like Andorra. Or the Samoan Islands."

"There's too many attractive people here," he had said, "so everyone's defensive because they're afraid of getting hurt. Did you know that earthworms have both sexes and that all they have to do to is find another earthworm, align next to it and then they impregnate one another. I kind of wish we had that system."

"That sounds way better," Alison had said. "They don't have personal preference. That fucks me up all the time. So much personal preference."

Alison had laughed her own comment.

"It's like I've built-up this imaginary boyfriend in my head," Alison had said, "to mythic proportions. The other day, I was like, who would be my ideal lover, and I didn't know what the answer was except I knew it wasn't anyone I could think of."

"Before I started seeing Meghan last year, the fiasco of that," he had said, "there was that one time where she described her ideal lover. She listed a bunch of things, like he needed to be a good cook and have a car and stuff. In my head, I pictured her shopping for boyfriends at the boyfriend supermarket, taking one from a shelf, checking the expiration date, putting it in the cart, crossing an item off her list or something. I was like, "That's not how it works." How it works is that we fit into each other's fantasy matrices for reasons we're not sure we understand. That's how it works."

"Not a lot of people fit into mine," Alison had said. "I've been mostly interested in people not interested in me."

"I feel like you probably end up a lot in situations where the other person is wowed by you and you're entertained by it but not wowed in particular," he had said, "so on some level it feels uneven. And if you try liking someone that doesn't like you, as soon as they do, you get bored."

"That seems about right," Alison had said. "What does that say about me I wonder. Something terrible I think. Something dark and sinister. Like dubstep."

Alison had laughed her own comment.

"You just want a relationship of mutual respect," he had said.

"People who like me make me intensely uncomfortable," Alison had said, "because I never think they really like me, I always think they like the person they imagine me to be. And that eventually they'll realize I am not that person and then ditch me. So I don't want that."

"You're easy to fantasize about I think," he had said, "in a sexual way I guess, but I mean it more like in a personal way. You don't come off as mysterious or guarded or whatever, so I can see people thinking that they know all they need to know about you and that they can just fill in the blanks in their heads with whatever seems convenient to them."

"That's unfortunate," Alison had said.

•

"Go away," said Alison to the cat, who disliked being yelled at, produced a face, a moan, but then stopped, as if resigning itself, being the mature one. It jumped over an obstacle and then ran away in an overly dramatic manner, like a horse escaping a barn fire. Ten seconds later, it was playing with a ball and a string in the living room.

"She's so annoying," said Alison. "That cat has some serious emotional issues. One second she's all sweet and then she farts in someone's face. Why would you do that? She responds to hate with love and with love to hate."

"You're projecting," said Lynn. "Responds with hate. I am quite sure that's not the cat now. That's you. That's you with men."

"You with men when you're in heat," said Joel.

Lynn laughed a little, heard Mark doing the same. They discussed the cat. On the laptop, she browsed to a movie-streaming website. Mark joked about which movie to put on. Lynn suggested a comedy and then Joel suggested a dramedy. She followed Joel's suggestion, wasn't sure she would like that movie but refrained from contradicting him.

A few scenes into it, she grew tired of staring at the screen and allowed her mind to wander. She had been living in Montreal for about three months now, had found this apartment on Craigslist and interviewed for it over Skype. She liked Alison, her roommate, but also Joel, and Mark, and the cat, and herself. She liked everyone, more or less, perceived herself as one of those terminally agreeable people, just like her mom, that would rather sacrifice themselves than risk group harmony. She wasn't certain she had a dark side. If she had one, it was a sasquatch: impossible to find, though presumably very angry.

She thought about how, as a child, she was absent-minded, would, on her way back from school, stop at every house and daydream about the kind of people that lived there, wondering if they, too, liked miniature golf, or else kept large photo-albums of family members, so large that some of the pictures were of the family members looking at photo-albums. Before moving to Montreal, she had explored the city using the street view feature on Google Maps, had stared at the buildings on her screen trying to imagine herself living there, on her own, wearing a wool sweater, green, her favorite color, buying an oversized pretzel from a small corner shop, leaving a dollar as tip.

In the bed, she was lying next to Joel but made no move or

gesture to suggest that she was interested in him, mostly waited there, paralyzed a little, hoping, somehow, to power-think her way into a desirable situation. Since arriving, she hadn't slept with or kissed or even been close to another person, wanted to experience a North American lover, just one, to see what that was like, how they compared, but didn't like to talk about it, felt shy a little, intimidated even, though wasn't sure by what. Joel was both older and taller than her. Next to him, she felt tiny, child-like, like something you could fold in half, preserve for later.

"Do you want Joel," Alison had asked her a week before. They were sitting on her bed, procrastinating, giving each other life advice, brainstorming feelings. "Whenever someone wants to get laid, I just send in Joel."

Alison had laughed her own comment.

"No, I mean, maybe," she had said. "I don't know, I am not, I don't know. I mean, he's very kind. What are you eating?"

"Protein bar," Alison had said. "My sister gave me a box before leaving for some unknown reason. She was like, 'Here are your bags, oh and this box of protein bars, don't use them as meals.' Sucka. I've been totally using them as meals."

Alison had laughed her own comment.

"I don't like it when they try to pretend it's a chocolate bar when it's really not," she had said. "It's dishonest."

"I had a weird dream last night that I kept mistaking for reality," Alison had said. "I lived with a bunch of jocks and they were eating protein bars. That's all I have so far. But this afternoon I had the thought, 'Remember that time you lived with those jocks.' It felt weird."

Alison had laughed her own comment.

"I thought Joel was interested in you," she had said.

"No," Alison had said, "I mean, kind of, he's been acting strange lately, but that's only because I thrive on making my life complicated. That way I don't have to make decisions. Because it's too complicated."

Alison had laughed at her own comment.

"You should be careful," she had said.

"Don't worry about that," Alison had said. "It'll go away. Joel only likes himself."

•

"Go away," said Alison to the cat, who disliked being yelled at, produced a face, a moan, but then stopped, as if resigning itself, being the mature one. It jumped over an obstacle and then ran away in an overly dramatic manner, like a horse escaping a barn fire. Ten seconds later, it was playing with a ball and a string in the living room.

Hearing the cat play, Alison thought about the day she had brought it home from a pet store. That afternoon, feeling despondent, like her clutter's clutter, she had lain in her bed for an unclear number of hours, as if testing the world a little to see if it would care enough to react, send help. Eventually, she had, somehow, convinced herself to go out, and buy food, and survive, had passed in front of a pet store she routinely ignored, deciding, instead, to go in and hold a kitten, a cream-colored one. Feeling better from doing so, she had purchased it on a whim using her credit card's theoretical money.

Now, several months later, she had mixed feelings about it, often imagined herself hosting a cat give-away party or, in an ideal world, replacing it with an advanced robot automaton, one that would brush her hair in the moonlight, provide unemotional, logic-based relationship advice, make pancakes in the morning for overnight guests and sometimes do handstands and cartwheels, trying to be cute. She was getting bored of the cat, felt she probably wouldn't have left the pet shop with it if it hadn't been so affection-prone that day.

"She's so annoying," said Alison. "That cat has some serious emotional issues. One second she's all sweet and then she farts in someone's face. Why would you do that? She responds to hate with love and with love to hate."

"You're projecting," said Lynn. "Responds with hate. I am quite sure that's not the cat now. That's you. That's you with men."

"You with men when you're in heat," said Joel.

Alison heard Mark and Lynn laugh a little, wanted to react but simply didn't, allowing the moment to pass instead. Though the cat had flaws, she liked to project her personality on it, pretend they had the same behavioral pattern, appropriate herself the cat's accomplishments. "The cat is less anxious this week, I am less anxious this week," she sometimes told herself.

"It purrs way too much," said Joel. "I don't even understand the sound it makes. It's this low-frequency noise, with a little thump at the end. It's weird."

Mark made a joke. Alison explained that the cat was in heat and that she would take it to the vet to get it fixed soon. This, she knew, had very little chance of actually happening, as she had spent most of the money allocated for that on herself and cabs and other unaccounted-for, intangible expenses. She felt she had very little control over her budget, which went up or down or violently in all directions at once, as if on too much caffeine. She disliked money, not so much the process of having and spending as much as being unable to reconcile the disorganized person she was inside herself with the structured person she had to pretend being outside herself to obtain it, a kind of epic struggle between an inward independence and an outward conformity.

She sensed Mark switching position and then his arm covering her body. She became aware that they were getting closer and closer to one another, establishing a progressive intimacy. She had stopped drinking a few hours ago, was no longer drunk but also not yet hungover, a kind of a buffer zone between those two states.

On the laptop, Lynn browsed to a movie-streaming website. Mark joked about which movie to watch. Lynn suggested a movie and then Joel suggested another movie. The movie they put on was about two families getting into a feud because of the parents being zanier than their children. Alison tried to pay attention to the movie but became frustrated with the dialog and lost interest about five scenes into it.

She turned away from the screen and towards Mark. She began playing with his hand under the covers. She saw him moving his face within close vicinity of her face. She paid attention to the sound of him breathing. They remained in that position for a few seconds. She liked Mark, esteemed him even, liked his inner life, especially in comparison to Joel, whose dialogue with himself was probably the sound outer space makes, but wasn't attracted to him, felt an inability to love him, or herself, or anyone, and yet was tempted, still, to make out with him a little, just to see what that would feel like.

She also suspected that, if she were to do so, Joel would witness it, take it as a form of rejection, grieve her a little and then move on, restoring their friendship.

"It's a plan," thought Alison. It felt like a plan.

She moved in and kissed Mark, at first in a soft, polite way, but then with added intensity. On some level, she felt a little disappointed that he was letting her do so, in how easy it was for her to manipulate people like remote-controlled plastic helicopters, that all she had to do was make them believe she was helpless to her problems. She wasn't sure she remembered how to empower herself, act differently.

A few minutes later, they stopped kissing, changed positions and then reverted back to holding one another. In the room, no one was saying anything, except the movie, which was saying things to no one. She closed her eyes and, shortly after, fell asleep.

In the afternoon, she awoke alone in her room. She wasn't sure where everyone else was. She looked for her phone around the bed and located it on the nightstand and then checked for time. It was two thirty PM. She saw the cat leaping onto the bed. It was purring at a higher rate than usual. "Can you imagine if you had babies," she told the cat. "You would be a terrible mom. A party mom."

She drank water and ate microwaved pasta. She googled, "Cat always in heat" and read on a website that cats can go into heat simply from arousal. "Everything makes you horny," she told the cat. "Great." She decided to clean the living room, though wasn't sure why. She rarely cleaned. "One of these days I am going to make some man very happy four times per year," she thought while vacuuming.

She looked at pictures of boats and then Facebook and then pictures of boats again. After googling something unrelated, she landed on the Wikipedia entry for Karpman Drama Triangle. She read about two thirds of the page. She looked at the time again and saw that it was now seven forty PM. She didn't understand how that many hours had gone by. The cat began repeatedly asking for food. She endured the cat's complaints for about an hour, until Lynn returned home. She opened a can of wet food and poured the contents into a bowl. The cat ate too fast and then threw up on the floor.

"So you begged for food and then you ate so much that you puked on the floor," said Alison. "You need to think about your life."

She fell asleep in her bed at about one thirty AM. Three hours later, the doorbell awoke her. She hesitated before getting up but eventually did so. Downstairs, she saw Joel standing there and about to ring again. She felt confused. She opened the door for him. They went to her room. They talked on her bed for a little while.

The following morning, she felt overwhelmed, her thoughts in complete disorder, like a crime scene. She walked to the kitchen but couldn't get herself to make anything, not even coffee. She went back into hiding. A few hours later, she approached Mark on Facebook chat. She said hi and then typed sentences before he could respond.

"Something weird happened with Joel last night," typed Alison, "and by weird I mean he ambushed me and then confessed loving feelings for me. So right now I am having a mental meltdown or a panic attack or a panic meltdown. I haven't eaten anything today. There was a yogurt in the fridge but it was mixed berries. I wasn't sure I could handle more than one berry."

"Hi," typed Mark. "Wait, what happened?"

"He showed up at my house at four thirty in the morning," typed Alison. "It was super dramatic. The first thing he said was, 'I wish you loved me,' and then 'I want you to be a part of my life' and I was like, 'Oh, but I am' as in, 'I am your friend.' Then there was this pause and he went, 'No, I mean' and he told me that I am annoying but that he loves me anyway. I don't know what a person is supposed to do with that information. It was madness."

"What did you say?" typed Mark.

"I said I wanted to talk about it but not when he's drunk in my living room at five in the morning," typed Alison. "But now I don't know what to say to him. That's a friendship-ruining conversation, that's what that was."

"Maybe, but maybe not," typed Mark. "I mean, it can either ruin or deepen the friendship. Did you ask him why now? You guys have been friends for a while. He's had forever to develop feelings."

"I did do that," typed Alison. "He said it was normal to develop feelings for your close friends after a long period of time, but I am suspicious of it. He didn't look at me twice the entire time we've been close friends and now I am suddenly all that he needs. That's weird to me."

"He could be confused himself," typed Mark. "Do you know what your next move is?"

"No," typed Alison. "In a normal situation I would just ignore him for a while, but we're good friends, so that doesn't seem right. I guess we should meet and talk about it in person, but that's so fake, I'd rather not do that. We're going to sit at a table and say aloud things we've rehearsed in our heads and it's going to feel kind of like a job interview."

"Write him a letter," typed Mark.

"Maybe," typed Alison. "I don't like it when people do love declarations. My first thought is always, 'Well, that's nice of you,' like they just told me I smell good. Then I think about it and it's like I am trying to figure out what delusions made them say they love me."

"Maybe he's just in a rut," typed Mark. "You always look around you and scan the pool of available women and pick the least worst one. That's what love is. I am a romantic."

"I am a romantic too," typed Alison. "I don't know what's going on with him. I know for a fact he's been going on dates."

"The other option," typed Mark, "is to be a good friend to him, by understanding that he's not really in love with you as much as maybe in hate with himself or something, for hitting a romantic wall, which is hard on his ego. I don't know, I am just speculating. Down the road, you rejecting him could be positive, if he wants it to be."

•

"Go away," said Alison to the cat, who disliked being yelled at, produced a face, a moan, but then stopped, as if resigning itself, being the mature one. It jumped over an obstacle and then ran away in an overly dramatic manner, like a horse escaping a barn fire. Ten seconds later, it was playing with a ball and a string in the living room.

"She's so annoying," said Alison. "That cat has some serious emotional issues. One second she's all sweet and then she farts in someone's face. Why would you do that? She responds to hate with love and with love to hate."

"You're projecting," said Lynn. "Responds with hate. I am quite sure that's not the cat now. That's you. That's you with men."

"You with men when you're in heat," said Joel.

Joel heard Mark and Lynn laugh a little.

"It purrs way too much," said Joel. "I don't even understand the sound it makes. It's this low-frequency noise, with a little thump at the end. It's weird."

Joel was tired, felt as if all his thoughts were occurring in slow-motion. He heard Mark say something funny about the cat and then Alison laughing. He wasn't sure what their relationship was. He had seen them write little messages on each other's Facebook wall, communicating there, out in the open, as if defying privacy, just to see if anything bad could happen, like peeing with the door open. Though they seemed to have synergy, he felt unable to perceive him as anything more than a distraction for her.

Alison said she was going to take the cat to the vet soon, a plan she then debunked herself. She laughed at her own comment with her usual laugh, he noticed, cheerful but with an underlying sense of urgency, like a distress signal disguised as a laugh. On the laptop, Lynn browsed to a movie-streaming website. Mark joked about which movie to watch. Lynn suggested a comedy and then Joel suggested a dramedy. He hadn't seen that movie but pushed for it, thinking that Alison might like it. Within the first few scenes, she looked underwhelmed by it and later, turned away from the screen entirely.

He tried to pay attention but kept drifting in and out, closing and opening his eyes. He noticed that Lynn was falling asleep also. An unclear amount of time passed. He became aware of movement coming from Alison and Mark's side of the bed. He overheard ambiguous breathing. "They're making out," he thought. He wasn't sure what was going on exactly. He tried to think of other explanations but couldn't come up with anything plausible.

He felt them stopping and then switching positions. A few minutes went by with him being unable to do anything. He felt hurt, or fooled, or humbled, or betrayed, or spiteful, or something. He didn't know how to describe the feeling. He got up from the bed and walked away from the room. He put on his coat and shoes and left without saying anything. He walked home alone and thought mostly white noise.

The next day, he awoke in his apartment around one fifteen PM. He showered and then made scrambled eggs and a fruit salad. He tried working on a song with his acoustic guitar but couldn't concentrate. "Closeness is not measured in miles but in heart beats," he sang. "My heart is shattered like a vase."

Everything he tried felt trite and unsatisfying.

While making coffee, he thought about texting Alison. He

changed his mind. He opened Gmail and tried writing her a long email. After thirty minutes, he felt frustrated that the email wasn't communicating what he wanted it to communicate. He saved it as a draft. He checked to see if Alison was on Facebook chat and saw that she wasn't. He thought about texting her again but then messaged Will instead. He thought about her again. If, in the past, thinking of her would occur in uncaring or normal terms, now he couldn't help himself being charmed, smitten by her, which felt like a kind of oversimplification, as if he was deliberately focusing on the aspects of her he found attractive, and forgetting what he found dangerous or impossible.

An hour later, Will let himself in. He was wearing a winter hat with ear flaps and carrying two beers in a plastic bag. "Leftovers," he explained. Joel said he had half a bottle of gin they could share.

"I didn't know I was going to see her last night," said Joel, "and then she was drunk so I just wanted to make sure she was okay. We all ended up in her bed watching a movie. Me and her and her roommate and this guy, Mark, do you know Mark?"

"I only met him that one time," said Will.

"She made out with Mark," said Joel. "I was right there. It wasn't good. She does that all the time, she drinks too much and then loses control, and standards, and logic, so I am not that surprised, it's just, I don't know. I really need to talk to her."

"She's bad at making decisions," said Will. "Her decision process is full of holes. It's like a normal decision process but dipped in acid. That's why she needs you. You just need to be honest with her."

"I know," said Joel.

They sat in his living room and drank until twelve thirty or so, at which point Will mentioned that he had to get up in the morning and couldn't stay. After Will left, Joel couldn't see himself going to bed, had invested himself too much in the idea of confronting her.

He put on winter clothing and walked out of his apartment. He improvised a discussion with her in his head: strong statements being made aloud, tension, someone hugging a pillow, a peaceful resolution. The closer he got to her apartment, the less certain he felt about the peaceful resolution. He panicked, made a sudden left turn and then headed to a bar, to think it out some more. This wasn't him, he felt. He approached things head-on, obtained results, rewards.

At four thirty a.m., he rang the doorbell outside her apartment. He waited a little before ringing a second time. He was fairly certain the door was unlocked but rang for a third time anyway. He tried readjusting his hair using his reflection in the glass. A light was turned on. He saw Alison walking down the stairs and then staring at him. She opened the door, looked confused and asked why Joel was there. He said they needed to talk and asked if he could come in. She replied, "Okay" in a businesslike tone.

They sat on the bed in her room.

"Look," said Joel. "I don't know why we're not together. I want you to be a part of my life."

"Oh," said Alison, "but I am."

"No, I mean," said Joel. "I just wish you loved me. You're annoying and selfish but I don't know, I just, I love you anyway. I thought when we made out that there was an underlying agreement. It was more than just physical."

"I don't know," said Alison. "I mean, I don't know what to say. I just don't understand where this is coming from. We've been friends for, like, six years. Why is this happening now?"

"It's normal to develop feelings over time for people," said Joel. "And once you do, it's like a switch. You can't turn it off."

"Okay," said Alison, "but we should talk about this when you're not drunk and it's not five am. Do you want to sleep on the couch?"

"Do you think we could give this a shot," said Joel.

"Maybe," said Alison. "I mean, I'll think about it. Just go sleep on the couch for now."

"You're just saying that," said Joel. He paused. He felt a kind of internalized anger. He thought about kicking the chair next to her desk but managed to repress both the thought and the urge. "I know you. I know when you actually mean something and when you just say maybe as a way of saying no but without having to disappoint people. You would rather make out with some guy in front of me just to piss me off and avoid having to have a serious conversation with me."

"That's not what that was," said Alison.

"Whatever," said Joel. "You're a terrible person. I am going home."

•

"Go away," the cat heard. It jumped and then ran. It saw a ball and a string. It began playing with it.

**JORDAN
CASTRO**

THE APARTMENT

When I think about those six months or so, there are certain things I remember and certain things I don't. I remember, for example, the name of the cat everyone liked—Darby—but not the name of the other cat.

When there are two cats living in a house, the people living there usually like one of the cats a lot and the other much less.

•

I mostly remember the drugs. Painkillers stolen from Cory's dad who was on hospice, dying of brain cancer. Weed from Jason, or Terry's cousin's friend in California—ounces weighed on digital scales, sacked and sold to kids on campus, smoked out of bongs, bowls, and blunts. Lean from doctors when our throats got sore, throwing up while driving past a cop car after drinking eight ounces in an hour. Adderall from that obese girl on campus, or my friends from back home who practically gave the stuff to me. Vyvanse from Sammy, whose doctor prescribed him 90 a month, or that kid in the dorms who sold beer to underage kids. Xanax from Tiffany, until she moved to China, or Blake who sold the yellow four milligram bars in bulk, shipped from India. LSD, staying up for three days straight and losing my shit until Kara showed up with some Klonopin, marching around campus at 4 AM thinking *this is my town* and *I fucking own this campus*, peeing my initials (JC) onto the side of a church.

I remember the junkies. The way their words seemed to slide from their slanted mouths, slimy and slurred or coughed up and short. The way their legs bounced anxiously as they waited—always waited—for Jason to come through with Opana or oxy or heroin or whatever they could find that day. The way their zombie-like eyes shone through eyelids like slits, pupils small as pins. The way they scratched their skin obsessively, like there was something underneath it.

The way I too eventually spoke from the side of my mouth, tapped my foot to that haunting, inaudible rhythm, hung pictures of past with the pins of my eyeballs, scratched unendingly at that incessant, incurable itch.

I remember sleeping on the couch, on the rare occasion that I slept, and the way I felt when people said "This is a sweet place, man" or "Oh, I thought you lived here." I remember searching "effects of un-cleaned cat pee and feces" on Google, wondering if that was why I coughed so much, was so sick all the time.

I remember the first trip to the hospital, the second trip, and so on.

I remember listening to Gucci Mane, Three Six Mafia, and that band we liked to listen to while tripping—the one with the singer related to Sammy's friend's friend or whatever.

I remember the cops parking directly across the street from the apartment, pulling over every car that left the complex for "running the stop sign."

I remember the tapestry in the living room. How someone looked it up online and said it stood "for home, love, and family."

I remember how empty I became. How nothing meant anything and there were drugs to be done and there was money to be made. Thousands of dollars counted on the cigarette-burned carpet; guns next to the bed in the living room; friends disappearing, disappointed, gone.

•

Some things I can't remember include the address of the apartment, what happened when, and everything I talked about doing but never did.

GABBY
BESS

POST-SWALLOW

I have a friend who keeps telling me that she just wants to be a normal girl but then changes her mind and continues to act strangely, which I like and admire.

(Specifically the part about indecision and unwillingness to commit.)

I guess it's true that there are different types of girls that you can be at any given time.

At most, I was probably twenty four different girls at once.

I'm not a callous girl, or an unfeeling one, but I'm certainly not a lonely girl.

Or a sad one.

In the hotel room, I just wanted to be one of many.

I wanted each individual act of living on our bed to be anthologized, highlighted in their glut.

There is something in being where so many bodies have been that I can romanticize easily.

The sheets were neither mine nor yours but I ate them anyway.

We stood the excitement of ruining that which belonged to no one.

There was nothing on the walls—just prints of flowers and fruits from some generic retailer.

The title of my memoir will be *Still Life*.

You know as well as I do that to entertain a new person is just an exercise in amusement.

I could perform all my faces for you and it would be a nu romance.

But tru love? I don't know about that.

A forgetful girl, I left comfort on some shore that I sometimes imagined returning to—though it seemed more like a fantasy now.

I could never return because, for example, I started dreaming of eating pussy in libraries, consuming bodies and swallowing human hair.

I'm ruined and I belong to no one now.

There are strangers whose hair I eat on accident.

And then there is my own hair that I chew on deliberately.

And then there is your hair that I patiently swallow at night.

And then there are always other things that can't be accounted for and unfortunately, there is this new sadness that hangs over us.

But I ate the sadness.

And when it wouldn't fall away, I ate your body with the sky still attached to it.

And when you called me a curious girl, the whole room took blueish tint.

We became so quiet.

Our own bodies towered over us in the absence of other images on the wall.

To replace genuine feeling, I started performing this person who marveled at small things and I just wanted to touch everything at once.

I just wanted.

I was a Good Girl.

I just wanted.

I guess it's true that I probably pout more now than I did in 2012.

I guess it's just the new thing that I do in the bathtub or at a restaurant when I'm subtly pushing my tits together and you're not noticing.

I just let the juice from the watermelon drip down my fingers and I licked them clean.

I threaded my wet fingers through the handle of the mug that said *#1 WIFE*, though I didn't deserve it.

Oh well.

I just hope that when you picture my body, I am two fingernail painting emojis and a knife emoji.

POST-BODY

After a while, it was harder to put our bodies together.

You became liquid and started falling asleep before midnight.

I liked you better when you pulled my arms toward you, accepting of what I wanted to give.

I liked you best when you gave my body direction.

   But I was also to blame for the unceremonious change of matter.

At the time, I was occupied with the skin on my face.

I was always occupied with some body part and then it happened to be the whole of my face,

I guess, due to it being summertime and the air being the way it is in summertime—

   Like spilled fruit juice, slow evaporating, sticky, unassailable once set in motion.

And similarly, there is no defense against this type of air, only damage control.

The humidity was hitting my face in flecks, bringing my mascara away with it.

   When left out in the sun for too long, the beautiful melts and becomes less beautiful.

Together we're learning the lifespan of things.

Like you, I became liquid.

I stopped wearing heavy makeup and every picture was a test of will.

I never felt clean.

I would move my body across the sidewalk while the air was wet, causing my hair to frizz and my body to affect a look of damp insanity.

In the summer I can look sexual and hungry; The men can tell that I am after something.

> Wait, let me figure out how to explain the summer,
> I was many places so it gets confusing.

> I was in Baltimore, Philadelphia, New York,

>> (My mother warns me of the city
>>> *Because it is my own fault.*)

Virginia.

Later I was in London.

> In London, we made a whole trip of visiting the house that Sylvia Plath died in—it was painted all purple with a plaque on the outside that said her name and the dates that she lived in the house.

> We just sat outside and talked about her being dead.

It was awful.

I was sweating in Baltimore, Philadelphia, New York, Virginia.
Later I was sweating in London.

Sometimes the sweat felt satisfying and perverted
underneath my shirt where it collected under my tits,
becoming my only strength.

I was sweating through my cotton underwear.

That summer you would close your eyes and become farther
away and I would do things just to feel nasty

Or to indulge in a character.

I took on the role of the exhausted narcissist,
Too tried to try to figure out whether I am understanding
concepts the way I am supposed to.

I understood the world in the way that I needed to.
For example, I read Gertrude Stein and it only confirmed
my own genius.

It feels great to be one of the most important artists of the
21st Century.

My childhood has something to do with this but I can't remember
my childhood so I won't bore you with those facts.

Not to lie, but I remember being a child and playing hide-and-seek.
I would just run to a wall, turn to face it and close my eyes.
I wasn't even hidden, but I really thought I was.

To be bodiless and unheld to expectations is my filthy, sexless

dream but I will always be the arm
>To which you hold yours against, to feel shocked at how pale
>you are,
>To make you wish for summer

So if I can't become bodiless, I will become the ultimate body 4 u.

>If I only try harder I can find the part of me that can unfold
>to stretch farther—like an unassuming wooden dining table
>that could seat four and then six, for parties.

POST-LABOR

I googled Henri Rousseau for no reason other than boredom.
    There was something to value in learning
    And the goal now was to cultivate a curiosity.

I was always drawing parallels to the past.
Stealing from artists became a lifestyle.
My biggest embarrassment would be to think that I was original.

I remembered looking at Rousseau's jungle paintings for the first
time in a museum, knowing that he had never left Paris.

I imagined him painting these foreign landscapes when he got
home from his job as a toll collector—dreaming of a more exciting life.

My fault is that I can't divorce the artist from the art object.

    I have this obsession.

I like to look at great art because I know that it was the result
intense longing.

Viewing them, Rousseau's jungle paintings took on the absurdity
of a Frenchman trying to imagine the Other.

I sat in bed, staring at my laptop, trying to remember what a
jungle looked like other than green.

Though he was poor and ignored until death, there are now
1,810,000 results that come up when you search for Henri

Rousseau.

I have these delusions of being known for my work while I'm alive but I'll settle for being missed.

I found comfort when I read the words, "The most important thing you should know about Henri Rousseau is that he had a completely boring life—with the exception that he became convinced, somewhere along the way, that he was a superbly talented artist."

I realized (I was always *realizing* and it was exhausting. I felt stuck on the hamster wheel of my mind, *realizing* that I was just a dumb animal.) that there is a point when we decide what to specialize in: ideas or labor.

When I started concerning myself with ideas every act of physical labor was suffering.

I wanted to quit my job and get serious about my art but I also knew, that practically, the valued labor of my body causes the money in my bank to increase with hours worked.

> It's sex work, an unfortunate reality.
> I can touch the effect of my body through the plastic.

The effect of my body is $8.64 an hour.

At work I learned that the mop goes through the rung of the bucket and expends what it can.

I know this motion and if you asked me what I felt when I watched the gush of dirty water release from the head of the mop I would say that I felt glorious.

And if you asked what glorious felt like I would say that glorious feels like my hand against the wooden mop handle, displaying all the ugly, incongruous shades of brown.

It is always surprising that two socks, matched perfectly out of the dryer, don't have a faint glow pulsating around them.

Something out of place is now where it belongs, you see *this* is glorious.

If the world has beauty to offer me, I will accept it.

I am interested in a different way of living.

The hues of brown that can infinitely exist will remain wonderful to me.

Every day that I go to my job the touch of the lonely arm increases.
It is exciting to work so thoroughly with just my hands.
I can bite into the juicy fruit of my labor.

At a party once, a writer friend of mine started pointing to girls in the room, other writers:

"You know how Emma makes her money? You know how Lindsey makes her money?"

Sex work.

We're all selling ourselves. Our ideas. Our labor. Our time. Our bodies. It doesn't matter anymore.

I felt sick that night and couldn't sleep.

ALEXANDER J ALLISON

A NEW PERSON

My admission was immediate, unchallenged. The facility made exceptions. I renounced my name, possessions and liberties. I was allocated a private room—it was proposed as a temporary arrangement. At that point, no ward would have me.

Information was fed back slowly, as fragments. I was not yet accustomed to being the exception. There was still much to learn. My new life was reluctant to reveal itself. I had to expose it.

I spent those first days nude, learning my new shape. I trained my hands to forget, to accept the new smoothness. Though the act was complete, it seemed important that my body should commit. I had betrayed it. Only now could it catch with the plan.

Within a week, my soreness had passed. Dressings were applied two, not five times a day. Ablutions became thorough and regular. The facility's nurses insisted on the importance of avoiding infection. They believed that I had suffered enough. The bathroom was my safe place. I learned a new method for peeing.

There, I would shave with a surgeon's hand, picking off every hair. From a distance, I looked to the mirror: a ghoul, ridiculous. I learned to do without eyebrows, to manage the subtleties of plastic expression. I was not yet a human.

In spite of our agreement, they subjected me to a rota of professional visitors: psychologists, psychoanalysts, psychotherapists, a dietician, two dermatologists and a plastic surgeon. In memory, these figures blend to a slurry of pitiful expressions, cheap assumptions and inappropriate questions.

Days merged. Through the nights, I throbbed. I trained myself to sleep in new positions. My limbs popped and groaned. New flesh wept through the creams and padding.

The professionals addressed me in careful terms, keen to honor the seriousness of my actions. They insisted on calling it sacrifice. I informed them it was progress. I was baptized Robin, on the emphasis that I was not expected to self-identify with the title. It was purely for their convenience, for the staff's charts and the ward listings. Robin: unisex, non-offensive and simple. They are always keen to simplify. They still insist on knowing what's best for Robin.

I embraced privacy, training myself to move outside of gender. I discovered how it had infected every muscle, every reflex. Gender shaped the way I ate, the way I stood, smoked, grimaced. I knew that all of this was evidence. I felt sure it could be conquered.

In that room, I sculpted a robot from flesh. The professionals recorded my development. Photographs were taken. They became comfortable in my naked presence. Before me, their genders swelled. I had much to relinquish.

I was informed of life on the wards, of mounting interest and suspicion among other residents. The professionals insisted that cohabitation was their most useful rehabilitative tool. I contended that Robin was still being established. In compromise, it was decided that a few residents should come to me.

I treated the meetings as practice. These were people who didn't know the details. The idea of me made them uncomfortable. But I felt prepared. My story was thoroughly rehearsed.

Before the first, they put me in clothes. Following sustained isolation and nudity, this felt foreign and abrasive. Through material, my skin ached for the air. Their clothes hung off of me, my figure indistinct.

Residents were seated at arm's length, taking turns to lead the interview.

"But, how did you manage it? On your own, I mean. Did you use a saw or a knife, or what?"

"I can't understand why you chose to eat it all. Surely that wasn't your immediate priority. Did you want to hide your old gender before someone found you?"

"Why is the facility treating you as a problem? Seems to me that you're no more fucked than the rest of us."

"So, what are you?"

JANEY
SMITH

FOR THE WINGS OF A DOVE

I dragged on the street a big bag of frozen french fries.

The night was cold. I wrapped my hands in blue plastic bags. I wrapped my sides with green. I put white ones on my shoes. I wrapped myself in all these bags. Red ones too. I was covered with bags. The bags felt warm to me. So, I sat in the bags. My pigeon looked at me. My pigeon looked out onto the street like maybe he wondered why.

A man came by. Another one. Then all these men. There kept being more of them. Then it stopped. It was lunch.

My pigeon had a bread. Not a big one but a little bread. A crumb or a part of one. My pigeon ate the little bread. I said "Oh, look." I pressed my thumb on a piece of gum, left a fingerprint that was dark and dirty—a blacked-out scene of birds in flight at night. My pigeon blinked at it, though there was no wind, studied it like it meant something.

I ran after my pigeon saying PIGEON! PIGEON! . . . I ran after him. I ran.

One day, a man gives me a dollar. I say "Thank you," and hold up my pigeon to him. The man says "No, thank you." I hold up my pigeon some more like "here, take it." But, the man says no, walks away. I turn my pigeon to me. It blinks at me. I scratch my head a lot. He makes sounds in his sleep, otherwise nothing. On that night, I walk around with my pigeon tucked under my coat. In the cool, I think maybe something's wrong with pigeon.

I wrap my pigeon in foil to keep warm. It blinks its eyes at me. My pigeon looks like baked potato. I wonder about that sometimes.

He hops on curb. He hops off it.

I live in a beautiful country. As you can see it is spring time. People think nothing happens here. It's so peaceful. But a lot happens here. In the rain, I hold my pigeon beneath stacks of soggy cardboard. He is not cold. I say to the wind that will hear me "Pigeon."

I say it again and again, to the wind that will hear me.

11.

MICHAEL
HEALD

THE GUY FROM SACRAMENTO

Looking down at myself, it seems, on the one hand, rather embarrassing that I could have expended so much nervous energy over the past few months, raised so many objections and made such a fuss about visiting Miss Ophelia; on the other, it seems equally embarrassing to finally be here, to be standing in a dungeon, wearing nothing but two nipple clamps and a condom which, despite Miss Ophelia's frequent reminder that safety is the first rule of play, seems to serve the purpose of mocking my state of complete unarousal. April, still wearing her work clothes—bright blue Chucks, slacks, and a comfy-looking hoodie—is off to the side taking notes. Miss Ophelia, who lives in an apartment upstairs, has agreed to start renting the dungeon to April on a per customer basis. Part of the rent, she explains, will cover her fee for supervising the sessions. She will be listening in via a hidden microphone, and won't hesitate to step in if things ever get out of hand. Miss Ophelia is in her mid-forties, and hasn't dressed up for the occasion. She's wearing a sweater and jeans and glasses, and as she reaches for the nipple clamps, she tugs playfully on one of my half dozen chest hairs. Her touch is tender, almost grandmotherly, and I'm having trouble imagining her clientele. If getting hurt is what gets you off, wouldn't you look for somebody a little more intimidating, a little more Cruella de Ville? Now she takes the clamps and pulls on them a little more energetically than she pulled on my chest hair. One at a time, she asks, or should we do them together?

Nothing much has changed since childhood. Instead of my mother nagging me to leave my bedroom and take advantage of the weather, it's April dragging me away from the computer because we have a responsibility to take advantage of the city. We're fresh out of college but she's already infiltrated a sizable community of sex-positive individuals, many of whom are twice our age. Whenever I join the crew at the bar she invariably reports back to me that they're surprised by how vanilla I seem, and no matter how many times she purrs *little do they know how dirty you are* I can't help but wonder if my kinks aren't a little traditional for her scene. One night she comes home from watching a movie over at her friends Luke and Ashley's, and I ask how the night went and she tells me oh, it was pretty mellow, everyone was just kind of hanging out on the couch drinking beer, but the movie ended up being kind of stupid, and at some point Ashley ended up lying across their laps, wearing less and less clothing, and eventually she ended up getting fisted. It was very sweet, April says, everyone was just lying there, chatting away. When it's my turn to account for my evening, instead of telling her that I powered through another hundred pages of Michael Chabon, I say hang on, I'm not sure I understand the physics—whose hand ended up inside Ashley?

I want to be okay with everything. I tell her I am okay with everything.

I can't stop looking back at the beginning of last summer. It's early June, just after graduation, and we are driving across the country. After three, four, five days, we are no longer lamenting the broken stereo or trying to read Michelle Tea over the roar of the semis. We are no longer buying ice for the cooler, no longer trying to get the cigarette stink out of the motel rooms. We are not stuck in Lodi again, we are just singing the song. We are almost there yet. All around us the suburbs are falling away. We are climbing up this final little rise and there, off in the distance, under a dollop of fog, is the city. Cue the string section, the high-fives, the discussion about the people we will become. The plan: to be so much ourselves, so full of whatever we are that the city will wrap us up in its pastel-colored heart and never let go. They don't know we're coming, I say. They don't have a clue, she says. I tell her it's

1967, or no, it's 1956, and I am Kerouac, Ginsberg, and Gilbert all rolled into one. I am a spliff, I say. You are ridiculous, she says. At eighty miles per hour, I merge into the carpool lane. For a moment the road is wide open, and it occurs to me that I could make an entire mixtape about this thing we are doing, moving to California, and as I begin sorting out the track listing, she begins, not for the first time, to tell me things that belong on a very different mixtape. I hear what she's saying but I don't really believe her. What I mean to say is that of course I believe her, of course I understand that she is interested in these things, but deep down I'm confident that this is all temporary, like she's talking about going to the Olympics or something.

Let's do them together, I say. Smart boy, says Miss Ophelia, and she steadies herself like a gunfighter and reaches back up. Finally, here's some of the flair I was expecting from a dominatrix. But when she yanks them off me, it's nothing special, I just feel like she's pinched me, and to be honest, I'm a little disappointed, but mostly relieved. I smirk at April, who is always making fun of my tolerance for pain, and she smirks back at me, and suddenly I'm on my knees. Pain blooms on my tongue, in my balls, on the soles of my feet. Pain is exponential, Miss Ophelia explains, it doesn't plateau. You did good, April says. Miss Ophelia tells me that if I'm going to finish myself off to please keep the condom on, and I'm like, does it look like I'm going to finish myself off? After I get dressed Miss Ophelia takes us out for spaghetti and April talks excitedly about her first client, a guy coming in from Sacramento this weekend. He's coming into the city because he wants to hurt her. My girlfriend is not a dominatrix yet. She will be learning the ropes as a professional submissive—she will be the one wearing the nipple clamps—and instead of Miss Ophelia in her sweater and jeans and glasses she will be sharing the dungeon with a guy from Sacramento in a three-piece suit. In my head the guy from Sacramento is always wearing a three-piece suit. Looking down I realize I've finished my spaghetti. As I push my plate away, I can't help but think about how the guy from Sacramento will be taking the same highway we took back in June and how the guy from Sacramento will probably need the condom.

April spends six months in the dungeon. During that time she has tons of cash and takes us out for fancy dinners and shows and hotels. Our sex is better than ever and, like the Olympics, often ends in tears. I never really see the bruises until afterwards. And then I do see them. They're all I can see, and they never seem to go away.

I wish I could tell you that I've finally learned my lesson, that I finally understand that people really do mean what they say. I wish I could tell you that I'm keeping out of the kind of trouble I got into in San Francisco, that things are different for me up here. And they are, in a way: these days, the trouble seems to happen in kitchens, not dungeons. The trouble starts because you and I have been drinking, we have been out, and now we are back at my place, in my kitchen, and you are telling me very carefully that the smart thing to do would be for you to call Radio Cab. The trouble is that when you do call Radio Cab, there is a recording that says there are sixteen calls ahead of you, *sixteen*, and something about the size of that number makes it feel okay—maybe even gentlemanly—for me to lean in and kiss you—and now there are thirteen calls ahead of you, eleven, ten, nine, seven calls ahead, how great is this countdown, it's like a spin-the-bottle moment right here in adulthood—and right around four calls ahead of you you gasp *but I can't be doing this* and I'm like *but you are* and the trouble continues until the cab arrives and big surprise, that's not the end of it, there's trouble the next day, and the next, and here you are, back in my apartment, and you are telling me that we really can't kiss each other anymore, there's someone else, in fact it's messier than that, and after telling me this we're both so relieved to have it out in the open that we decide to get high, and we finally leave the kitchen, and we go over to the bedroom window, and we slide open the window, and we press up against each other and blow smoke out the window until everything is brittle and just out of reach and even then, try as I might, I can't think of anything I would rather be doing than standing here not being with you. So I don't know. Maybe I do like pain.

JULIET
ESCORIA

DUST PARTICLES

Mom took the divorce money and moved us to a condo the summer before third grade. There were hardly any kids in the complex and school hadn't started yet so I didn't have anyone to play with. It was looking to be a really boring summer. She wouldn't let me go to the pool or the playground or anywhere fun alone.

But a couple weeks in and there was a girl at the pool. She was my age and real little with red hair. Her name was Katie. She taught me to do handstands at the bottom of the pool and later I showed her how to bake cookies. We both liked Ninja Turtles over Barbies, and knew how to ride our bikes without training wheels. We decided to be best friends.

Then one day after we'd just gotten back from the pool, Katie told me we were going to play girlfriend and boyfriend. I didn't know what that meant and she said that I'd find out. She said it in a way that made it seem like it would be exciting. Then she told me to get on the bed.

All of a sudden and she was on top of me. I asked her what the heck she was doing.

"I'm your boyfriend," she said in a growly voice, "and you're supposed to like this."

She put her mouth over mine before I could say anything else and stuck her tongue in. She pointed it around my mouth, swirling in circles, and it made my teeth feel cold. Her eyes were closed like they did on TV but I left mine open so I could watch her. It looked like she was an alien and she was eating off my face. Her hair was still wet and it tickled my shoulders.

"Okay," she said after a bit. "It's time to have sex now."

I didn't really understand how sex worked yet because I wasn't allowed to watch rated R movies, but I was pretty sure you needed a man and a woman to do it. I didn't want to say anything though, because I wasn't sure and I didn't want to look dumb. If she stopped liking me then I wouldn't have anyone to play with and I wouldn't know anyone when I started at my new school.

We took off our clothes and stood there in silence for a moment. The lights were off and the blinds were closed. One of the slats toward the bottom had broken, and the sun shone through the gap, the beam ending next to my foot. I watched the dust dance around. I'd learned last year in school that dust was mostly particles of skin, and I learned we breathed in a pound of dust each month. I figured out that both of these facts put together meant we were always breathing in people. I looked at Katie's naked body and told myself that the skin I was looking at would be dust someday. I looked at her naked body and told myself I was already breathing her in.

"Get back on the bed," she told me.

"How are we supposed to have sex?" I asked.

She looked at me like I was very stupid. "We're supposed to rub our privates together," she said. "How do you not know that?"

I really didn't want to play this game anymore but it seemed like it was too late to stop. I got back on the bed and closed my eyes. I wanted to pretend that I was asleep, or maybe not even asleep, but dead. I made my whole body limp. Katie crawled on top of me and moved around until one of her legs was between mine and vice versa. She started thrusting at me and making grunting sounds and something warm and strange started happening between my legs. I wanted to jump up but sleeping people don't move so I tried to stay there and I tried to stay still. But I couldn't. I just couldn't. I couldn't keep playing the game. I pushed her away and flew off the bed. My bathing suit was on the floor and I picked it up and ran into the bathroom and locked the door. I got dressed and then I stared at myself in the mirror for a long time, until my eyes became just eyes and my mouth no longer looked like my own.

When I got out, I expected Katie to be dressed but she wasn't. She was still sitting on the bed. "You kicked me in the stomach," she said, "when you pushed me off of you."

"I have to go home," I said, and then I went. I didn't look at her as I left the room and I didn't say good-bye. I didn't mean to be rude, it just happened that way. It wasn't until after I got home that I realized I hadn't even apologized for kicking her.

I decided I probably shouldn't play with her for a while but I didn't hold out very long. It was my mom's fault, I guess. She came into the room one day and I was just lying there on the carpet biting at my cuticles. It was one of my bad habits. I don't know how long I'd been there but it was long enough that they'd started to bleed. "Good God," my mom said. "Go outside and play or something. Go play with Katie."

I listened to her because I was really, really, really bored. I was so bored that I'd kind of forgotten why I'd decided I didn't want to play with Katie in the first place. I stopped biting my cuticles and went to Katie's house. We played Little House on the Prairie and I got to be Laura. Afterward, her mom made us quesadillas. It was all so nice and fun that I re-decided I liked her.

A couple weeks went by and school started. Katie was in a different class but I still played with her more than anybody else because she lived so close. When my birthday came, Katie gave me one of those necklaces that is half a jagged heart. Mine said *Best* and hers said *Friends*. I'd always wanted one of those. I had imagined the day I would get one for a long time. But this wasn't like I'd imagined it. In my head the necklace was silver like the moon, and the necklace Katie gave me was golden like the sun. In my head the best friend and I could talk to each other with looks because we knew the thoughts in each other's heads so well. In real life sometimes I would catch Katie staring off into space, completely unaware of anything going on around her, and I had no idea where she was in her mind or what she was thinking. All I knew was she was somewhere different than I was, and the place was somewhere I would never be, and that I didn't even want to be there.

I went to her house one day near Halloween. We were supposed to work on our costumes. Katie's mom had a big sewing machine and she was going to help us. We had just seen *The Wizard of Oz*. Katie wanted to be the Tin Man, but a Tin Girl, and I wanted to be a Wicked Witch.

Her dad answered the door. He was hardly ever home, and he scared me a little because he never smiled. "Linda's at the store, I think," he said. Linda was Katie's mom. I never called her Linda, though. It felt weird for her to be called that; it made her sound like a stranger. "I have no idea when she'll be back. Katie's upstairs in her room."

I walked up the stairs. I was feeling disappointed. I wanted a scary witch dress and funny witch stockings and now I wasn't sure if I'd get them at all. I pictured my mom and me going to CVS, looking for a witch costume, one of the store-bought ones that's itchy and doesn't fit right, except all that was left were some Power Rangers and a ninja. No Wicked Witch for me.

When I got upstairs I saw Katie standing in her doorway, waiting. She wasn't wearing anything except for big gold sunglasses I guess she'd stolen from her dad. Her hand was on her hip. "There's my little girl," she said in a weird voice. It was like she was acting something out of a movie.

My heart started pounding. It felt like something very bad was happening.

"Katie," her dad's voice came from behind me. I guess he'd followed me up the stairs and I hadn't noticed. He was talking in a quiet voice but even though it was quiet I still felt afraid. "What are you doing?" he asked her. He seemed really mad, mad in a way like this was something they had already talked about.

She hadn't moved, wasn't even trying to cover herself. Her hand was still on her hip. "It's so hot," she said. "I was hot."

It wasn't hot in the house and all three of us knew it. I was so embarrassed but I knew I wasn't doing anything wrong. Except her father was staring at me like I was. It was like he was trying to figure out what I was thinking, trying to figure out what he should do to me, how I deserved to be punished. I didn't know where I was supposed to look or what I should say so I kept quiet and stared at my shoes but I could feel my cheeks burning like they were on fire.

"Put your dress on," he said finally.

I heard shuffling and I imagined Katie getting dressed, but I refused to look away from the ground. It didn't feel safe yet. Suddenly I didn't want to be a Wicked Witch anymore. I wanted to be anything else, anything at all, anything that wasn't made by Katie's mom and also anything that wasn't wicked. I'd go be a Power Ranger. I'd love wearing my itchy store-bought costume. I'd love wearing my pink plastic mask.

I looked up again when the shuffling stopped. Katie was wearing clothes now, but the two of them were standing in the same spots as before: Katie in the doorway, with her hand on her hip, her father across from her, both of them looking at each other in a way that made me feel like things were being said between them that I never could or would want to imagine.

I looked down at the floor again. I just wanted to be safe. The carpet upstairs was fluffy and dark blue. I remembered how one day, when I'd first met Katie, back before anything bad had happened, her mother had gotten a new microwave. We took the box upstairs and pretended it was a ship and the carpet was a sea and we were sailors. I wanted to be sailors again.

The carpet had fresh vacuum lines in it, but there was a thin strip running right below the molding that was dusty and grey, which I guess was where the vacuum couldn't reach. The dusty strip was dust but it was also pieces of people. There was some of my skin in there, mixed with Katie's skin, mixed with her dad's skin, mixed with Linda's. Even if I left right now and never came back, some of me would stay right there in that carpet. Some of them would be in my lungs, and some of me would be floating in that air, waiting to be sucked in.

JEREME
DEAN

IN RETROSPECT, THE DAYS WERE FRESH AND EASY

- Born 1977 to seventeen year old Crystal Dean/Alfred Gomes (late twenties) at Chapman Hospital in Orange, CA. Alfred was in prison for armed robbery/heroin possession and not present for my birth. Iris Sexton, grandmother, was present.
- Lived with Crystal/Iris in several low income apartments located in Anaheim, CA.
- Cypress Community College magazine photographs me playing alone in the day care sandbox. Crystal was in class.
- Earliest memory was crying on an ottoman because Crystal was "going out." Iris tried to console me. I remember thinking, "You are not my mother. I just want my mom."
- Iris shared sips of beer while I sat on her lap before bed. Iris was an alcoholic. I remember thinking I felt loved.
- Visited my Great Grandmother, Velma Barkley, often at her house in Hesperia, CA.
- Velma had a blue kitty named Suki. I fed the kitty her wet food in the mornings. Velma painted a picture of me feeding Suki.
- First memory of my schizophrenic uncle, Michael Dean, at Velma's house in Hesperia. He clutched me in his lap causing Crystal to panic. Mike flung her across the room after she attempted to rescue me, bouncing her skull off the corner of a coffee table splitting the forehead open. Velma took us to a hospital Emergency Room. Sat in the sterile cold of the waiting room feeling helpless. Stared at the drying blood covering my mother's young face.
- Discovered a black widow in the bathroom of Velma's house. She captured the spider with a square of toilet paper, crushed it in her hand. I remember thinking she was mighty.

- Often hunted alone in Velma's backyard for desert rocks to paint.
- Friday was Bingo Night for Iris/Velma. They would bring home a box of Cracker Jacks if they won. The tiny prize inside the box made me happy. I remember feeling excitement trying to stay up until they came home.
- Crystal worked/schooled day and night. Almost always home alone. Panic attacks start.
- Played in the neighborhood until 11pm with no supervision.
- Mike began sleeping in an abandoned car in our garage.
- Velma diagnosed with brain cancer. Iris had been searching for hours when she finally found me playing with paint cans in a neighbor's garage. My skin was browned by the stain of varnish when she delivered the news.
- Family outings with Velma. Fished for the first time. Frightened by Velma and avoided her physical touch. I did not understand what brain cancer was.
- Velma dies. Crystal/Iris hysterical after hearing the news. I could not comprehend why.
- Velma's funeral. People kept asking me if I was okay. I felt apathetic. I was okay. I saw her corpse in the coffin. Started crying and thought "I will never be loved again." Tried to put my fist through a car window several times. People were laughing and joking at the wake. Sat in the back alley to avoid the liars.
- Began first grade. Walked alone to school. Made a wrong turn down a busy street and became lost. Felt intense anxiety and began crying. Arrived at school two hours late.
- Crystal moved frequently. Went to five schools in first grade. I did not have friends.
- Crystal forgot me in a Lucky's grocery store. I paced each aisle. She drove back to find me trembling in the dairy section.
- Cops swarmed my apartment courtyard on a Saturday morning. I walked outside to witness SWAT yelling at a Mexican man positioned on the second floor. The Mexican was shirtless, shoeless and covered in blood. He waved a large kitchen

knife. I ran back inside to window watch. SWAT shot him dead in the apartment he lived in.

- Mike baby sat me and another girl (daughter of one of Crystal's friends). Crystal went dancing at American Bandstand. Mike read Hustler on the couch and mumbled to himself. Played doctor in my bedroom with the girl. I did not see her again.
- Crystal and her friend Starla took me to a drive-in to watch *Children of the Corn*. They neglected to explain it was a horror movie. The final car scene terrified me. Had anxiety walking past cars at night until my middle twenties.
- Woke from sleep to hear Satan screaming and moaning. Crystal was watching *The Exorcist* on the living room television. This was the beginning of my insomnia.
- Mike randomly apologized for doing that "thing" to me. I didn't understand what he meant. I have no memories of abuse.
- Lit an apartment building basement on fire with some neighborhood boys. It was an accident. Sort of.
- Crystal/me would frequent the Anaheim mall. She would hand me a $5 dollar allowance to spend in the arcade while she shopped in the mall for hours.
- One mall visit I felt very anxious about being alone and shit my pants. Sat on a parking lot bench for three hours waiting for Crystal to return.
- Crystal dropped me off at a Filipino woman's house. She told me I was going to live there a while. I ate rice every night.
- Started wetting the bed.
- A goofy looking white lady visited me. I had never met her before. She said she was a friend of Crystal. Her name was Denise. We went to McDonald's every weekend. She talked about God the entire time.
- Denise stopped visiting without notice. I still had not seen Crystal in months.
- The Filipino family wanted me to leave. Crystal picked me up in her car. She was living in a Motel room five minutes from where I was living. She left me alone in the Motel room. I

took the cover off the air conditioner, stuck my finger against the rotating blade. The cut practically severed the tip off.

- Ninth birthday Crystal took me to Chino Prison to meet my father Alfred for the first time. I spent most of the time watching a vending machine rotate food. I was wearing a pin with the words "kiss me it's my birthday."
- Conjugal weekend at Chino Prison. Crystal/Alfred/me vacationed in a trailer on the prison campus. Made shrinky dinks alone while Crystal/Alfred had sex. Alfred taught me how to throw a proper punch.
- Crystal casually informed me Alfred was out of prison and I was going to live with him. She dropped me off at his apartment in Santa Ana the next night. My half-brother Alfred, Jr. and half-sister (I can't recall her name) were already living there. I didn't know I had siblings prior to our introduction.
- Alfred was not allowed to have children in the apartment. He would leave us at Hart Park in Orange every day before work (around 7am) and pick us up after work (around 6pm). We did not get money or food. Called random numbers collect from the park pay phone to pass the time.
- Alfred, Jr. informed me Alfred was present for his birth.
- Crystal arrived to take me back with her. Alfred dangled her over his second floor balcony and beat her for it.
- Crystal brought me to Iris's house to live.
- Enrolled in little league baseball. Walked alone an hour and a half to practice and an hour and a half back home. Families would drive by and wave.
- Iris's alcoholism worsened. Each evening she drank a cup of brandy and chased It with beer. Then the yelling would start. Most nights she would retire to her bedroom and moan cry for her dead mother.
- Alfred made an unannounced visit to treat me to ice cream. We went to a house to buy heroin instead. He drove back to his apartment. Instructed me to stay in the car. Four hours passed. I was shivering from the cold night when he came

down from his apartment. He let me lay in bed with him for about ten minutes to warm up. Alfred had never showed affection towards me before. I felt really happy falling asleep next to him. Then he told me to "get the fuck out of his bedroom and go to sleep in my own bed." This was the last moment of my life I shared with him. Iris retrieved me from the apartment in the morning while he slept. There was never any ice cream.

- Iris began working graveyard shifts. I spent my nights alone watching television. We only saw each other on the weekends.
- Crystal would visit once a month with her new boyfriend Dutch. Dutch was a 6'6 350lb biker.
- A few times I would stay with Crystal/Dutch at their biker house. There were nine or ten additional bikers living there. Constant drug use and leather clothing around me. First time I saw marijuana, it was packed in gallon size plastic freezer bags.
- Crystal/Dutch got married. Dutch sold his Harley motorcycle and bought a truck with a camper on the back.
- Crystal/Dutch decided to move to Oregon where Dutch had a machinist job waiting for him. They took me with them against my will. Listened to The Beastie Boys "License to Ill" twenty-four times during the drive to Oregon.
- Dutch's new job was graveyard shift. Crystal and I slept in a sleeping bag at a local Oregon park for the first three days while he worked. There were ducks in a small pond at the park. I would pretend I was one of them to fall asleep.
- Moved to a month to month motel in Gladstone, OR. The motel was owned by an Indian family. The smell of spice was strong.
- Watched *Spaceballs* twenty-five times on HBO during the summer. Walked around Gladstone alone.
- Moved into a house in a poor neighborhood in Southeast Portland, OR. We had no furniture and used an igloo ice chest for a refrigerator.
- Sat on the hardwood floor in my bedroom for hours after

school until I fell asleep.

- We got some furniture/refrigerator.
- Crystal worked graveyard shift. I did not see her often. Dutch started working the early day shift.
- Dutch became depressed. He would sit in the chair in the living room and glower at me. He would not allow me to turn the TV on or eat. Days would go by before he would say a word to me.
- Frequently in trouble at school.
- A boy on a bicycle rode past my school room and pointed a loaded pistol at the class. This was the first time a gun was pointed at me.
- Had one friend, Robbie Krietzer, who lived next to the middle school. I stayed the entire three months of summer at his house without going home. I did not tell Crystal where I was.
- Robbie and I played *Legend of Zelda* for 70 hours straight until we finished the game. Had a serious case of Nintendo thumb.
- Went back home the day before school started. Crystal did not seem to notice my arrival.
- Robbie attempted suicide because he thought boys were mean to him. I saw Robbie one time afterwards. He moved away.
- Started spending time with a boy named Wally. Wally's parents were separated and both heroin addicts.
- Played dungeons and dragons with Wally and his skinhead friends. The skinheads did not like me much. I fought a lot with them.
- Wally's dad paid me to rip apart wood pallets in his backyard.
- Started getting bullied by a kid who lived on my street. My house sat on a dead end with a cemetery behind. He lived at the front of the street. I had to walk past to go or come home. At school he left me physically alone. He would punch me in the face when he caught me walking to or from my house. I would try not to leave my room and would cry from the anxiety of getting beaten.
- Wally attacked me over a joke I made at school. I did not fight back because I was scared to lose the only friend I had. Wally

and I were not friends for a long length after.

- Crystal and Dutch would fight the nights they were both at home (think it was Tuesdays). Crystal would scream at Dutch and hit him until he would show emotion. I watched Crystal punch a plate glass window and cut her arm in several places. Another night, Dutch broke Crystal's toe trying to drag her outside to prevent Crystal from hitting him anymore.

- Existential terror started. When alone, often while in bed for the night, had panic attacks over my imminent death and resulting nothingness. I could stop the panic attacks by crying, shaking my head violently left to right, and screaming "no no no" repeatedly. I began elaborate escapist fantasies in my mind to distract myself from the realization of my death. Many hours of nights/days were spent pretending I was someone or something else while hiding in my bedroom.

- Thanksgiving was spent alone watching television and eating food Dutch cooked. I remember Dutch sitting silent in the dark living room staring at the wall. He didn't move until 10am the next day.

- We had no Christmas tree because Dutch/Crystal were fighting and "punishing" each other.

- Crystal took me to Damasch Mental Hospital where she worked. Crystal wanted me to "see and meet the really neat patients she worked with." The place felt cold and evil and the schizophrenics scared me by saying random words about killing me or stare and whisper towards me. Crystal was infatuated with the mentally ill. She showed more interest in them than me.

- Started my first of many round trips from Oregon to California to visit Iris. Rode an Amtrak train alone for twenty-five to twenty-six hours. I would go to the bottom floor to be alone and watch the country speed by through a little window next to the bathroom.

- Steve Reedmer, Iris's brother, came to live with her. I shared a room with him when visiting. Steve was an alcoholic like Iris. Steve would often scream and flail in his sleep. The severity depending on his drunkenness.

- Steve gave me $20, told me to "wash my balls, armpits and face but not in that order" and left me at the train station. I remember feeling sad and did not want to go back to Oregon to live with Crystal/Dutch.
- Crystal was not at the train station when I arrived. I sat there and watched people come and leave the station for three to three and a half hours. Crystal arrived in a new car and said she was sorry.
- A mentally ill woman, Karee, escaped from the hospital Crystal worked at and arrived at our house. Crystal talked with Karee for a few hours then had the police pick her up some time after I fell asleep. I don't remember how Karee knew where we lived. Crystal had a cat she named Karee.
- Crystal became pregnant and gave birth to Montana Sue Karee Betzhold.
- Crystal would leave Montana with me for hours every day. I became very protective of her.
- Mike had been committed some time during the past few years and was incarcerated at a mental hospital in Norwalk, CA. The hospital was more like a prison. Crystal and Iris conspired to help him escape. They flew him up to Oregon. Crystal committed him to Damasch Hospital where she worked.
- Started hating my birthday. Crystal would promise to take me some where every birthday then forget or be sick. I got a Supersoaker from Toys R' Us the next birthday and had a friend spend the night. It was the happiest birthday I can remember.
- Rode the Greyhound bus to California. Played *Street Fighter II* at 4:00am with a crack addicted male during a layover in Sacremento, CA. I remember it was the only social interaction I had had in the previous twenty hours.
- Eighth grade teacher confided she was a Wiccan and that she did not cast a curse towards me because she was scared it would bounce back on her.
- Started high school at Marshall High in SE Portland. I was

put in the "high risk" freshman class.

- Enrolled in football because it would be a reason to see Dutch sitting silent in the living room at home. Did very well at football. Played starting offensive/defensive line. I felt "accepted" and remember being happy.
- First time masturbating. It made me feel nauseated afterwards.
- Befriended Rick Curry and his younger brother Robert "Little Bob" Curry.
- Crystal would provide me $2 a day to ride the bus to/from school. Some days I would get too hungry, spend the money on lunch and walk home after football practice.
- Started shoplifting from grocery stores to feed myself.
- Stole *The Anarchist Cookbook* from the library.
- Stole *The Satanic Bible* from the library. Returned it. I wasn't impressed.
- Joined the wrestling team. The coach, Monty, had a giant scar over his right eye brow. He received the scar while chainsaw cutting a door frame above his head. The saw bounced off the frame and went into his skull.
- Rick and I befriended James, a thirty year old black man who worked at a gas station. He would often invite us to his house in NE Portland to drink 40's.
- Rick, Bob, some other people and myself went to James house in NE Portland. I noticed we were the only white people around. I watched two black women fight in the street until one pulled out a steak knife from her purse and stabbed the other one. The stabbed black girl ran back to her apartment and reemerged with a butcher knife. The cops came. We ran inside.
- James had a naked roommate sleeping on his couch who would not stop talking about Prince. We drank 40's of Old English and St. Ides. James and his roommate were closet gay. They frequently tried to lure one of the teenage boys to stay alone.
- Began graffiti tagging with a few boys from high school. A

couple of them were in a tagger gang named "DK" short for "Devil Knights."

- Three of the boys I associated with died by the end of the school year. Dean, the leader of DK, committed suicide by shooting himself in the head while sitting on his girlfriend's lap, Richie was murdered while sitting in his car and I never heard the details of Tom's death.
- Rode the Greyhound bus to California again. Read Stephen King novels and X-Men comic books.
- Iris and Steve would get drunk every night and scream argue. Spent most of my nights alone at the $1.50 double feature theater at the Orange Mall. Iris/Steve would (usually) pass out around 11pm. I always tried not to be home until 11:30pm.
- Arrived back in Oregon the day after Labor Day. This caused me to be late for the start of football. The coach and I did not get along. He refused to allow me play in games as punishment for not starting practice in mid-August with every one else. We argued a lot. I ended up crying on the sideline of a game and quit the team.
- Stopped going to school. Spent most of the days at the mall playing *Street Fighter II* or *Mortal Kombat*.
- A senior from high school named Brian pointed a laser scoped pistol at my chest while I was eating at McDonald's one night. Rick noticed the glowing red dot on my torso. I saw Brian in his car smiling and pointing the gun towards me. I ran towards traffic to escape.
- Rick left Oregon to live with his father in Washington. Bob was my only friend. We became very close. I spent the entire Christmas break at Bob's house.
- A few nights before Christmas, Bob and I went to the liquor store late at night to play *Street Fighter II* and buy soda drinks. Inside the store two other boys said "hello" and waved at us while leaving. They didn't look familiar. Bob and I left fifteen minutes later to start our walk home. When we cut down a dark alley the two boys from the liquor store were waiting.

They started to hit Bob. Bob ran away and shouted something incoherent. I got punched in the mouth which broke my front tooth. Then a gun pointed at my face. I realized Bob was trying to convey that the boy had a pistol. I immediately ran.

- Bob called his eldest brother, Phil, to explain what happened. Phil dealt drugs. He drove to Bob's house, picked us up and we found my broken tooth on the asphalt. Bob said he recognized one of the boys from a tagger gang. Phil drove around a neighborhood by my house describing the kids to people on the street. We found where they lived and went to their house. The boy would not come out. Phil took us home, drove back with a friend and threw bricks through the front windows. He then physically beat the boy when he ran out to see what was going on.
- I phoned Crystal and told her I needed to see the dentist. The root in my tooth was exposed and the pain was very intense. Eight or nine days later Crystal scheduled a dentist appointment. The root was dead and the dentist made a fake tooth to replace the broken one.
- Won a trip to Disneyland from a radio show. Spent the entire weekend alone at Disneyland. I saw Crystal, Dutch and Montana once for about twenty minutes. We flew back to Oregon on July 4th.
- Moved to a small rural town called Sherwood, OR.
- Crystal pregnant with Cheyenne Ryen Betzhold.
- Kicked out of my house for the first time. Crystal was depressed and told me she hated me. She wanted me to leave. She punched and screamed until I left.
- First time homeless, I slept in a playground fort in a park. I was wearing shorts and a t-shirt. It was late fall. I shivered most of the night. I watched Crystal drive by the park on her way to work. Found a closed gas station with an open bathroom and took to sleeping on the toilet. Pan Handled for bus money to get back to Portland. Stole food and clothes.

- One night it was freezing and windy. I slept behind a hand-ball court at an elementary school, slept another night in the grass under a freeway overpass, another night on a rattan chair sitting on a random person's porch, and a couple nights at Rick's. The police found me walking by the side of the road, arrested me, told me I was a runaway. They took me back to Sherwood where Crystal and Dutch scolded me for running away.
- Read *Catcher in the Rye*.
- Crystal would lock up the house and not provide a key. I started breaking in to sleep in my own room.
- Dutch became increasingly confrontational and began threatening to beat me.
- The day after Christmas I told Crystal I was going to Portland for the night. She forbade me and became very upset. She started hitting me and screaming. I let her do this for about five minutes until I couldn't keep the anger in, grabbed her by the shoulders, shook her and begged her to leave me alone.
- Stayed in Portland sleeping at various people's houses for a week.
- Visited a friend named Wayne. We were in his father's bedroom when he unexpectedly pulled a revolver out of the closet, aimed it at my face and said, "I could shoot you right now and no one would miss you." He lowered the gun after a couple minutes.
- Crystal was to check in at the hospital to give birth to Cheyenne. I took a dollar in pennies from a friend and rode a bus to the hospital.
- I could not find Crystal in the normal maternity rooms. I found her in a back room. She explained she gave birth to Cheyenne the night I left. She had him on a friend's couch. They could not make it to the hospital.
- Saw Cheyenne for the first time. He was very small and looked sickly. He had just had surgery to repair scrotal hereneas.
- Crystal and Dutch did not talk to me much. I sat alone in the hospital waiting room for hours.

- Dutch pushed me around a little one day. Told me never to touch his wife again.
- Dutch pushed me while I was doing dishes in the kitchen. I grabbed a large carving knife and pointed it at him. He backed off. I threw the knife in the sink and fled to my room. I grabbed a metal ring measurement gauge waited behind the door for Dutch. Crystal stopped him on the stairs leading to my room.
- Homeless again.
- Shoplifted to eat. Oreos and coca-cola mostly. Slept in parks/public bathrooms. Wally let me sleep in a camper on his property a few weeks until his mom found me. Smoked hash for the first time with Wally. The session lasted five hours straight. His mom said I couldn't stay there.
- I was walking at 2am looking for a place to sleep when my friend Blue saw me from his bedroom. He told me to climb in through his window. I slept on his floor.
- Blue's parents allowed me stay a week. Blue told them I was homeless. They wanted me to call Iris.
- Iris paid for me to fly back to California to live with her.
- Enrolled at Villa Park High School.
- Made friends with Steve Critchfield and Aaron (forget the last name).
- Steve and I would write humorous stories during class and exchange them after school. My best story was about his stepfather, Perry, who had a high pitched voice and a smooth hairless region where his penis was supposed to be.
- Iris purchased a computer for my school work. It was an IBM PS/2 25mhz 486 with a 1200 baud modem.
- Introduction to the online world. Started dialing into BBS (Bulletin Board Systems) around Orange County. First introduction to the words: Hacker, Warez, Phreak.
- School became a dead place to me. I found no value intellectually or socially and would not attend for 2-3 week intervals. A classmate would forge my sick notes.

- Convinced Iris to buy me a Unix shell account to the Internet. Everything was text. Began using Internet Relay Chat (IRC) to communicate to other internet connected individuals. #ansi was the channel I normally frequented It was a meeting place of the BBS clique. I would spend my days and nights online instead of learning in school.
- On random occasion would show up at school to see actual human beings. My English teacher Mr. Corradino realized I was not interested in school. Instead of homework or class work, would ask me to take a book from his shelf, read it and return it the next time I decided to come to class. He introduced me to the book *1984*.
- Began reading the hacker journal *Phrack*. The dark side of computing was exciting. Began reading every hack/phreak journal I could find on the internet.
- Transitioned to the IRC channel #hack. A meeting place where hackers would boast about exploits and shit talk each other.
- Steve showed up one night and explained he was homeless. I hid Steve in my closet every morning until Iris left for work. two weeks passed and he departed.
- Built a "beige box." Used the beige box to illegally set up 1-800 ATT teleconference bridges. The conference bridge was a past time of the hacker.
- A school counselor, Mr. Edwards, pulled me aside one day to inform me I was a fuckup and wouldn't graduate—ever. I felt underestimated.
- Enrolled in Richland Continuation School under my own volition. The school was easy. I finished most classes in one to three days. Shop class was the worse.
- Entered in a Scholarship Contest. The assignment was to write an essay about why a person should get a scholarship. I wrote about my life. The Rotary club scholarship awarded me as winner of the contest. Two years of paid community college.
- First of the headaches. A strange pressure would fill my head.

My brain would feel like it was folding or flapping until I thought I would die. I was terrified it was cancer. I didn't want to know the day of my death. Avoided telling people about the headaches. Every day after my thought was rife with death.

- Graduated Richland high school, not on time but early. I finished my last class, English, met the principal at the front office, was given a weird smelling robe and cap, a Polaroid picture was taken of me, then posted on the wall. Gave back the robe and cap and walked out the door.
- Iris bought me my first car: an early model 1970's Volvo with beige exterior with a faux red plush interior.
- Two guys from #hack—El_Jefe (Zak) & Ap0calypse (Bob)--befriended me. We shared mutual feelings on humor. El_Jefe and Ap0calypse were in a hacker gang named Phone Losers of America (PLA). El_Jefe and I would spend 4-6 hours daily prank calling and social engineering.
- Used "war dialing" to find interesting phone numbers.
- Started dumpster diving at Pacific Bell. Found some informational technical manuals. The entire summer was spent online. I had no concrete interactions.
- Inducted into the PLA.
- Began working for a friend's father, Vernon Van Winkle, in his video production business. We recorded weddings and cable commercials.
- Enrolled at Rancho Santiago Community College. My classes were: Creative Writing; Algebra; Asian History; Speech. I hated the writing class. The teacher was all ego.
- Wrote PlA099 under the screen name dr. hate. Released it to the internet.
- The Volvo's transmission went defunct. The car stayed at the mechanics for the next three months.
- My speech class was cancelled. I decided to drop out of Community College. Spent most of my time online.
- Began talking to a girl, Amy, I met online. She was a friend of Zak's.

- Broke into payphones to talk to Amy. My usual spot was at Shaffer Park. Most nights I sat under the phone booth talking with her until 2 a.m. The park was always empty.
- Steve and Aaron were now homeless and sleeping in my community laundry room. I gave them sleeping bags and blankets.
- Decided to stop working for Vern. Didn't show up for work again.
- Amy wanted me to come visit her in Illinois. I didn't.
- Got my car back. It worked for five days and the transmission died again. I was too scared to tell Iris. She was getting meaner with the drink.
- One night I stole the car keys from Iris' work uniform. She always hung her nurse's apron in the master bedroom bath. Pulled her Mitsubishi Galant out in neutral and foot pushed it down the alley way, started the engine and sped away.
- The Galant was a stick shift. Something I was not used to driving. I took the car up into the Anaheim Hills. Suddenly the front driver's tire exploded during a turn on a hill. The area was rural, the car was in a blind spot on the road. I had no idea how to change a tire and decided to coast the machine down the hill to a payphone where I would call AAA for assistance.
- Halfway down the mountain the car's electric system started to short out. Every light, bulb and diode sputtered. The car's wire harness was caught on the ripped wheel rubber.
- A half mile from my home the car completely died. I pointed it towards the curbing and parked it with the emergency break. The engine wouldn't turn. Everything electrical was dead.
- Called AAA from a payphone. They wouldn't help me because I was not Iris. It did not matter if my name was on the account. Ran home and borrowed Iris's ATM card. Got out $140 to call a tow truck to bring the car back to the condo parking.
- Saw Steve and Aaron wandering around the area. Explained what happened. We decided steal a replacement tire.
- After hours of searching, found another Mitsubishi, but not a Galant. Removed the tire with a jack where the car was parked.

Left it on three wheels.

- Soon realized cars have different bearing configurations. The stolen tire was useless. Tossed the stolen wheel.
- Pushed my Volvo next to the Mitsubishi. Vandalized both cars with eggs, mustard, toilet paper and other condiments. Ran upstairs right before dawn and jumped into bed.
- Iris woke to find the vandalized cars. Later that day the mechanic would explain to her what actually was wrong with her car. I am a really bad liar. I confessed.
- Got my car back from the mechanics. Now functional.
- Iris left to gamble in Laughlin, Nevada.
- Picked up Steve in Orange. Drove to Silverlake to pick up Aaron. Drove back from LA with the two smoking from a bong in the rear.
- My neighbor, Jeff, bought us a fifth of cheap whiskey. By the end of the night I had been thrown out of a local Lucky's for wandering in their boiler room and Steve was vomiting, repeatedly. Took Steve home and fell asleep on my living room couch to Aaron sucking in a massive bong load.
- Woke up late in the afternoon. Wrote Iris a letter telling her I left for Oregon, took Aaron back to Silverlake, drove to LAX, left the Volvo in short-term parking and stepped on a flight for Oregon. It was a flight no one knew about other than my mother. She bought the ticket for me.
- Arrived in Portland. Crystal, Montana and Ryen greeted me at the terminal gate. Dutch had abandoned the family. His whereabouts unknown.
- Crystal pleaded for me to stay and help her raise Montana and Ryen.
- Avoided Iris's phone calls. Decided to stay in Oregon. Did not speak with Iris until eighteen months later.
- Woke up in the morning to discover a golf ball shaped lump on the left side of my throat. I started weeping. Soon after I was hysterical with thoughts of brain cancer.
- Crystal drove me to a hospital. The doctor placed his fingers

on my throat and diagnosed me with globules. I was told to go home and not worry so much.

- Crystal's demeanor changed after two weeks of living with her. She began criticizing me for her hardships in life. I was given an ultimatum to get a job or sign up for welfare by the end of the month. She threatened me with homelessness if I did not soon help with money.
- Made an appointment to apply for state welfare.
- Stopped to buy a Jolt cola at a Plaid Pantry on the way to the welfare appointment. The store was conducting new hire orientation for four prospective employees. I asked if they were hiring. Four hours later I finished training and was the new graveyard shift.
- Crystal's face turned swollen red while she screamed at me for not bringing home food stamps. I went to bed feeling very confused.
- My first night working at Plaid Pantry. The other graveyard shift worker, Jamie Cunningham, showed me how to stock the beer cooler. We went to his manufactured home during a lunch break. A five foot marijuana plant was growing in his closet. Jamie removed a black leather kit from a shoebox. I could see a glass syringe and a spoon. I declined the offer to shoot up.
- Agreed to cover Jamie's shift that night. He drove off. I never saw him again.
- Maggie Reynolds began working the morning shift. She had recently moved from Orange County to Oregon. Flirted with her every day. I was terrible at it.
- Seven night, sixty hour work-weeks became the standard.
- Slept on the carpeted floor in Cheyenne's bedroom.
- Received an $800 paycheck every month. Crystal demanded $350 be forfeited for rent.
- The district manager of Plaid Pantry informed me I possessed a black aura. I had never met the man previously.
- Crystal became more abusive. I was accused of being selfish by not helping the family. Crystal was very angry I was not

babysitting my brother and sister so she could catch up on her sleep or go out shopping alone. She yelled me into submission. I didn't sleep much after.

- Befriended a neighbor Shane Heavyrunner, a mixed-blood native American heavyweight boxer.
- Freezing rain desolated the city. It was a vicious winter.
- Ate LSD for the first time. After pressuring me to drop the acid with him, Shane suddenly left to run errands. Sat at home alone talking to Ryen's *Casper, The Friendly Ghost* pillowcase for the majority of the drug experience.
- Purchased a radio frequency scanner to eavesdrop on cellular phone calls. Listened to a conversation between a medical doctor and a father debating to keep the latter's son on life support. A decision was made. The doctor provided the death itinerary. I cried a little.
- The February floods of 1996: Days of heavy rain punished the city. The temperature suddenly rose causing the mountain ice packs to melt. The lower end of town was immersed in ten to twelve feet of water. I was trapped. Cars, houses, trees and a mall disappeared. A boat drove in circles over a parking lot of drowned vehicles.
- Lydia Ramirez, a co-worker, offered her couch to me. She felt bad after hearing how abusive Crystal was.
- Packed my belongings into my backpack and moved in with Lydia. Didn't tell Crystal I was leaving or where I was going.
- Stole the entire stock of beer from Plaid Pantry's cooler with the help of Shane. Unofficially quit by not going back to work.
- Lydia's ex-lover, Rudy Gonzalez, arrived from Oxnard, CA. Rudy was fleeing from a handful of felony arrest warrants.
- Met Cory Kalteich and his mulatto cousin Jay. They lived in the same apartment building as Lydia.
- Lydia worked two jobs. She often wouldn't sleep.
- Slept on the couch. It wasn't so bad. Lydia had a sister, Anitra Nunez, living there too. Anitra was feminine and beautiful; she had skin the color of old pennies.

- Began drinking every day.
- Some fat bitch thief came over to Lydia's. She lived in the neighborhood. The fat bitch thief stole money out of my wallet. She ran home.
- Rudy/me showed up at the thief's house. She wouldn't come out. Her man wouldn't either. Rudy started kicking in the door. He heard sirens and fled home.
- Popped all four tires on the fat bitch thief's car. Used a cordless dremel.
- Anitra would often invite me to her room. We would sit on her bed and talk to each other. She told me she had a dead baby son while pointing to a small picture of a smiling boy. I had an emptiness after.
- Maggie/me still saw each other. Awkwardly. We would usually go park somewhere public and drink until dawn.
- At a party with Cory and Jay. They confide they steal Volkswagon cars. We decide to find some automobiles to pilfer.
- Stole my first car from a church parking lot.
- Helped steal a second car. This one belonging to the Sheriff's daughter.
- As I stood in line at Plaid Pantry, a boy made a throat slice motion with his hand and pointed at me. I had never seen the kid before.
- Jay and I followed him up the hill. When I was close enough to ask him what he meant by the threat seven teenagers circled me. Jay was gone.
- A girl I knew from Cory came out. She got the guys to back off long enough for me to run away.
- Came back with Rudy, Shane, Cory, Jay and myself. We all had weapons except for Shane.
- Shane knocked on the door of a mobile home. A man in his late fifties answered and told us to "fuck off." Shane threw an uppercut to the man's soft head knocking him out.
- We moved back to the street. Teenaged boys were pouring out of apartments. Cory sliced one from the corner of the eye to

the bottom of the cheek with his blade. Rudy was clubbing several boys with a cue stick. A man was pleading for Shane not to hit him again. I went to stab the man but Shane flashed an uppercut. The man started weeping on the asphalt of the street. Sirens came. We fled.

- Talked to Anitra about Death. It was the first night I didn't have a panic attack over the subject.
- Got a job working the janitorial graveyard shift at Fred Meyers. Spent nights vacuuming, cleaning, mopping. The entire time worked I thought about death. Masturbated to the smell of menstruation while cleaning the women's bathroom.
- Shane gave me a ride to SE Portland. He dropped me off in Rick's neighborhood.
- Went to Rick's house. Talked for a few hours. He told me Bob was in the urn above my head.
- Earlier in the year, Bob had fought back against two bullies. The agitators were ex-friends of Rick. Bob beat both of the boys with a mop stick. The cops were called. Bob was worried because Oregon had recently passed the minimum sentencing law and assault was a felony. He was going to get five years in prison for defending himself.
- A friend came over with a revolver tucked in his work boot. The friend tried to convince Bob and Rick to shoot the two boys to mitigate the looming five year sentence. Bob refused. The gun was muzzle up and tucked back in the boot. It accidentally fired a bullet bounced twice against the cement walls of the basement. The bullet exploded Bob's chest. He died in Rick's arms mouthing the words "it's okay." And spitting up blood.
- I felt contrite about Bob's death. I could have protected him.
- Drank all night with Maggie, Cory and Jay for my birthday. The night ended in daylight with Maggie leaving. I felt really sad about death. Laid down in a gutter to watch the cars pass by.
- Rudy confided in me that he had killed a woman then melted her corpse with gasoline.
- Drank a fifth of tequila. Maggie dropped me off at home.

Three hours later I woke in the abandoned field next to the apartment building. Rain was falling on my head.

- Rudy/Shane had been snorting cocaine for months. They suddenly became paranoid towards me.
- Anitra drunkenly admitted one night she liked guys like me. I was too dense to understand what she meant.
- Rudy pointed a butcher knife and threatened to kill me while I slept on the couch one evening. Lydia panicked and called the police. Rudy's last words before incarceration were, "I'm going to murder you!" I slept through the entire altercation.
- A lean and muscular man wearing camouflage pants came to the apartment looking for Anitra. He introduced himself as Ron, her husband. He had been training for six months with the US Army Rangers.
- Anitra avoided me. She refused to talk to me intimately anymore.
- Felt extreme sadness.
- Had been drinking heavily with Maggie and her cousin Sara. Maggie's car was parked next to a black Volkswagon Cabriolet. I pretended to break in to the car to scare Maggie and Sara.
- Five police enforcement vehicles descended on us as I drove out of the apartment building. A neighbor contacted the Tualatin police department after witnessing the drunken prank. I was handcuffed, verbally abused, handed a ticket to appear in court and released.
- Lost my virginity with Maggie. The sex was horrible. I was too busy thinking, "I HATE MYSELF," to enjoy the act.
- Moved to an apartment building, Todd Village, with Maggie, Cory and Brian. Brian worked with Maggie at Plaid Pantry, coated white makeup on his face, and proclaimed to be goth. I hated the guy.
- Worked several temporary jobs as a telemarketer. The jobs would last one to four days, paid $5.25/hr typically. The workspaces were all the same: a makeshift desk, a phone, a pencil and paper. I frequently thought about suicide.

- Brian loathed his mother and father. He told Maggie about his plans to steal a few grand from their house the next time they were out of town.
- The following weekend Brian's parents left for a fourteen day vacation. Maggie drove to their home and convinced me to help break in. We took $6,000 in cash. I felt terrible afterwards.
- Bought a computer. Also, a shopping mall engagement ring.
- Used stolen credit card numbers to order pizza for pick-up. Had a surplus of three thousand plus card numbers from a hacked website. Fraud was our source of nutrition.
- Thanksgiving dinner with Cory and his mother in Washington state.
- Brian ended an argument with Maggie by shoving her. He had left for his parents after the altercation with her.
- Cory/me arrived home from Washington State to find Maggie in Brian's room. She had the eyes of a destroyer. Maggie poured bleach in the television, slashed the waterbed fifteen different directions, scored every compact disc, dented, crushed, and flattened anything with more than a $10 worth.
- By morning, Maggie moved everything in Brian's room to the dumpster outside. I never saw Brian again. The subject of the disagreement was never disclosed to me.
- Met Maggie's alcoholic grandmother, Barbara, and her schizophrenic aunt, Pati.
- Got a job as a data entry clerk at Oregon Title Insurance Company. The position paid $6.50/hr, but the placement agency forced me to sign a contract (otherwise I wouldn't be hired). According to the contract, I owed the placement agency $250 a paycheck/$7000 total. I made less than minimum wage because of the fees.
- First ultrasound image. My son was beautiful. His predicted birth date was May 22nd—my birthday.
- Maggie/me moved to an apartment in Lake Oswego owned by Barbara. Had to pay full rent.
- Made an extra $150 a week by shoplifting/returning mer-

chandise from/to Fred Meyer & JC Penny.

- Adopted an Australian shepherd dog from the pound. Her name was Stormy. The placard on the cage indicated Stormy was two years old but had never been inside a home. She pissed submissively when I knelt down to pet her. Her sadness hurt me a little.
- Stormy was abused badly by her previous owner. She had severe abandonment anxiety and couldn't be left alone. Anywhere. The first night home from the pound I pad locked her in a dog crate before leaving for dinner. I came home to a living room of broken things.
- Maggie was diagnosed with toxemia and gestational diabetes. Her body wanted to nullify the baby.
- Maggie/me went to the doctor's two to three times a week. She would randomly vomit four or five times a day. Her body was getting sicker.
- Called Crystal to let her know she was going to be a grandmother. It was the first time we spoke since my departure. She had a selfish excitement about being it.
- Called Iris. She was very drunk. I couldn't explain much to her without getting angry.
- The work placement agency was threatening to garnish my wages because I had not been paying the monthly fees.
- Maggie's sickness worsened. The doctors committed her to bed rest/hospital observation for two weeks.
- My son was at risk. The doctors decided Maggie needed an earlier birthing date. They planned on inducing labor the next day.
- Early morning hospital arrival. I brought Stormy. Left her in the car. My Toyota was the only place she felt comfortable alone.
- Maggie had gurgle tubes attached to her in various places. The nurses were not letting her eat. Her blood sugar crashed twice causing the nurses to go into a panic. I fed Maggie some stolen peanut butter when the idiot nurses were out of the room.
- The induction medication was not working as quickly as

planned. Maggie's cervix hadn't dilated at all after five hours. We watched television to pass the time. A black lady on *The Price is Right* yelled, "I'M NOT MAD AT CHA BOB!" All of a sudden I felt empty and alone.

- My mother arrived by nightfall. We went to the cafeteria together. It was the first break I had had all day/night. I got pistachio pudding. We didn't talk much.
- A mechanical breathing device was fastened over Maggie's face when I returned. I asked the lead nurse why the breathing apparatus was being used. She responded with, "Don't worry about it. You don't work here." I was removed from the room for telling the nurse to go fuck herself.
- By the next morning, Maggie was dilated. Her water broke suddenly, within twenty minutes she was lava faced, slurp sucking the air. Her pussy was bulging from a round object pushing out from within.
- It happened quickly. A cut from asshole to vagina, screaming, pushing, then abruptly the doctor yanked him out. I started to panic. The baby looked like tethered death, he wasn't moving or making a noise.
- My knees buckled but I caught myself. All I could do was stare at the silent baby. My stomach began to spasm and my eyes were paralyzed but I couldn't cry. Fear kept me from talking. I was mortified.
- The doctor smacked the baby slightly. Then a huge stream of piss erupted from my son's penis in response. It hit the nurses, the doctor, and Maggie. I began to cry hysterically; my son had arrived.
- Cut the embilical cord with scissors. Asked the doctor if I could keep all of the cord. He didn't take me seriously.
- Held my son and smiled.
- Went home for the night. The next morning I would pick them up to bring home.
- Got a call before leaving for the hospital. Steve and Aaron where wired on LSD and driving from San Francisco to see

me in Portland. They expected to be there tonight by 8pm.
- Left for the hospital.

14.

NOAH
CICERO

EXCERPT FROM *GO TO WORK AND DO YOUR JOB. CARE FOR YOUR CHILDREN. PAY YOUR BILLS. OBEY THE LAW. BUY PRODUCTS.*

I called my parents and told them I got the job. They were excited for me. They told me to come over and they would get pizza and cake. My parents were very big into positive reinforcement. When I scored my first goal in soccer when I was seven, they bought me pizza and cake. When I was in the eighth grade talent show, playing guitar very badly, they bought me pizza and cake. When I got straight A's on my report card, I was for sure going to get pizza and cake. Pizza and cake are the ways Americans celebrate triumphs.

I drove into Deer Valley Estates. My parents lived in a beautiful suburban development. Which means I grew up in a suburban development. All the houses were relatively new and clean-looking. The yards were perfectly mowed and the hedges were trimmed. There was no crime except for teenage boy vandalism. There were no broken-down cars in the driveways, not a single shingle was missing. It was perfect. There was even a cul-de-sac.

I went into my parents' house. I had spent the last five years living in a dorm and then in an apartment right off campus, then recently, after college, I had moved in with my grandpa. Going back to my childhood home was not exciting to me. I walked into the house and it looked "nice." Everything in the house was ordered and clean and boring. We didn't live in an old country farmhouse or a mansion with paintings on the walls or spiral staircases. I really liked the old apartment I lived in by campus, with its old sinks and flaking paint. There was something human about it. You could tell that humans lived there. You couldn't tell that humans lived in my parents' house. They had the house remodeled once every five years. They would redo the kitchen and living room and bathroom, so people would think they were normal and up to date.

There were ceramic plates with pictures of horses on the walls and cabinets with strange teapots and figurines in them. My father was into photography. His nature pictures of hawks, the Grand Canyon, and bull moose running through the Rockies were all over the house.

My dad worked as a cameraman for a local television station. He stood behind a camera and filmed local news anchors for money. It provided good money and made him happy. My mother worked as a second grade teacher. It provided good money and made her happy. They had enough money to pay for things like remodeling their house, new cars, and vacations. They had worked the same jobs my whole life. They were determined people. They were determined to work the same jobs and be the same people from the day of my birth to the day they retired.

My father got up at four in the morning, put on his clothes and drove to work at the television studio. He had been waking up at four in the morning for so long that he didn't even set his alarm anymore. When my father got home he went straight to his bedroom and took a nap for an hour and a half and then got up to start his day. My mother woke at six, took a shower, put on her makeup, and drove to teach little kids cursive and times tables. When she got home, she would exercise on a treadmill for an hour and then cook dinner. After dinner, she would work on the next day's lesson plans. This routine was repeated every day.

My father had hobbies. He took a loan out five years ago and bought a sixty-thousand dollar camera to film movies and commercials for local businesses. He would go to a car lot and film a car lot owner wearing a cowboy hat or go to a lawyer's office and film a lawyer talk about disability insurance. Sometimes he would get to be on a movie crew. He especially enjoyed filming horror movies. The man loved horror movies and movies in general. Ever since I was little, whenever we watched a movie, he would tell me about the camera angles and the lighting. He would obsess over movies with bad camera angles and never stop talking about movies with good angles. My mother ran short marathons, not like twenty-eight mile marathons, but little five mile races for charity. She had won several events in her age class. She had a little shrine to the races she had won in the living room.

Sometimes I would think about their marriage. They had been married for twenty-eight years. They had my sister in their second year married and me in their fifth year. Then they stayed married while half their friends and family members got divorced. They stayed married and committed. Some years it seemed like they loved each other and some years I don't remember them even speaking to each other, but time passed and they would love again. There was a year when my mother got terribly depressed and wouldn't leave the house, but my dad said nothing, then one day my mom went to a counselor and she started exercising and doing marathons. About five years ago my dad had a small thing of cancer on the back of his neck, but they were able to fix it. I remember my mother crying a lot then. When my sister and I were little, we would take family vacations to Disney World and the Colorado Rockies, but when my sister and I hit our teens, family vacations ended. My father would go to a national park out west and take pictures and my mother would go to Spain, England or France for five days with her friend Donna. My mother loved Europe and couldn't get enough of it. She would sit and read books on European castles and their kings and queens. My father cared nothing for Europe. He didn't like cities or even the suburbs, but he knew he had to live there to have a job and maintain his family. Their marriage was full of compromises. I never knew when these decisions were made about vacations or about my mother's depression. I always assumed they took place at night when they were alone in bed, hiding away from their children. They never discussed their life plans with me. I had to discuss my life plans with them, but they were not obligated to discuss them with me.

When I came in my mother was wiping down the kitchen

counters and she said, "Mike, you have a job. Give me a hug."

I gave my mother a hug. I felt nothing. I don't know why I felt nothing. We were never close, I don't think we ever had one real conversation our whole lives. We had lived together for eighteen years and I had known her for twenty-three years. The conversation was always the same. She would ask me about my life, she would tell me positive things, and she would tell me about the accomplishments of my relatives and kids from the suburban housing development. We never discussed movies or how we felt about politics. The conversation was always determined by her and what she thought was important to talk about.

She said, "This is so exciting, your first grownup job!"

I looked at the kitchen table, where there sat a pizza box and a cake with the words 'Grownup Job' in frosting.

Then she started, "Is grandpa all right? Are you taking care of him?"

"Yes."

"Are you washing the dishes on time?"

"Yes."

"Are you taking the garbage out every week?"

"Yes."

"But you aren't treating him like a child, right?"

"No, I'm not treating him like a child."

"But you can't let him just do things. He is old and needs to be taken care of," said my mother.

"Yes, I know."

"What temperature do you have the house at?"

"I have it set for sixty-eight."

"Oh no, you need it to be at seventy. Your grandfather will be cold."

"It seems pretty warm in there," I said.

"No, that isn't warm enough."

"I think I know when something is warm."

"Are you eating right?"

"Yes, I have been eating a lot of salads and spinach."

"Spinach? You eat spinach now?"

"Yes Mom, I eat spinach now."

"You never ate spinach when you were little."

"I'm trying to eat healthier. I even started taking a flaxseed supplement."

"What the hell is flaxseed? Why don't you take a multivitamin?"

"Because multivitamins don't contain flaxseed," I said.

"How much are they are paying you?"

"$11.30."

"How are you going to get married and start a family with that?"

"I put out like forty applications. They were the only place hiring."

"Did you try your cousin Tony? He's got a political science degree and does the government contracts for constructions companies. Did you try him?"

"Yes, Tony said they aren't hiring."

"I thought you wanted to become a political consultant. Did you try the local consulting companies?"

"Yes, they aren't hiring either."

"What about the local non-profits, are they hiring?"

"I called all of them and none of them are hiring a political science major. They want like geologists and chemists."

"Oh, why didn't you just become a nurse like your sister? She makes twenty-four dollars an hour and put a down payment on a house, and did you hear about your cousin Carrie? She has an accounting degree and just got a big time job making fifty-thousand a year to start. Oh, why did you choose political science?"

"I don't know. I get the best grades in it. Shouldn't you do what you get the best grades in?"

"No, you should do what makes money. I became a second grade school teacher because that was a good job for a woman back then and I was able to pass the classes. With that job I was able to raise two children and pay off a home."

Then my father came in the room. I looked at him. I could see my nose on his face, my forehead and my mouth, all on his face. I couldn't look into the mirror without seeing that man staring at me.

Like a good Italian he walked over to the pizza, picked out a corner piece and started eating, and said, "Michael."

I didn't want to hear what he had to say. I said, "Yes."

"You really want to do this job, I mean I've never heard you mention wanting to work in corrections before. You are really nice, a bit too nice in my opinion. I don't think we raised you to be a person who yells at prisoners all day. I remember that one time we were in the city you saw that homeless black woman standing in the snow with those open-toed shoes on. You made me stop the car, then you took your sister's gym shoes from the backseat and gave them to her. And how you went to all those volunteer events in college helping poor people get food and Christmas presents. You're really friendly. This isn't really a job for friendly people."

I sat there wanting to leave and said, "I don't know what else to do. They were the only people that wanted to hire me. And like, the job is helping people. They told me in the interview that it was a treatment center, not a jail."

My father said in a firm voice, "Sounds like a jail to me. They are locked in there, right?"

"Yeah."

"Well that's a jail, not a treatment center. They might be giving them treatment, but it is inside a jail."

"I don't have to carry mace or any weapons, we don't have riot gear."

"Yeah, but my job has led me to meeting a lot of cops and people in corrections. Those people are all power hungry nutballs."

I sat there confused. Maybe he was right. I didn't know what I was getting myself into. I had never known anyone who worked in corrections. I wasn't even friends with criminal justice majors in college.

My father ate another piece of pizza and said, "See, I like my job. I like cameras, I like talking about cameras, I like getting new cameras, I like thinking about cameras, and camera angles. I love cameras. I don't even care about the local news. The local news can screw itself for all I care. I wouldn't mind filming birds or action movies, it doesn't matter as long as I'm surrounded by cameras and other people who love cameras. But I have never heard you express any love for corrections or criminals."

"But I've been told if I do this job for a year it will be a great reference."

"A great reference to what, being a cop?"

I sat there defeated. I didn't want him to talk anymore.

Then my mother said, "What happened to that girl you were dating in college? Linda?"

"Linda went to law school."

Then my father said, "Why don't you go to law school?"

"There are enough lawyers. The world doesn't need another one."

"But how are you going to make enough money to raise a family," said my mother.

"I don't know. The economy is really bad. What do you want me to do?"

"We want you to have a good job," said my father.

It had never occurred to me that I was supposed to have a good job. I still had no kids and no wife, which to me meant I had no reason to care about such things. I just wanted to have enough money to live and party a little.

My father said, "I think you were screwing around your senior year of college and didn't take the GRE or LSAT, and now you have to work this shitty job."

It was true; all I wanted to do was graduate and get on with my life. Everyone was talking about going to grad school or moving to Chicago or New York City to start incredible careers, but instead I would smoke weed and drink a few beers and go to sleep. People would ask me what I wanted to do after I graduated and I would tell them that I just wanted to start my life. It was true, I was tired of school. I was tired of showing up to class and listening to lectures, I was tired of doing assignments, I was tired of going to school all week and working on the weekends. I wanted days off, I wanted two days off a week to lay around and read a book, watch YouTube videos, and maybe get good at golf.

To keep them quiet, I said, "How about I take the GRE and LSAT this winter and apply for grad schools in the spring?"

My father nodded his head in approval and then my mother said, "You better start working on your math now. You know you aren't good at math."

"Yes, I will start working on my math."

I eventually left my parents' house. It was the same thing every time; all they wanted to do was discuss my life. My life was a huge issue to them. We never discussed their lives. According to them their lives were great. I believed it was a political stance that parents took, a nice, noble lie parents from the middle-class told their children. They told their children their lives were great and that if they did what they were told then everything would turn out great. I didn't know anything about my parents; they never discussed their personal feelings or childhood memories with me. I had no idea if my father was a drunk during his college years or if my mother was a slut in high school. I didn't know if my parents ever had suicidal thoughts or what kind of women my dad was attracted to. My parents had sex, but what kind of sex, I didn't know. As you grow older, you start to realize that your parents have lives of their own, separate from you, but by that time your parents have formed the habit of keeping you out of their lives, and no matter how old you get they will never let you get to really know them.

On my way home I wondered if my father was right. Was I making a good decision about working for NEOTAP? I knew it wasn't my dream job but I still hadn't figured out what my dream job would be. I had applied for jobs I actually wanted but they weren't hiring. It was either work for NEOTAP or work for a factory for $8.50 an hour or keep serving at a restaurant.

MIKE
BUSHNELL

This poem is dedicated to Stephen Michael McDowell

BLACKHOLE GOSPEL

I'm really touched and brutal sway and whatever
reason to go online
I'm just bored so I clicked
because I've clicked not because I want to
I taste a sentiment then all the salt pours
I done something wrong
what happened
my heartfeel is nothing more than nothing pulling in
I do this thing
I beluga right between two social media apps
my fingers been bleeding
I put my phone away
I just want to say hello
I'm still there in the morning
I Listen for the orcas
what's going on
right now I'm trying return
oh it doesn't seem to be working
It's just a life on the fritz
I pull my heart out of my mouth
all the veins are still attached
I slap it on the kitchen counter
I look out the window for your eyes

the gravity is absolute
black holes have become meaningless
secondary to invented interpretations
the archetype of a hero in the belly of the whale
and I wanted laughing
anyways I don't

I'm holding my hands
I had my hands in my hands
I'm holding my fives I am just touching my palms together
above the water
as I start the boat
anything that gets too close is doomed
oh the blackhole
you know
solar systems don't know a damn about keeping a friend
or about the other day when I saw you on the platform
or it wasn't you but I wanted it to be
blackholes can come out right behind you and gobble you up
and they won't even bark

I'm on the sands
with the seashell memorial
stone of a fallen seagull
digs a wide passage
deep kind of night
bright star
basic conception of philosophy
understood to be I don't know
I'm avengers like a diamond
was trying to get somewhere
I feel like an idiot
want to say anything out loud
to hold me to be true
I listen to myself all day long
I will see you
all along I work I work
I work in the moon canoness
people and soda grasp the value of myths
it must come down

Oh you watch me

go look around with me
I say the world is just as big as my body
the world is as large as my body in the world is as large as my body
and my prayers are as large as my body in the sky as large as my
words in my prayers
and the seasons are only as great as my body and my words in my
prayers
and it's the same and waters boiled is read by the tyrants hair I
killed them sadly
and sings were delighted
the Kings lives come

Mother do not grieve
no one can live and not die
to imagine oneself is possessing anything is to be mistaken
only the continuous round of birth and death
the hero yesterday becomes the tyrants of tomorrow
unless you crucified some self today
world redeemer curtain no longer

here is the temperature of a kiln
how are you

understand and retain the selfies firmness
turn away from the sound
another object is abandoning love
Eating in solitude
eating so little
controlling speech
cultivating freedom from passion
the crowd in concert
this power prided
lost possessions
free from ego
becomes worthy of becoming one with the imperishable

the pattern is that of going and coming
of the universe manifest
taking the step of the renounced from which there is no return
not the paradox of the dual perspective
but the ultimate claim
that the unseen is here
intended

Oh I'll answer that
one bring me a call
or four times a day asking for me
working
let me sleep
I has to put me out of my misery
I bring extraordinary news and some official dreamboat water
was pretty hilarious when your daughter says that she comes in
is just like the rest
because I know the thunder and the figurines
I use encyclopedias for making my stools
there she goes
never heard of him

I want to step in the chains and we're serpents
I want to step on the panther
where serpents on my solely yodel like a serpent
I will tailless
I want things to be Sorkin
stop bleeding
now bleed some more
I want to tip the sales
to show the children the goodness of the night
to be an instrument of peace
I dreamed we don't fire
I saw in striver thorns
I'm known as I am on the crown of the lake

in the rivers and only serpentine rivers
And suddenly I am a Mall
I'm foldable info
living in my death

See light sucked in the point
the camera forward at first
it only sees black
what's in mind
the update status
a new photos as a funky chicken
as a machete
as Batman
As shut up
damn straight I texted
I'm going back
to go to my life of being alone
it's the only thing I'm good at
wish you were here
Only Beyoncé could pull this off

Yeah I don't really know
but a relationship for a long time
and now I'm looking back on everything
I'm saying what I was actually doing all time
you know
it's hard
backdoors are swaying
I never know exactly how to tell
Which stars are very close to the center of the galaxy and position
your incredibly accurate
and this would be the equivalent
of me in Los Angeles
looking for you in New York
and seeing you move your finger

I hate like the mass
not the general force of frescoes of wrestlers
panting dancers
not despondent figureheads
imagine longboats
oh repeater pain with the warden's instinct
my feeling I am a survivor
time is grass on fire
I suspect this life
I still have the address
I wrote it on the paper
I still have that address
open the black medical bag
Inside a clarion
walking downstairs
Selecting a Color theme
footsteps
something to look burns downs

Supermassive black holes live the supercenter of many galaxies
because the stars around them are drawn in
millions of miles per hour
but there still might be a way
to take the picture of The very edge
that event horizon
teams are trying to capture images
give me the outline
show me a little bit
or looking for something
looking for the silhouette
we want to find a black hole
I'm looking for the black hole
where is it
feel it

I know it's inside the sent

I'll un-sentence the dice
So I may be hung from the neck on the rearview mirror
over the water
was cold in the casket
left by the window to swell
and I lifted my head like a lost would not
I'm from the car
new cancer or the mud
I was driving down the street
I thought about setting fire to the cold fields
I want to hurt on the stick
Apologies to my mirror
I will live in the old ball
vine and a burden
I will envision the deserts laments
I go down the road
damn I'm drawn to them

I'll use optical telescopes
is all I can't
I can't see it directly
as a black hole that somewhere inside of me
and is also in the center of the galaxy
is also moving through space
and it's also forty thousand light years away
I have this feeling that I am forty million light years away from us
and it's beeping
and it's the warden
and it's sucking the stars
and I feel I felt the collapse I know

We need to take multiple copies placed around the world's cannot
We will create a vision the size of the earth itself

I'm an appointment
Your the telescope and the whole network is connected
We'll be a virtual dish
over ten thousand miles across
with five hundred times the power of a single telescope

Because I don't know what's going on
I'm scrolling through Facebook
someone else posted something
vine someone else's wall
just wanted to find a friend
someone says oh yeah I like that
what is the username
we got someone looking at some pictures
we got the pictures of naked people in different poses
that all like yeah execution
yes there's a bird on the piano
inside someone's house

I've never
God I don't know
no I didn't even try to talk about it
a try started talking about it
my mind is bridge stones and I feel the blackhole
you feel the buckle
on what is it
that thing
that person I loved that I now know nothing about
I will never forget is no escaping
my past has been
what I've done and scrolling through Facebook
the bunch people I don't talk to anymore of downtown nothing
for the people I love I can't help it really
I'm sorry if I have loved you
I'm sorry it's all my fault

2013 and it's all my fault
from the start of another really

Alright long distances with the neurons
climbing buckwheat on the end or through the night sweats
and I am known as a braggart of dreamers
I feel well with the moon
I went to the garden of loving a cradle met like a hearse
I stole my spirit
I was two weeks
I have no name
I dedicate my powers to the fish
I love my life in the dark eyebrows
and spread the word of the stone to test kilos with the martyrs
I loved in the bedrooms of the older sisters vanished
what the piper
it's not a living
I slouched in the lawns
I knew the loins introduction
I perished in the shipwrecked born

You doing a airplane dance
Flying around saying
intense swag
swag culture
someone else is talking about books that are stupid
and someone posted eating pizza bagels
comment section
Beyoncé
Kimye
Kanye kissing Kanye in front of the sunset
perhaps the matter is blown out
like doesn't sound like a big bang
you know the sound
like anything

but all the matter is just blown out into existence since
To be our own universe
we formed the mass of the universe
the size of the universe
bingo
find our universe actually solves that equation with blackholes
in other words we could be inside an event horizon
perhaps living inside a black hole is not always new
sometimes you just feel it
sometimes you learn about it and you feel it
I know that it's there
I don't forget that it's there
I hope I don't forget

We figure out later
we know now
that black holes even bigger in size
the more critical to the evolution of the universe
than we ever imagined
I don't know what to do with my hands
I mean my understanding of the universe is that it's important
universe is visible to telescopes
black holes are fucking everywhere
what's mountain people thought about it

I would rather go unknown inward with that affect
the standard ease like a clock weatherboarding
child I trouble
road of the germ beware as I'm easy
and Swiftly you will not touch me
AI authentic moving slow is Backwaters
If you are afraid to die then cover up the tracks
the countryside wounded
really good book
a kindhearted unfolding

the dark down of my broad lifers
soothing my living death
I land of the dark
woodbound for the lamp of ashes your soul and sex
I kiss the black of the piano
I have fears that I may cease to be called

But now I know little bit
something about black holes you know
I don't goosebumps are
I know what dogs look like when they run next to the lake
with a run on the dock and jump in the lake
I know it heights look like when they do various things
I live the part of the life of seen part of the universe
I am a part of the universe but I might wave bye
this is the black holes

But I've been here before
it's not something new and I know there's still hope
I'm on the wagons I see the good memories of my life Pass by
was still so much hope
there's still so much hope
this still so much
hope regardless
No matter what I feel
That hope in the world remains
waiting for me
says find me motherfucker

And I'm in a look and I think I might find it
I don't know where
I cannot see it out
alright now
I must change everything
but I've seen it happen before

when there was no choice
I've joined it

16.

TARA
WRAY

FLATBED, SEABED

We drank purple grape wine till dawn, then drove to the water and parked the truck just at the edge of the beach. Some waves came up the tires. Hello tires, they said. We laughed with our heads thrown back, kissed for a minute with forceful lips, and then passed out on the flatbed, sleeping bags and cold wheelwells pinning us ever closer.

First light came after a long black sleep. The truck had drifted into the sea. We must have been out there for hours; it could have been days. I had some chocolate covered mints in my pocket and ate two and so did Jack. We hugged frantically, then wondered aloud about the state of things.

Water is a very beautiful thing if you are not afraid, said Jack. Are you afraid?

A little, I replied, because I was. There was so much of it and just the two small bits of us.

Don't worry, he said, and climbed into the cab through the back window.

I'm not so much afraid of the water, I told him, climbing in myself, I'm more afraid of what's inside the water. There are jellyfish and stingrays and sharks and Fungleharder fish and, I'm sure, some eel.

Jack tried to start the engine but it was flooded. There are all those things, he said, but if you do not bother them, they will not bother you.

I had no intentions of bothering them, so this relaxed me. But then… What If I accidentally bother them, I said, you know, we accidentally run into the head of a baby shark and the mother gets mad, what if she calls her poisonous friends and they jump out of the water and fly into the truck and sting me or chew me dead or…

Jack stopped me and said: Let's listen to the radio.

We picked up only one station, and the reception was poor. It was someone named Roy and he was playing a banjo. It was a very beautiful distraction for about twenty minutes. I held Jack's hand, ate a sandwich from the night before, rolled down the window and let me hair blow back all salt-water tangly. But then the plunk of the banjo started to get on my nerves and I picked a fight.

I told Jack if he hadn't won the lottery he wouldn't have been able to buy the purple grape wine we drank till dawn, and he certainly would not have been able to buy the truck we drove to the beach; and he told me not to worry (don't worry, he said) because the money was all spent anyhow and as soon as we got back to shore, he said, I'm gonna give up the bottle and trade the truck for something smaller, a two-door maybe. Something red.

I folded my arms in a pout. Jack turned to me: What? What, goddammit!?

There was no time to be reasonable. It was getting dark and the sea kept folding itself over and over like a giant green bowl of batter. It reminded me how frightened I was, and how hungry I was. How delicious a cake would be! Then Jack pulled from his jacket a package of spongy sweet snacks and in that instant I forgave him for everything. But he must not have forgiven me because he did not share. And so I was still mad. Turned to face the window, away from his gnawing maw.

That's when I noticed something up ahead. Not far in the distance. Just right there. I looked, blinked, Jack was eating his cakes, not paying attention, but for sure, it was, indeed…. holy shit! A four way stop! Signs and everything. And a small bobbing car of teenagers. It was terribly exciting. It was people, other people! Oh how nice, I thought. But then we realized, and they realized, that we had no brakes, that neither of us had brakes, and we were coming to the stop at exactly the same time. We put on our seatbelts, braced.

Bump.

Impact was slight due to the speed at which we were traveling. Nonetheless, we needed to take down their names and insurances.

Hello, they waved.

Hello, we said.

Purple grape wine? they asked. They knew.

Yes, we said, a little embarrassed.

Us too, they motioned.

Because we could not stop and they also could not stop, we did not have a chance to get their information. They drifted through the intersection, noses pressed to the glass, then fell out of view.

Jack…I said.

He handed me the last bite of his cake. I stuffed the sweet thing into my mouth and apologized for earlier, for the accident, asked was he ok, did his neck hurt or anything, was he sore?

No, he shook. No. But, he said, I feel as though we're sinking.

Sinking? I managed to say, the cake being very thick in my mouth. We're sinking?

He stuck his head out the window to put a chalk mark on the tires. We waited several minutes in relative silence. There was a noise of considerable lapping. Then he stuck himself back out the window and saw that the mark had disappeared.

Yes, he said, we're sinking.

I cried for a good amount of time. So did Jack. I looked to the rear of the truck and found it was many inches thick with water. Small sea frogs backstroked across our bed from the night before. When I could not cry any longer… I stopped. We tried a little to make love, but decided it was neither the time nor the place.

It got darker and darker until it was full-blown night. Jack turned on the headlights. Frosty pockets of sea shone bright. My eyes were gummy from the salty air and also from the crying. There was nothing left to eat and only a little time before the weight of the water in the back of the truck would pull the machine down, including us.

So this is what it feels like to be doomed, I said.

Jack was too preoccupied with his own gloom to comfort me in mine. I thought: this cannot possibly get any worse. Then it did. A swarm of Fungleharder fish surrounded us. These are the smiling kind of fish. They smile when they are about to eat something. They circled our sinking selves like big black non-winged buzzards of the sea, and I think they were more leering than smiling actually. They glowed a little too.

They nipped at the truck, taking small bites at first, then moved onto larger chunks: tires and hubcaps and wheelwells at once. They got into the engine. Metallic clatter came from under the hood. It was the sound of fish teeth on spark plugs and it was horrendous. Some wires must have shorted or crossed because the radio came back on, and it was Roy, and he was playing his banjo, and it was the sweetest saddest song I'd ever heard and I wanted nothing more at that moment than to hear him play. I asked Jack would he like to dance and he sulked and said I was an idiot.

I love you, I said. Love, love, love you.

Then I unbuckled my seatbelt, rolled down the window and squeezed my way out. The water was choppy and cold, but no more so than Jack. I swam very fast.

Goodbye, I yelled. Goodbye to you! I saw him look out the window. I saw him look. He did nothing else but this. The truck bobbed for a little while more. I could hear Roy strumming on the old banjo, I could hear Jack cursing me and the lottery and the sea and the truck and the snack cakes and those Fungleharder fish biting into his body—he cursed as much as I'd ever heard him curse before. Goodbye, I whispered. Goodbye to you. And then he was gone. The truck was gone completely. The tinny banjo, silent. Jack, silent. And me, out there by myself, surprisingly, welcomingly, unafraid.

SPENCER
MADSEN

GOING OUTSIDE FEELS LIKE CALLING MY PARENTS

Televise this: two people walking home ten feet apart
TV is a crude medium that funnels the outside in
my doctor told me to meet new dogs everyday
I didn't have the heart to tell him that he isn't real
we'll try again, I thought
it will take a year for me to comfortable talk about
what living now is like
and in five years I will get tired
and in ten years I will only remember what I said five years ago
the bowl I eat cereal out of
has a Chinese print on the sides
it is made out of plastic
it's function comes from its shape
the relationship we are in is like that
I stand alone in the shower
and the way I stand is beautiful
like a commercial too sexy to air on TV

OUR DISTANCE IS SOMETHING WE HAVE IN COMMON

I pull my cock to the left
so that it slingshots back
and hits you in the cheek
you smile like you are on vacation
I stood in the shower this morning
and thought about becoming a sex poet
I imagined myself hosting retreats
and writing articles on the various blogs
about misconceptions concerning the body
and the truth behind projected signals
I thought about how I need less shampoo
because I have less hair now
I thought about how I could be more attentive to sounds
and anticipate a change in water temperature
after I hear the flush of a toilet upstairs
I thought about *Courage the Cowardly Dog*,
home movies, and how quickly your ass gets red

LAURA MARIE
MARCIANO

HORSE GIRLS DON'T GO
TO THE MALL

No I never had a pony
not a horse girl
who are you to judge
the value of my childhood

I WANT TO DROWN IN THE PAST AND CALL IT THE BEST DECISION OF MY LIFE

All of the missing plastic is in the garage. When you ask to write inside of my writing. When you drop me off in the K-Mart parking lot and say you will be back later. The mini-mall is close by a horse farm. At birthday parties he would pull me on his lap. I wanted to be on the swings. No one was watching. Lift the window and let the snow come into the room. Play in the snow. Make angels in the snow. Now I am walking home from dance class on the main road. I am seven. You were late picking me up. I am wearing close to nothing and every step feels like his lap. The best possible place to be now is the ocean. This problem we have. Let's call it the way that it is. And ever shall be. I am wearing my Swavorski crystals. I cost $99. I am floating in my black Baby Phat sweater like an olive in your martini. I am at the mall. I am watching cheerleaders at the mall. Look at that brat. Look at that mall brat. I want to drown in the past and call it the best decision of my life.

BUT YOU LEAVE ANYHOW

In the basement I watched you snort coke. What were the starter jackets doing on our small shoulders. When the moon is full above mom's Toyota and we are talking about life. I admire your fingernails and blushing cheeks. Can you imagine what it might be like if I took you behind this day and said "let's start over?" There aren't any second chances. Rain will come through the moon roof. I want the world to stay in one tab so I don't have to keep clicking over. My hands are developing carpal tunnel. When he beat his wife she would run across the street barefoot crying. We would call the police. I walked around barefoot because I wanted to feel the earth and I wasn't worried about glass. I didn't need to run. How many times can we watch all seven seasons of Sopranos on my bed? I want to be like Adriana. Missing for two years. But really dead. I want to get my nails done. I want them to be so long that when I stick my hand out the car window on the highway I can reach back to before you left. It's raining. I am barefoot in my yard. I am wearing my Italian American for you. I am tan and glowing. And saying fuck you. The moon tells you not to. But you leave anyhow.

19.&20.

JACKSON
NIEUWLAND
&
CAROLYN
DECARLO

TWILIGHT ZONE

I lock the
door. I close
the window.

This room has
no door and
no window.

I close the
curtains and
make the bed.

There are no
curtains. There
is no bed.

I set my
alarm for
six a.m.

I do not
own a clock.

I lie down.

I can't sleep.

Close your eyes.

When you wake, look through the slats in your window blinds. The sky will appear one of two ways: blue or white. If it is the former, consider making french toast and raising the blinds. If the latter, shut the blinds quickly. Do not leave your home for at least six days. Spend all free time scrubbing the dirt from your socks in the bathtub and avoiding empty closets. Listen for the man who says "woodchips." Open the blinds and check again.

I have ink
in my veins.
It is not
blue, because
I am not
royalty.

I cut off
my finger
and use it
as a pen,
severed end
to the page.

It rains ink.
It fills the
bathtub so
I pull the
plug and the
ink spirals.
I look down
the drain and
see a ladder.

I climb down.

I am in
a goldmine.

Goldmines are
just as dark
as any
other mine.

Every mine
is the same
color once
you get deep
enough in.

I look down.

My foot is
on top of
a landmine.

I notice
that I am
surrounded
by deep holes.

Rainbows do
not end in
pots of gold.
Rainbows end
in black holes.

A mine grows
the more you
take away.

I cannot
stop shaking.

Silence is
invisible.

Stalactites
drip ink. I
hear the cold
infinite
echoing.

It sounds like
a ticking.

You sit on the gold looped carpet in the hall and watch your sister through the crack in the bathroom door. She reaches between her legs for the string that's been there all day that's finally ready to come out. When she pulls the string, you expect it to be beautiful. You hold your breath and wait. You see color where there was none. The red spill is bright at first, then darker. Your sister clenches the muscles in her pelvis as thick black clots drop from her hole into the toilet water. When it stops, she wipes until the color is gone, then flushes. You hide behind the bookshelf when she opens the door. When you check, threads of red lift toward the surface of the water from the black stones she left behind in the bowl.

I fall and
keep falling.

The   darkness
from the trees at
the sides of the
highway eats at
the edges of your
headlights. You
passed the last of
the cars hours ago,
and now the only
thing to remind
you of the road is
reflected on every
white dash that
forms the line
that curves toward
the distribution
center, where men
in small hats will
unload your truck
while you eat,
shit, shower, and
then fall asleep in
the cab so you can
repeat it all again
tomorrow night.

I put a
blank white sheet
of paper
inside my
printer and
print a page
of black text.

I put the
same sheet of
paper back
inside the
printer and
print a page
of black text.

I do this
until the
sheet is black
all over.

Ghosts are not
blank white sheets.
Ghosts are holes.
You do not
simply walk
through a ghost
and out the
other side,
you walk through
a ghost and
into a
brand new place.

When you were small, your mother poked two holes in a sheet and put it over your head. She stood you in front of the oven next to your little brother. You found a plastic orange basket on your arm but it was empty. You held your brother's hand. His hand was sticky. He was dressed like a chicken. He kept quacking even when you told him he was supposed to be a chicken. You could see your mother okay through the two holes in the sheet, but you could see her better when you hooked your fingers in the holes and pulled them down. She said, get together now. She said, stand still. She said, now say boooo! Your brother said booo! You smiled. She held down the button. you said booooo! The camera flashed. You disappeared.

Keyholes come
in only
one color.

All holes are
keyholes.

I use a
key to carve
a keyhole
in my chest.

I push my
finger in
the keyhole.
It comes out
the other
side of me.

There is a
black treasure
chest inside
my chest. I
have the key.
I swallow
it. I am
now unlocked.

Cats are grey but you aren't, in the afternoon in the light from the window. You are always clean, cleanest in the afternoon, your fur shining and unpigmented. You are licking your nose and ears and paws all pink and luminous. Your brothers, dark and tabby in the shadows, couldn't have done what you did, licking your paws after like it had been any other morning. Poor Baxter, brother said, poor dumb doggy.

My first word
was dog.

I do not
enjoy white
chocolate.

I never
learned to count
syllables.

My posters
always fall
off my wall.

I bought glow
in the dark
underwear
that did not.

Whenever
we play chess
I always
go second.

I could spend
my whole life
failing to
describe the
color black.

There is an installation at the museum so pure that your shoes have to be covered to walk on it. We do as we're told, sitting on a bench and putting the booties over our shoes. Inside the installation, red and purple and blue bulbs flush the walls with artificial light. Inside, the floor looks dirty anyway. So do our shoes. We grin at each other through the green fluorescent lights making alien smiles. We hear and then we see them, the teens who fill the empty spaces, their voices so loud. They don't like the booties either. We stand still while they crowd around us, then we sneak out, return our booties. The next part is blue cords hanging from a ceiling, row after row. You can go in, the guard tells us, but you can't run. We push against the cords. They slap our faces and arms. We hold hands. We run.

All holes are
bottomless.
Black holes are
the only
type of hole
that exists.

There is such
a thing as
black light, so
is there such
a thing as
white darkness?

I travel
back in time
until I
come out the
other side

Every
planet does
not have a
sun, just like
every
parent does
not have a
son.

Tattoo a
bottomless
hole on my
right forearm
for me to
keep treasure
inside of.

You are hiding in the red tube in the back of the Mc-
Donalds Playplace castle because when Lindsay tried
to tag you in the ball pit, her blonde hair brushed your
cheek and you tripped her. There isn't anyone else in the
red tube now and you sit with your back to the curve.
The light outside makes the walls almost translucent.
Your zipper is undone and your left hand is inside your
undies. Lindsay's hair is long and straight and blonde.
You've never seen her hair with anything in it, not a bow
or a barrette or a scrunchie. You think her hair must be
too smooth for anything to hold. You think about Lindsay running toward you except with no clothes on, just
her hair gliding across her body as she runs. You touch
yourself until it leaves a stain on the inside of the tube.

Plant a seed:
Dig a hole.
Climb inside.
Dig a hole
in the floor
of the hole.
Climb inside.
Fill the first
hole with the
soil from the
second hole.

I am tall.
I only
fit halfway
in the hole.

I did a
handstand in
the hole, so
I could see
the bottom.

I saw a
cave down
there.

In the cave
I saw a
skeleton.

In the cave
I saw a
great black
shark.

Down in crater valley there is a sock, and in that sock there is a tooth. If anyone ever bothered to look in crater valley, they would find that tooth. Then they would see that the tooth buried in that sock belonged to Mary Beth Dean, and then, if they had any sense in their head, they'd be able to solve the case. But no one has gone looking for anything in crater valley in a very long time, and you have nothing to worry about.

A grave is
a hole in
a graveyard.

A cave is
a hole in
a mountain.

A window
is a hole
in a wall.

The sky is
a hole in
the clouds.

Stars are holes
in the sky.

Halos have
holes in them.

My head is
full of holes.

My teeth are
full of holes.

You watch me
through the eyes
cut out of
a painting.

I will search
the deepest
cavities
to find you.

You are not a lunar deity. You wake up under green sheets every morning. You carry a Jansport backpack to school. You paint your toenails every Sunday. Your mom won't let you wear mascara yet even though Gina's mom has let her since the sixth grade. You have long legs and a short torso. You like to read books with talking animals for protagonists, but you hide them under the bed when your friends come over. You keep a lot of things under your bed when your friends come over, including the moon, which you have stuffed inside your old Lisa Frank backpack from elementary school. The moon has been hanging around ever since you found it in Peter's tent when your class went camping last may and it followed you home. The moon never says much during the day, but at night it is a constant whisper while you sleep. At first, it was impossible to sleep with the moon there. But now you've gotten used to it. You've never considered trying to make the moon leave or asking it what it wants because you know that wouldn't get you anywhere. Anyone who reads anything at least knows that. The best you can do is try not to think so much about mascara, paint your toenails every Sunday, carry your Jansport backpack to school, and no matter what, whatever you do, never stick your head into the bag where the moon lives at night.

Fire is more
dangerous
during night.
The smoke is
invisible.

I started
a fire with
black matchsticks.

I murdered
the fire. I
buried it
in coal.

Moths are not
attracted
to flames. They
are searching
for the dark
that always
comes after.

Fire always
leaves blackness
behind it.

"Don't look at it," she says, covering your eyes with her hands. They smell like dandelions. You pull them off and look. You can feel your eyes swelling, little red lines zigzagging across your vision until the water rises and you have to blink. When you do, tiny black suns etch into the backs of your eyelids so hard you can still see their negatives when you open them. "What did I tell you?" she asks, pushing the toe of her trainer into your father's lawn. But you don't hear that, you're too busy watching circles dance on her legs.

This isn't an
infinite
universe.
If it was
there would be
infinite
numbers of
stars in the
sky. Looking
up at night
I would see
only fire.

I stare at
the spaces
between stars.

Light is an
optical
illusion.

There is no
light in space.

We lie on
our backs on
the deck of
a boat that
floats on a
sea of ink.

We watch the
invisible
black fireworks,
black chalk on
a blackboard.

You are dressed from head to toe in a color of green Wikipedia identifies as jungle, except for your hands. Your hands are bare and brown and, from the way you are holding your arms, they seem to protrude from your chest. Once they help you into your gown, your hands will be gone. You will wait until the gloves have been unrolled onto the cuffs of the gown. You will thrust your fingers into the gloves. Then your hands will not be brown any more. The gloves will look cleaner than anything else in the room. You will be sterile.

Medical
diagrams
of human
bodies are
completely
unrealistic.
There is no
light inside
a body
until you
cut it open.

Inside my
body there
is no sun.

When we hold
hands there is
no light in
between them.

Hold my hand
while we watch
the movie.

I always
stay until
the end of
the credits.

From your lounge chair, you watch Max Sanders's perfectly tanned arm as it extends toward the wall, cutting the water wet and shining, feet flutter kicking behind him. When he stands, his back is slick with it, the water he shakes so casually from his hair, beads of the stuff actually hitting Annalee's goggles, that lucky bitch. The plastic straps of the chair cut into the backs of your thighs and you push harder with your elbows against the arm rests, peering over the top of your library copy of *Reef of Death*. Max pulls himself out of the pool, palms flat against its concrete edge. You watch the water peel off his back as he emerges and think about biting into its milk chocolate surface. When max lifts his knee up onto the concrete, the book slides from your fingers onto the lycra belly of your one piece. If you had any sense, you would keep yourself from staring at the line where his tan ends and the flesh of his ass peeks from the gap of his board shorts. Instead, you are fidgeting with the thick straps of your own suit, doing your best to expose a similar line of flesh on your chest and shoulders despite the less impressive reddish tone of your skin, willing him to look in your direction while the warm tingling spreads between your legs. When Max turns, you squirm in your seat so hard *Reef of Death* falls to the wet concrete beside your chair, but you leave it, the hard plastic cover giving you at least a five minute window before any water damage sets in. Max is really looking at you now and you smile, you can't believe it, and then you're giving him a little wave just with your fingertips when Jessica Whitely, that awful slut in the triangle bikini, sloshes over in her flip flops and wraps her stinky pale arms around his shoulders and you know he'll never look at you like that again.

My shadow
ran away.

Sometimes I
stand in the
dark and I
pretend my
shadow is
still with me.

Sometimes I
think I see
my shadow
following
behind me
but it is
only my
ghost lurking.

I look in
my mirror.
I see my
reflection
dancing with
my shadow.
My mirror
has stolen
my shadow.

My ghost gives
me a hug.

I look in
the mirror
and see my
whole body
frostbitten.

I shatter
the mirror.

A broken
mirror is
a doorway.

I step through.

You are standing in a field at night but it isn't really night or it isn't really dark because the field is covered in snow and the moon is full. Where are your fingers, you ask, where are your toes. What do you think of frostbite, he replies. You push your fingers down into the snow and wait. I think it is beautiful, you say.

HEIKO
JULIEN

WHY 'MATT DAMON' AND I ARE NO LONGER ON SPEAKING TERMS

'Amanda Bynes' and I first meet on the Internet.

She's 20/f/in. I'm 26/m/il.

'Amanda Bynes' likes a story I wrote about accidentally drinking too much cough syrup and going to the mall.

It's 2 p.m. on a Wednesday afternoon and I'm drinking whiskey in the kitchen with my roommate and next-door neighbor when 'Amanda Bynes' requests to video chat.

I accept and she sends me a link to what she calls her 'nude blog.' I ask if it's ok the show my friends and she gladly gives permission. Everyone approves of the blog and we all agree that 'Amanda Bynes' seems pretty cool before packing up our liquor in a tote bag and heading to the park to fly kites.

It's summertime and I just don't give a shit.

'Amanda Bynes' asks me for my number and I give it to her. We text each other a lot over the following week.

I like texting 'Amanda Bynes.'

She's playful and I'm curious about her. She seems to think everything I say is funny. Her sense of humor is pretty vulgar but she seems like a sweet person.

She doesn't seem dumb.

I'm drunk again, this time on the front stoop at night with friends, sending her a series of messages bragging about an 'iced-out Livestrong bracelet' that I don't have.

Now she wants to drive from Indiana to see me.

I agree and three hours later 'Amanda Bynes' arrives in a red coupe with a trash-littered floor and a sticker that reads 'Take Yo Panties Off' on the windshield.

She's all smiles and they're all good.

They make me do the same. We bounce off each other all night.

'Amanda Bynes' ends up staying for three days. When it's time for her to leave, I don't want her to go. She says I should come back with her to Indiana where she shares an apartment with her ex-boyfriend until the lease ends in a month. It's possible. I only work three days a week and have the next four days off.

"Is he going to be cool?" I ask.

"Yeah, of course. 'Matt Damon' is really chill. He's really busy with work most of the time anyway."

I'm skeptical.

"He's had girls spend the night before and it was fine. If I have someone over he's not going to bother me."

I agree. 'Amanda Bynes' and I listen to trap music and chain smoke in between tollbooth stops. We pass a black-and-white sign on the side of the road that reads 'Hell Is Real.' I take a picture and we laugh and laugh.

Then it's silent. Neither of us speaks for a bit.

We exchange glances, seeking assurance that it's ok to be quiet. Trap beats vibrate the speaker and rattle the trunk. We share the stillness through Indiana.

On arrival, I'm surprised 'Amanda Bynes' lives in an actual house rather than an apartment. She parks in the garage out back next to the shell of a hollowed out vehicle. There's a mattress covered in mysterious stains propped against the wall but I don't want to solve the mystery very badly.

'Matt Damon' works on cars for a living, 'Amanda' explains, gesturing at the shell. He's 28, she tells me. I didn't ask.

'Amanda Bynes' invites me inside and shows me around. All of her things are in boxes in her room. The bedroom floor is covered in magazine cutouts. There's the disembodied head of a muscular black man along with a speech bubble that reads 'are you ok?' They're for a project she's working on, she says. It's not finished.

'Matt Damon' comes home early. He is super chill, as promised. Possibly too chill. He walks right up to me and shakes my hand. Firm.

"You're that writer from the Internet, right?" he asks.

"Yeah," I reply.

"'Amanda' made me read that one story, the one about you getting high on cough syrup at the mall. Funny stuff, man."

"Thanks."

"Did you really do that?"

"Yeah."

"Haha. Wildness. That's cool though. I used to robotrip in junior high when I couldn't find weed."

"I was just really sick and drank too much on accident."

"Oh. Haha. How?"

"I was chasing NyQuil with it and I guess I wasn't paying very close attention."

"Huh. Well, I guess that's pretty funny too. Ha. Yeah. Oh man. You must have been surprised as shit."

"Yeah. Didn't see that coming."

"Oh man. I know. Totally."

This is going better than expected. 'Amanda Bynes' is in the other room playing with her pet rats through the bars of their cage.

'Matt Damon' announces he is going to bake some chicken nuggets and offers me some. I politely decline and he smiles at me for what feels like a long time. He reaches into the freezer and produces an economy-size bag of nuggets without breaking eye contact.

I ask 'Amanda Bynes' if we can go hang out somewhere else for a while and she cheerfully agrees. She says goodbye to the rats in a baby voice and we pass through the kitchen on our way out.

"Hey, you guys," 'Matt Damon' shouts after us.

"Have a great time tonight, alright? Be safe."

I assure 'Matt Damon' that we will and he waves goodbye, whistling what I believe is the Andy Griffith Show theme song while greasing up a pan with a stick of butter.

"I'm probably going to die tonight," I think to myself.

'Amanda Bynes' slams the screen door shut.

"Bye, little shit baby," she shouts back into the house. She grins at me.

I could die tonight, yeah.

I'm thinking we'll just see how this plays out.

Later that evening, 'Amanda Bynes' and I are sitting on her floor admiring her collages. There's a cutout of a malamute and a speech bubble that reads "chillin wit dogs." I can hear 'Matt Damon' moving things around in his bedroom. I ask if it's ok if we close the door and 'Amanda Bynes' says sure. She shuts it and I take my pants off immediately. I ask if it's ok if we lock it too and she says that she would but it doesn't have a lock.

I'm considering putting my pants back on when 'Matt Damon' enters the room with his laptop and a big old smile. He wants to show us a youtube video he's got all loaded up. In it, the singer performs a song about how he can't measure up to the ex-boyfriend of the girl he recently started seeing. It's supposed to be funny.

'Matt Damon' sets the laptop on the floor on top of the magazine cutouts and presses play. 'Amanda Bynes' is laughing throughout and 'Matt Damon' keeps looking over at me and laughing in my direction even harder during the parts that seem like they'd be the funniest. Hahahaha. Haha. Yeah. I don't think it's funny.

'Amanda Bynes' thanks 'Matt Damon' for sharing but I'm not so grateful. Once he leaves, I ask if it's ok if he doesn't hang out with us anymore tonight. She says she's sorry; he just gets excited about videos and probably won't be back.

'Matt Damon' returns ten minutes later. He's holding a pair of yellow basketball shorts.

"Heard you didn't have any pants," he says with a smile and tosses them at me.

I say thanks. No problem, he says. 'Matt Damon' asks me if I like acid. I look to 'Amanda Bynes' and she nods vigorously. I say yes and he goes into his room and brings back a plastic sandwich bag containing a sheet with various *Peanuts* characters on it. He hands me two Snoopy tabs and tells me they're 'on the house.' His house. Because this is his house, he says. 'Amanda Bynes' laughs at that one. Not funny.

I thank 'Matt Damon' for letting me spend my vacation in his house. He says I'm totally welcome and asks 'Amanda Bynes' if he may speak with her for a minute and they step outside. I put on the shorts and think I'm probably not going to take this Snoopy acid but put it in my wallet anyway.

'Amanda Bynes' returns ten minutes later and apologizes, saying everything is fine now. I ask her what is going on and she reassures me it's fine now. We won't be bothered again.

'Matt Damon' returns fifteen minutes later. He's holding construction paper and a handful of sharpies. He says he noticed the cutouts on the floors and was wondering if we wanted to do some arts and crafts with him.

"Fuck yeah," 'Amanda Bynes' shouts and grabs some paper. I reluctantly take a glue stick and a sharpie from a beaming 'Matt Damon.' It's almost three in the morning. We get right to work.

I'm absent-mindedly gluing some of magazine cutouts onto construction paper while 'Matt Damon' carefully cuts little shapes in his construction paper. He's looking over at me periodically. I don't look back but can see in my peripheral that he isn't smiling anymore.

'Matt Damon' mentions offhand that, while he did have a girl over to spend the night once, they didn't have sex because the walls here are paper-thin and that would be really uncool. I nod and glue a cutout of a model's head onto an SUV.

We all finish our crafts and present them to each other. 'Matt Damon' declares that 'Amanda Bynes'' is the best before announcing that he's going to play video games. As soon as he leaves, 'Amanda Bynes' and I hop into bed. I really don't want to have sex here. She gets right on top of me and starts grinding away in vain on the softest possible dick.

"I am going to die tonight," I think to myself.

The TV 'Matt Damon' is playing on is adjacent to the wall next to the bed we're lying in. He's in there pretending to shoot aliens and the sound of gunfire and explosions is creating an effect similar to what feels like a pretty decent war zone.

'Amanda Bynes' says I should just relax and that 'Matt Damon' won't hear us. The game is so loud, he can't hear us. She takes off my shirt. She grinds some more and the bed squeaks like a cartoon.

The volume of the gunfire increases.

'Amanda Bynes' grinds.

Squeak. Squeak. Squeak. The gunfire stops. A brief ceasefire. I'm next.

We are both about halfway undressed when 'Matt Damon' bursts into the room pointing at me and shouting. 'Amanda Bynes' whirls around and positions herself in between us, naked, guarding over me like a mother lion.

'Matt Damon' is taken aback. Nonetheless, he presents his argument: what we're doing isn't cool. Therefore I must leave immediately. It's after 3 a.m. and I'm hundreds of miles from home.

This doesn't appear to be going as 'Matt Damon' planned. He is breathing heavily. His face is red; his eyes are watery. 'Amanda Bynes' won't budge. Her glare is fierce and I'm her cub.

'Matt Damon' looks hurt. He asks 'Amanda Bynes' if I took that acid he gave me. Apparently he and I are no longer on speaking terms. She tells him I did but that's not true. She's lying so he won't start a fight out of respect for the assumed fact that I'm on drugs. After some debate, he convinces her to leave the room so he may speak with me alone. I sit up and he takes a seat next to me on the bed.

'Matt Damon' somberly presents the facts: he welcomed me into his home and I violated his trust. I'm still wearing his basketball shorts even. The nerve of me. I feel kind of guilty but not really and then I don't feel guilty at all because fuck 'Matt Damon.'

I prepare all of the knowledge I can remember from grade school karate lessons but what I tell him is that I was just a bit confused because he had treated me so nicely today. He smiles and shrugs.

"Well, yeah."

And that was that. 'Amanda Bynes' and I leave without incident. She spends the next half hour apologizing. She says she'll take me home if I want her to but I don't want to make her travel that far this late.

We decide to take a few of her Adderall and go to a park where we swing on the swings and chain smoke until sun up. She's quiet and I don't need to look to her for assurance to see if it's ok. She seems like she wants to cry and I expect her to. Instead she tells me that she's glad I came. I tell her I am too. And it's true.

She smiles at me and it's a good one.

It makes me do the same.

STEPHEN
TULLY
DIERKS

SERIOUS EUROPEAN ART FILM

Sven lies frozen to death in a ditch by the side of a road. His nostrils and lips are pale blue, jacket, pants, and boots encrusted with ice. His eyes have rolled back in his head.

I sit alone in a theater.

Sven wakes up in bed. He stands, revealing his bare ass, calves, shoulders, and penis. He puts on a sweater and stares at a mirror, touches his stubble.

Outside Sven's house the air is a smoggy gray. We lurk behind various trees as Sven walks to his car with a decidedly grim facial expression. We are at a zany angle directly below him as he opens his car door and gets in. We are in the passenger seat. We are drifting in an aimless, perhaps symbolic fashion outside the cracked dashboard, looking in at Sven's eyes. Once again we are inside the car. He seems to be having trouble starting it. He slams the steering wheel and mutters an oath that translates into English as "fuckers of shit."

At a café Sven sips an espresso and stares vacantly at the street. We anticipate but do not actually see a single tear dribble down Sven's cheek. Five to twenty minutes pass in silence.

A balding man with a thick beard sits down next to Sven. They talk at length about aesthetics, Foucault, Nietzsche, Faulkner, Jerry Lewis, the economy, the balding man's wife, his students, and his mistress, who is one of his students. Sven mentions that his car is dead. The balding man mentions the recent deaths of his cat (postal truck) and youngest son (seizure, swimming pool). The balding man invites Sven to his lake house for the weekend. Sven says no, he has to work. The balding man asks Sven if he needs money. Sven says no and thanks him. He tells the balding man not to worry.

Sven exits the café, crosses the street, enters a patisserie and buys a croissant. He carries the croissant down the street.

I fidget in my seat. My eyes are tired and dry.

Sven is in his bedroom wearing long underwear. He gets into bed.

Sven enters a factory. A woman in grease-covered overalls waves to him as he walks by. Sven is working in the factory, operating a machine. The loud, grating noises of the machines begin to sound rhythmic. We see various other factory workers with grins on their faces. Sven begins to sing in time with the machine music. His voice sounds like a studio recording playing in sync with his opening and closing lips. Some kind of factorywide dance number is underway. Workers are doffing their hardhats in time to the music. We hover above the workers as they dance in rotating formations that seem choreographed.

After a few minutes, the music and dancing stop. The workers return to their machines. Sven frowns a little, breathes deeply, and returns to his machine.

Sven waves to his friends as he leaves the factory.

He is walking down a highway.

We see snow on the ground and his footsteps in the snow.

He moves away from us until he is a shadow on the horizon.

We are right alongside him and can hear his heavy breathing.

He is walking. His boots are cracked and a toe is visible.

It is snowing. We can hear the wind.

Hair blows in his eyes.

He is staggering. He moves slower and slower and slower. There are no buildings in sight.

We wonder where he is going and he drops to the ground.

He pants and tries to move his arms and legs.

We see his face and try to interpret his expression.

His head sags, and his body slumps over into the ditch and is still.

Everything ends and we are sitting in the dark. Names scroll and music plays. Lights come on.

I open my phone and see a message from Natalie: "hey can

u come by and pick up your stuff tomorrow? i have your bluray player & your clothes & that book hopscotch."

23.

LUCY
TIVEN

WHAT IS REAL

The sand vs. the beach

the nothing that you talk to
that can't talk back

I'm embarrassing myself

Try to be so specific
and everything goes

the end

NOTHING TO TALK TO

When I was younger a dream I had was to disappear myself
into sewers. bulimic is the most municipal thing   you can be

The further you get into life   the more distances to compare to

It used to amaze me how when you close your eyes
real hard   you see eye-shaped light
even after

How   you can hear the voice saying
     you are fine just the way you are
in anything

when I was younger, I was so patriotic
I would let anyone into my body

SHIT TO THROW IN A POEM

Ailment, apology, comparison, one grandparent, appraisal of reality, audience, moon, questions, dead anything, stating the obvious, dialog, feeling afraid around strangers, *specific knowledge*,
gross stuff, lists, jokes and familiar sayings, fruit, famed illustrated
fruit, fools, endings, a self defeating attempt to explain, in English, non-English language concepts as reminder of medium as
inherently limited— while also, paradoxically, affirming status of
medium at the same time, grieving women, women from myth,
myth generally, back and forths, a mistake committed on purpose, complex rudeness, accidents, spills, or missed appointments,
someone appearing from some place else looking lost, numbers
and other signs from math, transgressions of interest, reverence
that is also regret, pairings, kinds of things, a lament evolving
into admiration *or* admiration deflating followed by lament and/
or acceptance, food/ordinary things, lies, quizzes, peoples actual names, strangely saying the colors of rooms, rhyme, passing
thoughts of celebrities, things that flicker, cars, to put many words
where there could have been few, movement, pastoral shit, find-
ing something lost, knowledge acquisition, bruised objects, a man
from the past, a casual observation of something obvious ie "time
passed" "it is funny", Latin things, music, consideration of sexual
or romantic love for women friends, ventriloquized experiences
other people, making fun, unexpectedly placed happiness or grief,
mirrors, halls, interesting/uninteresting weather, presidents like
not really for their own sake but mostly just like to take mark of
time, the word like, triteness that is also sincere, sound effects, in-
truders, a computer desktop, thoughts of future children, glances
away/glances toward, something happening in the background
that distracts, feelings, a disappointing museum, goals, dumb
stories, bad advice, the not knowing how to live a life, chang-

ing the words from a line by Mary Ruefle but keeping the same relations between the words on purpose and not knowing how to feel: guilty or proud or wrong about it, love, dispersal, accusation, the time we sat in his childhood room on just the mattress after the bed frame had been gutted and taken (I am unsure what that had to do with) declining to have sex and instead masturbating closely facing each other like in school All of this while light poured in which even while it happened I couldn't help thinking would be so beautiful in a picture and how very sad to be able only to think up pictures and never paint them and wondering too if this sadness of being unable to do a thing was less or greater than the other (of loving someone an amount through your whole body and that moment being able to look right at him from a great height of physical pleasure that makes everything slow and further away all the while being so close you could hold any part of him and instead you are touching yourself) maybe, too sadness of measurement, sadness of naming, sadness of not knowing the names or that the right names come up during a bad example for instance the example of how as a moment happens where the rest of everything stops for it to distend into numerous, separate illuminations too scatter-y and vague to hold up but it goes too so even in the bright middle when it should be good there is also that part that hurts happening to you at the same time how even during this weird light's non-stop spreading through everything it is never really not dark.

24.

TIMOTHY
WILLIS
SANDERS

CAT STUFF

Jared called Michelle to invite her to Patrick's party. He joked about all the "cat stuff" in Patrick's parents' house. She said "maybe" and hung up the phone. Jared went to the mall. He stole a bottle of Cool Water cologne and a Tommy Hilfiger shirt. Jared went to 7-11 and paid a homeless man to buy him two cases of Natural Light. He walked home and hid the cases of Natural Light in the tall grass behind the backyard shed. Jared heard Nathan's Camaro pull in the driveway. He walked to the driveway and saw Nathan. Jared looked at Nathan's Camaro and thought, "I hope Nathan dies and I get his Camaro."

"What're you doing in the backyard?" said Nathan. "Smoking," said Jared.

"Well you need to mow. Dad wants you to mow," said Nathan.

"Yeah, I'll mow tomorrow," said Jared.

"You said that last weekend," said Nathan.

"Hey, will you give me a haircut?" said Jared.

"Will you promise to mow tomorrow?"

"I told you yes. I'll wake up early," said Jared.

"I'm serious. Dad's going to make me do it if you don't," said Nathan. Jared looked at Nathan's Camaro. It's red and has a blower on the hood.

"When are you going to get a bra?"

"When I can afford one. I'm saving for a system now."

"Your car looks kind of shitty without a bra."

"I just got it last week." Jared looked at Nathan's Camaro. He remembers his dad saying, "If you can get your grades up, we might consider doing something for you." Jared had no idea how to get his grades up.

"Give me a haircut," said Jared.

"Get inside," said Nathan.

Nathan cut Jared's hair. Jared took a shower. He rubbed gel in his hair and parted it down the middle. Jared looked at his hair and face. He popped two small zits on his cheek. Jared looked at his shoulders and chest. He made a promise to begin lifting weights. He sprayed his body with Cool Water cologne. Jared ironed the Tommy Hilfiger shirt. The shirt was blue with red stripes and had a white collar. Michelle said he looked good in a collar.

Jared paged Michelle at 7:45. She didn't call. Brad and Russell picked Jared up at 8:30. They arrived at the party at 9:30. They stood in a corner and drank Natural Light. Jared looked at cat stuff. There were cat paintings, cat throw pillows, and cat figurines. Jared looked at the party. He saw Curt Fernandez ash his cigarette in a glass filled with dark water. Jared thought "Curt Fernandez. What the fuck was she thinking? He's a sophomore. He's five feet tall. Fuck that guy."

Jared drank Natural Light with Brad and Russell. Russell talked about a GTO they were rebuilding in his Vo- Tech automotive class. It was 10:42. Jared wanted to rebuild GTOs. If he dropped out and went to Vo-Tech, he wouldn't get a Camaro. Jared wondered if he could rebuild a Camaro in Vo-Tech. He thought, "If I had a Camaro, she'd be here." He drank Natural Light and looked at the party. He focused on Cassie Kerns. Jared thought "Cassie Kerns is pretty hot." She was sitting on the couch talking to Curt Fernandez. Jared looked at her purse. It was open and sitting a foot behind her. Jared walked down the hallway to the other living room entrance. He reached into Cassie's purse and took some cash and a green pager.

Patrick stood drinking Natural Light with Jared, Russell, and Brad. It was past midnight. He looked at the party and bit his nails.
"Guys, there are too many people here," said Patrick.
Jared thought, "Too many sophomores. No Michelle."
"You want us to tell people to leave?" said Brad.

"Maybe soon. I just hope nothing gets burned or spilled," said Patrick. "My parents don't smoke."

"It'll be okay. Just chill," said Russell.

"I will. I just. I think people need to go soon." Patrick walked away.

Cassie Kerns knocked over the glass while looking for her pager. Dark water spilled on a tiger-print throw pillow and a stuffed cat. Jared remembered Patrick saying the cat died in 1983. Her name was Sigourney Weaver.

"Oh my God. Sorry. Anybody see a green pager?" said Cassie.

"Everybody out!" said Patrick. The party looked at Patrick. Patrick said "Everybody out!" and punched a hole in the wall.

"You heard him," said Brad. Jared and Brad ushered people to the door.

Patrick looked at the hole in the wall. Jared, Brad, and Russell looked at the hole too.

"Nice rage out Pat," said Brad.

"My mom's going to shit," said Patrick.

"Don't take much to fix," said Jared.

"Let's smoke," said Russell. He held up a joint.

"Let's go to the garage," said Brad.

Patrick looked at Jared.

"You really think it's easy to fix?" said Patrick.

"Yeah,"said Jared.

"Cool. Sorry Michelle never showed," said Patrick.

"Ah, whatever. I'll see her soon enough."

"Well, you smell good, fag," said Patrick.

"Fuck you," said Jared. Brad and Russell laughed. Patrick and Jared traded slap-punches and laughed. They walked to the garage.

Russell handed the joint to Brad.

"Check what I jacked," said Jared.

Jared showed them Cassie Kerns' pager. "This, and seventeen bucks," said Jared.

"Why would you take her shit?" said Patrick.

"Why?" said Jared.

"I had people at my house, they should be comfortable, not look and find their shit is gone," said Patrick. He kicked the floor and looked at his foot. Jared rolled his eyes. Brad cracked a knuckle. Russell blew out smoke and coughed.

"I don't care about sophomore girls," said Jared.

"Still," said Patrick.

"Everybody's drunk, she'll probably just think she lost it. Chill out." said Brad, cracking a knuckle.

"I gotta piss," said Jared.

Jared went into the house. He saw things doubling. He thought of paging Michelle "666" for no reason.

Jared peed a little on the leopard-print mat around the toilet. He looked in the mirror and clenched his teeth. Jared left the bathroom without flushing. He remembered Patrick punching the wall. Jared walked down the hallway. He glanced at a painting of a bobcat. The bobcat was sitting on a rock next to a waterfall. Jared opened the door to Patrick's parent's room. Two cats ran past his feet. Jared peed his boxers a little. He stepped inside the bedroom and shut the door.

Jared opened a nightstand drawer. He saw a jewelry box. The jewelry box had a latch in the shape of a lion's head. Jared opened the jewelry box. He took a diamond ring, gold earrings, and a cat pendant and put them in his pocket. He closed the box and the nightstand drawer. Jared walked to the garage.

"I have Vo-Tech tomorrow," said Russell.

"A Saturday? Fuck," said Patrick.

"I'm sleeping in," said Jared.

"It's cool. We're putting custom seats in the GTO. Plus, only have a half day on Monday," said Russell.

"Still though. Saturday? That's weak," said Jared.

"If you want a ride home, I'm leaving now," said Russell.

"Yeah lets get out of here," said Jared.

Patrick patted Jared's shoulder. Jared tensed his arms.

"Sorry for busting on you for taking Cassie's shit," said Patrick. "You know, you know, I don't care."

"It's cool," said Jared. Patrick put out his hand. Jared saw drywall on Patrick's knuckles. Jared shook Patrick's hand.

Jared sat in Russell's car. The cat pendant stabbed into his leg. He looked at the side mirror for a long time. He relaxed his face. Michelle said she can't trust his face sometimes.

ANA
CARRETE

PIANO

My mom took piano classes when she was little and her parents bought her a piano so she could practice at home. My mom stopped playing at some point. The piano is still there.

When my mom got married she asked my grandma if she could take her piano to her new home. Grandma said no. She said she could take the piano when she died.

When my sister and I were little we always tried to play the piano and my grandma would yell at us because we didn't know how to play it right.

She died and my uncle changed the key to grandma's house. We can't go in anymore.

1. A key is a thing that can open a lock.

2. I'm really afraid of touching musical instruments in public.

3. Human skulls are frequently used as a symbol of death.

4. When you think about your dead loved ones do you imagine a skull too?

POKE MY EYEBALLS
I WANT TO FEEL ALIVE

Can I get brain liposuction

somewhere in Beverly Hills

is it cheap

can I get before and after images

am I going to be dumber

can you suck the fat and inject it

in my ass

THE CULT OF ETERNAL YOUTH

If I shaved my head would people think I'm like
Britney or would they think I'm like
Natalie Portman or would they not care at all

and would you stop loving me or
would you point and laugh but still
kiss my forehead

MACARENA:
THE SCREAMO VERSION

My anger grows faster than me

it never goes away

I cry desperately and put my hands
in front while hitting the steering wheel
with my wrists

of course people stereotype and think
I'm just crazy about the Macarena

CHRIS
DANKLAND

THE CITY VERSUS *GODZILLA*

The crowd turned and burst screaming down the street. No single person was the first or last to run—they all did it together, at once. Something awful had happened. They were in incredible danger. They could be killed at any instant. As they ran, the people made howls and cries like tortured animals, covering their faces in their hands. Flickering street lights snapped and fell down on them like fly swatters. Only moments ago, a great and unprecedented wrath had announced itself. Above the buildings his huge lizard face appeared, dark and horrible, breathing fire. Men pleaded for their lives, children wept, mothers clutched their children and screamed. Nothing to be done. The shoes of the hysterical crowd made a sound like thunder as they ran, like applause at the end of a show. It was the end of everything.

Down the block, a small Japanese man in a gray suit pointed franticly at the sky. "A monster! How could one have predicted that I would meet such a sudden, horrific fate? I regret everything! All those hours wasted in vain attempts to taste success, the years of perpetual false beginnings and mistakes! I never visited South America! I never felt truly proud of anything! Last week I could have kissed Ms. Akimoto in the cold midnight air while we waited for the taxi…I know that she likes me, she kept brushing against me all night, oh…those dark, beautiful eyes! That smile, those lips! That gorgeous ass—"

A horrible high-pitched scream pierced the air, and a gigantic lizard foot came down, smearing him across the street.

GODZILLA VERSUS THE CITY

The monster screamed, raising its arms in the air. He kicked a hole into a hospital—seconds later a huge crowd of people came swarming out of the hole like ants, their tiny arms and legs flailing. The monster saw a naked little girl crying in the street, so he squashed her. He saw a city bus packed with people, so he breathed fire on it and screamed as it exploded, scattering bloody limbs and torsos fifteen feet into the air.

"Fuck this city," the monster thought to himself, pushing over a skyscraper. "All this god damn city cares about is its own god damned stupid self." He came across a bridge, ripped it apart. "They spent three hundred years putting this city together, building it up, filling it with false dreams and desires. Telling each other lies. Chasing glory." He punched a hole in an apartment building, pulling out a handful of people, gripped inside his giant monster fist. "But I am the only true glory. I am devastation, I am horror. I am the shadow that swallows everything. I am Hell," he said, throwing the people down his throat.

GODZILLA QUIETLY MUSES OVER THE CITY'S BURNING ASHES

The monster sat on a heap of rubble, looking over the smoldering city. The city was unrecognizable, utterly wrecked. Millions were dead, or dying. He didn't see any more people around, they were all gone now. He picked bones from his teeth with his sharp monster claws. The rampage finished, his anger sated, the monster felt strangely empty inside.

"Why do I only feel happy when I'm smashing things?" he wondered.

THE CITY WEEPS

Below him a woman appeared, wandering through the empty streets. Her shirt had been torn off and she was almost naked, covered in dark bruises and lacerations. She was screaming for her child, searching for him. The monster could tell that she would die soon.

"Monster," screamed the woman, beating her chest, pointing, looking up at the horror which stole everything she loved. "Monster," she screamed, collapsing to her knees.

"That is the only word you ever need to speak again," said the monster. "There is nothing but monster. Look upon me. I am monster. I throw into obsolescence and ruin all other words, all other thoughts. I am great, I am unconquerable. I am eternal. I come to kill everything. MONSTER," he hissed, baring his teeth. The woman moaned and fell on her face, sobbing.

MOTHRA TO THE RESCUE

Suddenly a giant monster moth appeared in the sky, as bright as the sun. The moth spoke:

"I AM MOTHRA, THE DIVINE MOTH. A DYING ALIEN RACE CREATED ME, GENETICALLY FUSING THE LAST OF THEIR LIFE FORCE WITH A COMMON EARTH SPECIES, THE WINGED LEPIDOPTERA. I AM METAMORPHOSIS INCARNATE. I AM EGG, I AM CATERPILLAR, I AM MOTH, I AM DEATH, I AM EGG AGAIN. I SPEAK WITH A SILENT MIND THAT TOUCHES ALL. I FLY AND FILL THE AIR WITH MUSIC. I SHOOT BOLTS OF LIFE ENERGY WITH MY ANTENNAE."

"Oh shit," said the monster, nervously.

"I WRITE POEMS IN THE FIRE WHILE BURNING ALIVE! I SPEAK LOVE WHILE THEY RIP MY BODY OPEN! I CLUTCH MY HEART AND SCREAM! I TOUCH THE

ANGUISHED SKIN AND CANCEROUS SORES! I THROW MYSELF UPON CORPSES! I WAKE THE DEAD!"

A yellow beam of light shot from the moth's head. The monster was paralyzed, grimacing in obvious pain. The yellow beam burned into the monster's scaly stomach, melting him. His body dripped and bubbled until nothing but a lake-sized puddle of green slush remained.

Shrieking, Mothra flapped her silver wings. "I AM MONSTER! I AM MONSTER!" she cried, as she flew around the ruins of the city in victorious, maniacal circles.

THE BASIC LAWS OF THE UNIVERSE

It was three in the morning and the Denny's down the street was about half full. I'd smoked a joint a couple hours ago to try and help me get to sleep, but it didn't work. I was frustrated. I didn't think I would get any sleep before having to go to work the next day. My bedroom was driving me crazy, flying around in endless loops like a swarm of tiny fruit flies. I had to get out of the house.

To my bloodshot eyes, the customers and table lamps and walls and white tables all blurred together into one delirious fog. And here I was, just one more dingy blur. One more peripheral smear in the corner of somebody's half-dreaming eye. Fuck my life, as the saying goes.

Who are all these people, I thought. What the hell are they doing here. "IT'S THREE IN THE MORNING," I felt like screaming.

Killing time, probably. Sobering up for the long drive home. Giving their wives and husbands some breathing space, so they could stop hating them. Chewing bacon and slurping coffee. Slurping bacon and chewing cups of caffeinated mud. Waiting things out.

I plopped down into a nearby booth and a fine mist of sandwich crumbs plumed up around me.

I felt an intense sensation of disappointed camaraderie with the human race. All these people. I'm not any different, I thought. I'm not special. One more ship passing through the night, as the saying goes. One more invisible heart. One more tired spelunker, hunkering down in some greasy all-night hole.

I ordered a milk and a piece of cherry pie, and opened the book I'd brought with me. I read it for a long time.

"Hey!" A girl I didn't know slid into my booth on the side opposite me. Her face beamed at me so hard I almost had to shield my eyes. She looked crazy. "I hope this is okay I just saw you sitting over here and I was sitting over there and I'm just waiting for my friend to come pick me up cuz his phone isn't working so I'm stuck here for awhile and I just saw you reading and I thought 'I wonder what he's reading' and you seemed like a friendly type of okay guy so I thought I'd just, is this okay? Am I bothering you? Jesus, I'm bothering you. I'm bothering you, aren't I."

I've been a druggie for long enough to know when someone's cracked out and wants something. Her dilated pupils stared at me like two black moons. Her jaw twitched. Her head jerked around like a bird's. She was on a mission.

"It's okay," I said, closing the book.

"I'm Tracy," she said, tilting her head to the side. I tilted my head to the side too, but she didn't notice. "Hey do you have a cigarette?" This was back when restaurants in Houston still had smoking sections.

"Sure," I said. I even lit it for her. "How's your night going?" I asked, after she took a deep puff, sighing endless curls of smoke.

"Oh…" She took another long drag and leaned back in the booth. "Thanks for the cigarette. Damn." She suddenly looked like she'd aged a couple decades. At first I'd thought she was in her early twenties, but now I was thinking early forties. Maybe she was old and just looked young, or maybe she was young and just looked old. She was skinny.

"You look like you needed that," I said, smiling.

"I need everything," she said. Her hands were shaking. "Just kidding I'm just waiting for my friend to come pick me up but her phone isn't working so I've been here for the last three hours waiting for her dumb ass and I told her I would be here at this specific Denny's but I don't have anyway I can get ahold of her cuz her phone is broke and now it's coming up real late and I'm not even sure where I'm gonna stay tonight cuz the manager's about to kick me out—" She pointed at a bald Hispanic man on the other side of the restaurant, staring hateful daggers at us. "That asshole he'll probably come over here in a minute or two that asshole."

Maybe he could hear us, because at that exact moment the manager came walking toward us. He walked toward us like he was planning on shooting someone. He stopped at our table, glaring at the woman.

"I already called the cops," he said. "I'm sorry about this sir," he said, glancing at me. His gaze almost immediately pulled back to Tracy, who was rolling her eyes and waving her middle finger at him. "Keep doing that, you just keep doing that. The police will be here any minute. Leave this man alone and let's wait for the police in my office."

"It's fine with me if she sits here," I said. "I want to order some french fries for both of us." The manager stared at me. "If you have chili cheese french fries, that would be awesome." The manager stared at me, and in his eyes I could see the reflection of gigantic all-caps curse words scrolling through his head. "Please," I said.

"I'm sorry, but I'm not serving this woman. This woman is a prostitute and a drug addict. The only reason she's here at all is because she doesn't have anywhere else to go. She's in here all the time. I'm not running a hotel. I've already called the police and they are sending a patrol car immediately. I understand how this might seem to you, but this has been an ongoing issue for a very long time and I'm at the end of my rope. I'm just trying to do my job."

"Fine, we'll leave then," I said, grabbing my book. "Let's go," I told her. I put a ten dollar bill on the table. She beamed, silently flicking off everyone in the restaurant as we left.

As we walked out to the car, I started instantly regretting my decision. I've been a druggie for long enough to know that you don't just take strangers home with you. If she saw where I lived, she'd follow me forever.

"Look," I said. I stopped walking. "Okay. First off, don't take me for a mark. I'm not a mark. I don't want that. I'm not even a good person, that manager was just being an asshole." She started to say something, but I held up my hand. "If you have a friend that's somewhere nearby—somewhere you want me to drop you off— that's no worries, I can do that. If you want me to drive you to another restaurant or a hotel, that's fine too. All I've got is twenty bucks, you can have that. But you can't stay at my place. I can give you a ride, and twenty bucks. That's everything I've got to offer."

"What's your name," she asked. I told her my name and she repeated it several times, like a mantra. "Chris. Chris." She leaned forward and grabbed my arm. "I'm sick, baby. You seem like such a nice guy. You're the nicest person I think I've ever met. You're so kind. I don't think you're a mark. It's just that I don't feel good. Okay? Do you understand? All I need is…" Her fingers were digging into my arm like eagle claws. "I need you to take me to… take me…" Suddenly she burst out sobbing, her body going half-limp. I caught her and held her, hugged her and stroked her hair.

She smelled like a whiff of air from an open manhole.

Through the restaurant window, the manager was staring at us with a couple other employees, laughing their assess off. "I don't know, I don't know, I don't know, I don't know, I don't know…" she moaned, openly weeping. The manager waved a couple people over and pointed. A couple of tired looking waiters showed up. They looked through the window at us and burst out laughing, clutching their stomachs.

I held her in my arms and petted her hair and said, "It's okay, it's okay, it's okay, it's okay, it's okay."

Forty minutes later I dropped her off at an apartment complex and gave her the rest of my money. She tried really hard to go home with me, and when that didn't work she tried really hard to get my phone number. I said thanks but no thanks.

By this point, the sun was coming up and I would have to be at work in two hours. As we drove, she started telling me everything that had gone wrong in her life from age ten to the present.

I told her I know how it goes. At the end of the day, nobody's really in your corner. If you're lucky, you might find some good friends or a couple of nice people, but the bottom line is that when all the propriety and generosity burn out and fade into the vague air like a twisting ribbon of crack smoke, you'll learn the basic laws of the universe. When you've got the world by the balls, an endless line of people show up to give you presents. But when you get to the point where you need everything, nobody will be there to give it to you.

When we pulled up to the apartment complex she crumpled the twenty-dollar bill in her fist, leaned over, and gave me a kiss on the cheek. She looked happy. I said, "I hope that things get better for you," but before I could finish my sentence she'd already jumped out of the car, hustling toward the apartment gates.

**OSCAR
SCHWARTZ**

HOW TO WRITE AN
EBOOK OF POETRY

Be part of the unchanging collection of mass and energy in the universe

Become manifest as a tiny fetus created out of the unchanging collection of mass and energy through the process of your parents having sex

Get born

Spend approximately twelve years vaguely experiencing things

Spend approximately four years becoming aware of experiences

Become self-aware

Start reading

Spend time reading

Feel for the first time a sense of not being part of the unchanging collection of mass and energy in the universe and slowly contemplate how this feeling is like what you've read about, that you are experiencing loneliness for the first time

Feel lonely

Spend time alone

Find a book that allows you to dissociate fully from past conceptions of yourself

Read that book many times

Carry the book with you everywhere

Buy a backpack

Put the book in the backpack

Try to become a character in the book

Try to become the writer of the book

Try to write exactly the same book but in "your own voice" and fail

Feel frustrated and worthless

Feel doubt

Feel inconsolable doubt one night in particular

Go for a walk

Suddenly realize that you have confused your ability to read and "enjoy" or "appreciate" a book with your ability to write

Make some money doing a job

Start writing

Slowly realize that you might be able to write something

Join the internet

See many people writing

Make a tumblr devoted to the books you read

Gain 24 notes on a funny review of a book in which you compare reading the book to sipping on a can of Diet Coca-Cola

Feel confident

Feel funny

Feel intelligent

Feel sense of entitlement

Spend full days in front of the internet

Feel part of the ever-changing collection of information on your screen

Get rejected by literary journals

Make a blog post about how many times you have been rejected by literary journals

Get 12 notes

Feel depressed

Feel jealous

Feel inadequate

Feel doubt and fear that you have "come nowhere" since you started writing

Reach out to people on the internet

Make an internet friend called Joanne

Tell Joanne about your grandparents

Read Joanne's emails about her earliest memories

Travel to where Joanne lives to meet her

Have sex with Joanne

Spend three months having sex with Joanne

Spend one day alone when Joanne returns to university

Spend one afternoon messaging Joanne while she's at university

Feel insecure

Spend one night awake while Joanne lies next to you and decide you do not want to feel insecure

Leave Joanne and go to your parents house

Live with your parents for three weeks

Go away for the weekend with old friends

Return to the city

Find an apartment

Start a new tumblr

Start writing about your experiences on the internet

Start using the language of the internet to write

Write a poem about twitter and use words like "IRL" in a way that is sincere in the sense that you use the word "IRL" all the time but also slightly ironic in that poetry is supposed to be a place where internet acronyms are not allowed

Feel freed from convention

Handwrite a poem about the internet

Read it fourteen times in one day

Decide that it is the best thing you've ever written, that everything else has been a lead up to this point, that it would be a good idea to delete all other poems you've ever written

Delete old poems off hard drive

Start writing a handwritten poem about the internet every day for seventy two days

Read them to your sister

Laugh insecurely when your sister isn't amazed by your poems and say yeah maybe they're not that good but secretly think that your sister doesn't spend enough time on the internet and couldn't understand them anyway

Start taking pictures of your seventy two handwritten internet poems and posting them online

Start getting followers

Get two hundred and fifteen followers

Get featured on #poetry on tumblr

Receive 1400 notes in twenty four hours

Type up your seventy two handwritten internet poems

Get a friend from high school who has since become a successful graphic designer to help you lay the poems out in a design that is easily readable but not boring

Collate the newly designed poems into a pdf and give it a title

The title should be "*72 handwritten internet poems*"

Start sending the pdf to various small press publishers

Start an excel spreadsheet that documents all the places you send your pdf

Get thirty four rejections

Get an email while sitting on a toilet in a bar while drunk that says your pdf has been accepted by a publisher of online eBooks

Be happy and relieved

Read the email another two times

Flush the toilet

Tell your friends

Promote your eBook online

Get interviewed by a few small literary blogs

Get a girlfriend

Start calling your girlfriend your "partner"

Feel happy

Feel good

Feel anxious

Feel dissatisfied

Go for a walk one night and panic when you see a broken chess-board on the sidewalk

Become obsessed with the fact a pawn in the game of chess doesn't have to move in the way it does, that it could move in any direction, that it could be replaced the any other material or shape, and that language and words are exactly the same and that your poems, your writing, are meaningless

Watch your partner's disinterest in your existential crisis

Watch you ruin your relationship

Travel

Meet someone in India

Come home

Train to become a nurse

Become a nurse

Start working as a nurse in a hospital

Feel sedated and part of the unchanging pile of mass and energy pulsating through the universe

Die

Get buried

Decompose

Become diffuse among various organic materials on earth

Be there as a collection of diffuse organic materials when humanity ends

Be there as a collection of diffuse organic materials when planet earth ends

Explode outwards into space with planet earth

Become diffuse among the various chemicals in the universe

Become more and more dispersed

Undergo unknowable transformations over unknowable lengths of time

For a brief time become part of the consciousness of some super intelligent life form

Observe that all previous intelligent data on earth has been accumulated by this super intelligent life force

View your eBook of poetry again amidst the troves of intelligent data

Be there when the super intelligent life form disintegrates for a reason beyond your comprehension

Become diffuse consciousness in the universe

Become reduced entirely to hydrogen atoms floating billions of light years away from each other

Spend many eternities doing unknown things

Start vibrating rapidly

Become infinitely fast and infinitely hot

End in a way that is, by definition, unknowable

STEVE
ROGGENBUCK

MY EBAY BUYERS RATING IS
THROUGH THE ROOF

my natural singing range is an octave and a half
with lessons i coudl sing over two octaves
thats why im prioritizing voice training in the year to come

yes, i am familiar with the scent of over five hundred plants
i can discern the age of your average tree by scent

my house contains treasures i have acumulated from
years of searching
i have decorations from every continent except antarctica

while perusing my home, u may be overcome by the beauty of a
given piece

my ebay buyers rating is through the roof

SOMEWHERE IN THE BOTTOM
OF THE RAIN

the news said that a family got lost in a corn maze
and was still in there at night and
they called 911
to get out of the maze
the news said that most people finish the maze in twenty five
minutes but this
family was in there for four hours and
i will kis you sitting on the pier of the
shalow river and
i will kis you in your
cars back seat on the gravel turnaround in the
rain and i will even kis you
another time
pushed against a dead tree in the back of a graveyard

im sory i like you better than everything
i want to whisper into your smile
come watch cops
with me
you make me need to write love poems
this is what i might whisper in the rain
come over and
nap with me i want you
i sleep like a raccoon in you
i sleep in you
like i am a raccoon somewhere
do you ever want
to climb into a birch tree with me
somewhere
in the bottom of the rain i want you

i turn you with slow animals
i turn you in the
dark trees
i have you with me in the dark trees
i am tryig to put you somewhere else in the
dark trees too
i am like the giraffe of you
wow
i am kising twenty five birds when I kis you

four hours of rain in the corn
i kis you and i dream that i am a raccoon

you trip and u
fall and
instead of geting up you stay down and
i kis you on the ground
in a corn field
at night

in december michigan there wil be a snow bank
somewhere of u and me and
your warm
legs and i am in between kising u
sweet drems you are very beautiful
i wil sing to
you justin bieber with my lips
on you and
my hands on you so
thank you i am far into the warm tunnels
of you
i will bring to
you my warm dark we are under a pine
tree and
it is mid night so
thank you i am deep into the rain of you

29.

LUNA
MIGUEL

YOUTH

Little prostitute,

carnivorous birds
ejaculate on your wings

and nevertheless you fly.

Translated by Jeremy Spencer

POEM AND CIGARETTE

One hundred hours under the cricket call of daisies.
Fingers crossed for a quick return.
Curtains closed until the sun reclaims me.

One hundred hours where Venus does no damage.

Take the scissors and look away.

Translated by Jeremy Spencer

MUSEUM OF CANCERS

(That's why they'll cut off your feet. That's why they'll seal your eyes with bits of ancient maps. That's why they'll say your name in celebration of the pancreas. Got it? That's why the uterus is darker - intestine and cornea-. That's why they'll cut out prayer. Got it?)

-Luna Miguel Santos: living / sugar cancer

-Ana Santos Payán: living / mom cancer

-Pedro Miguel Tomás: living / health cancer

-Chus Tomás: living / patience cancer

-Pedro Miguel: dead / grandpa cancer

-Mercedes Payán: living / loneliness cancer

-Manolo Santos: living / family cancer

-José Ángel Valente: dead / light cancer

-Roberto Bolaño: dead / probabilities cancer

-David Foster Wallace: dead / economic cancer

-Marcel Schwob: dead / syphilitic cancer

-Antonio J. Rodríguez: living / Europe cancer

(That's why it hurts me, you know? That's why my blood hurts:

because it's outside. And inside it doesn't hurt and outside it kills. And inside it doesn't ache and outside it frightens. What intense blood. How dangerous. That's why it hurts me, understand. Do you understand?)

-Daniel Clowes: living / ghost cancer

-Clarice Lispector: dead / audacity cancer

-Alejandra Pizarnik: muerta / cage cancer

-Miguel Hernández: dead / moon cancer

-Jorge Luis Borges: muerto / widow cancer

-Michel Houellebecq: living / penile cancer

(That's why I don't exist. You're leaving already? That's why we all escape once healed. Who stays behind? Or worse. Where?)

-Antonin Artaud: dead / insane cancer

-T.S. Eliot: dead / phoenician cancer

-Eduardo Cirlot: dead / Astarte cancer

-Édmond Jabés: dead / Egypt cancer

-Antonio Machado: dead / Leonor cancer

-Vladimir Nabokov: dead / gut cancer's fire cancer

-Thomas Pynchon: living / face cancer

-Sharon Olds: living / satan cancer

-Dorothea Lasky: living / milk cancer

-Virginia Woolf: dead / water cancer

(That's why I drown. That's why I don't understand love. That's why I don't fall ill. That's why I only sicken. You know? I only sicken.)

-Charles Baudelaire: dead / ugly cancer

-Arthur Rimbaud: dead / elephant cancer

-Paul Valéry: dead / marine cancer

-Joyce Mansour: dead / woman cancer

-Paul Éluard: dead / blue cancer

-Lysiane Rakotoson: living / snow cancer

(Thus these stains. And this skin. Like an eternal scar, long and white, my skin is scar, my skin is umbilical cord between tongue and armpits. Thus these red stains. Thus these black stains. Thus this smell of fruit: tongue, armpits)

-Emily Dickinson: dead / cunt cancer

-Anne Sexton: dead / cunt cancer

-Anna Akhmatova: dead / cunt cancer

-Sylvia Plath: dead / cunt cancer

-Marina Tsvetaeva: dead / cunt cancer

-Javier Marías: living / heavy cancer

-Enrique Vila-Matas: living / Enrique Vila-Matas cancer

-Gonzalo Torné: living / spy cancer

-Rodrigo Fresán: living / troubling cancer

-Tao Lin: living / MDMA cancer

-Ben Brooks: living / deer cancer

-Unai Velasco: living / 1990 cancer

(That's why I vomited, do you understand? Thus the bulimia of those months trying to slim down to draw pity, trying sickness impregnated with who knows what. Trying literature. That's why I vomited, do you remember?)

-Ana Santos Payán: living /

-Ana Santos Payán: living /

-Ana Santos Payán: alive /

Translated by Kevin Cole

CRISPIN
BEST

IO OR LET'S GONNA FUCK

When i die
stomp three thousand alabaster skateboards in my memory
kickflip my corpse into a ditch
eat pizza
sing

when i'm alive
every morning i am still me wishing
i was in a sleeping bag with you
on a jovian moon

i am dropping a frisbee with everyone watching
if we ever talk and you don't smile
there are hills in you and i am on them

o greyskull
o solemn wall-hung portrait of a kangaroo
o digestive biscuits in the spring

there are hills i am on
i love you is like sitting on a bench
if you think about it
everything is like that

when i die
remember us
it's cold
i can only hug your legs one way
and they can only hug me another
i like both

i am beside myself when i am beside myself
i am beside myself when i am beside you
o goatse in the snow
o tubgirl in the rain
o modern american poetry

it is truly okay to want to let me smooch you
knock my legs off with a plastic cricket bat
I'm ready

o besunglassed sun in the summer
o party rings
o life
o Des'ree
o Sonique
you

when I'm alive
feed me ex boyfriends' foibles
your thoughts on films
past moral lapses
let me be your ginger hard drive

listen I think of you while eating pizza

o dragostea din tea
o thudding in the electric lumber of my chest
o Fisher price
o feet

motherfucking Teresa
truly I could cry in a bathroom
I want you on Google street view

o brookside
o blobby
o burmese cliffbuilt monastery in May

my big idea is basically just the X-Games
but for dogs

we're listening to ace of base
in our winter coats

when I'm alive
I love you like soup
and want to fuck you the same way

o Bison
o Balrog
o Blanka
o Guile

by the way I've never kissed someone
this close to a plug socket
before
so thank you

girl
is your daddy Archimedes
because you're 3.1415 FINE

girl
is yr daddy a film director
because jean-luc goDAMN
that ass leaves me breathless

girl
I saw you

looking over at me
from across the bar
and i couldn't help noticing
that here is a picture
i'm holding
of a very beautiful dog
aw look

o earthquake
o savage
o hitman
o hulk

when i'm alive
it is strange to be naked in one room
and then walk to another room
and be naked there instead

we have raised this wild invisible animal
alone together
came home to it
what did we expect

you hate that metaphor though

when i die
know that i died how i lived:
not wanting to die

when i die:
know that i lived doing what i loved:
your mum

when i die
scatter my ashes on the internet

o puzz 3-d
o crystal maze
o mood-lit silk-bound aubergine

this poem is my petition
for every film in history
to be renamed
"*the mighty ducks*
[and then the next available number]"

when i'm alive
i am the first person to ever use sarcasm
everyone is so confused
did i enjoy the rice pudding or not

we are in the wildflowers again
throw your spanx into the distance
you are the barefoot me

o haunted toaster buried in a panic and the woods
o kerplunk
o huggies pull ups
o cloud cap over mount cleveland

when i die
roll my corpse down an up-escalator
i feel like my skeleton might enjoy that
eventually

let's watch cool runnings in the bath
sitting like they do
let's listen to big willy style in bed

when i'm alive

find me topless in your dreams
screaming i love you like white people love *mambo #5*
whispering i love you like a bike

o curly wurly wrapper
o crepitating autumn leaf
o nokia 3210
o mars bar ice cream in september and the rain

we like each other and vice versa

when i die
endorse me on linkedin
for the messed up sex things i wanted to do
but couldn't

o distance
o abandoned fairground
o tamagotchi
o gentle choad poking meekly out
o blue corn tortilla on the ground

let's gonna fuck

when i die
i will miss watching a sad magpie try to get through a window
i miss looking at a fucked up magpie with you

if u read this poem your life will be better
let's go bowling to celebrate

it's friday with you even when it isn't
especially

LUCY K
SHAW

ROBERT BURNS

I read the details out loud to Jimmy as we stood at the base of the statue on literary walk in Central Park.

"He died in 1796 at the age of thirty seven... The statue was put here in 1880... Oh wow, five thousand people came out. Can you even imagine? I don't even have that many followers on Tumblr." Jimmy was eating an ice cream. I had just learned where the phrase, "What would you do for a Klondike bar?" comes from. An instance, which had reminded me, cruelly, I felt, that I hadn't grown up in America like the rest of my friends. "I just knew it as a Kanye lyric," I had said sheepishly. *"...Or some girl who looks Christina Milian like..."*

Jimmy was edging away from the statue and I was still standing at the base, staring up. We were on our way to the Whitney gallery, but I kept getting sidetracked and looking at statues and buskers and squirrels and people in rowing boats and everything else that was happening at the center of the universe.

"Don't you think it's weird though, Jimmy?"

For some reason I said his name a lot in conversation. It just felt necessary. He had said it was something to do with our dynamic, or the fact that I was seven months older than him. I just really enjoyed the way it sounded.

Jimmy wasn't interested in the statue.

"Jimmy, don't you think it's crazy that a poet could have an enormous statue in Central Park? It seems insane. The plaque says he was a national hero. How distinct does one have to be as a poet to become a national hero? It seems impossible."

Jimmy was laughing at me. "I think," he said, "that's what it's about, probably. The *national* part. It would have been five thousand Scottish immigrants who came out to stand in the park and meet each other in 1880. They probably didn't really care about the poetry. Do you even care about his poetry?"

"I never read any of it." I said, smiling. "I have literally never read a poem by Robert Burns."

Jimmy dropped part of his ice cream on the ground. We both watched it fall in extra slow motion.

"Okay, let's go." I said, laughing. "I'm sorry about what happened to your ice cream."

It was our first time doing something together while serious and sober, and we were getting along much better than I would have expected. Our relationship had moved from random hook-ups to rejected hook-ups to new acquaintances to very good friends, and I liked him. He looked like the all-American man, with his good height and broad shoulders, always dressed in a way that made me think he'd just returned from the Second World War. He had a 1940s kind of Hollywood image, and he was, I thought, almost movie-star good-looking. A recent development, I had decided, because he was much nicer than anyone I'd ever known who had grown up so beautiful.

Initially, we had become acquainted because, one day, a few months previous, (when I was in another country) I had asked my Twitter followers to email me about how they were feeling. It was something that I did sometimes, whenever I felt a specific type of loneliness. And it was fun for me. I usually received ten to fifteen emails from people who didn't know whom else to talk to.

On May 25ᵗʰ, Jimmy wrote;
I have this headache; I don't what's wrong with me because I never get headaches. But now I have one. I'm eating an apple because that's what I do to feel better. I live in New York. New York is ugly today, but it's okay because I can feel good about not going outside and just lying on my bed. How are you feeling today?

An hour later, I replied;
Maybe you should have a glass of water? Sometimes dehydration can cause headaches, and sometimes when it's been hot or something, or you've been in a place with AC for too long, you can get dehydrated without even realizing.

I doubt it would hurt to try anyway.

Thank you for asking how I am. You didn't have to do that. I just wanted to know how other people are feeling. I'm feeling okay. A little sad but it doesn't seem like there's a specific reason. This will probably change soon. I think that's how it works

Another hour later, he wrote;
Somehow I forgot all about water... Just had a nap and some water on your advice and I feel all better. Hope you feel better too. I can never tell someone how I'm doing without asking them after, but also I'm generally curious. Vague sadness can be okay sometimes, like when it feels like you're holding something very delicate and you feel especially alive... but maybe that's not at all what you are feeling!

Somehow I forgot all about him until a month later when I was in New York too, and he introduced himself to me at a party. He was funny and interested in the same things I was interested in. He was unassuming and receptive to absurdity (which was all I could see); so from then on, I would spend my time with him as often as

I could. I consistently felt happy to see him, which felt completely unusual for me around new boys.

After the few nights I had stayed at his apartment, before we knew each other well, he would insist on walking me home in the morning, or on walking me to wherever I was going. A couple of times we stopped at a supermarket by the park so that I could buy myself a good morning Redbull.

Both of those times he bought a shiny, red apple and it seemed so amusing to me, like he was playing the character of himself in the scene I was already writing.

I was always busy making people into characters, and Jimmy was good at providing his own motifs.

One night, when we were drunk and failing at buying drugs from somebody in another part of Brooklyn, we lay down together in the park and looked up at the stars because they were there. We didn't know anything else about stars besides the same things that everyone knows. Orion's Belt. The Big Dipper. Ursa Major. Ursa Minor. And we were in New York anyway, so we could see only a handful of them, and very faintly. But it was quiet and we were alone, and there was something comforting about being in close proximity to him, because he seemed to have a similar kind of sadness to the one that I had.

"Are you happy with what you've achieved in your life so far?" He asked, confirming that he was one of those people who couldn't enjoy the moment for worrying about the next one. I am, of course, also one of those people.

I imagined an owl watching down on us from a treetop, listening closely and shaking its head at our naivety. "Just shut up and kiss her," the imaginary owl was whispering aggressively, almost falling out of the tree for peering over.

I didn't know if owls really lived in Brooklyn, but as everyone else did, it seemed entirely possible.

"Yes, I think I am." I told him, after thinking for a few seconds, feeling surprised that I could truthfully answer yes to that question.

"Are you?"

"I don't know... I guess, I don't know."

His voice trailed off to a very quiet volume.

"Your life is really good, in my opinion." I told him. "You live here. You live right next to this park. And you have really good friends. I think you're doing well. It seems exciting. A lot could happen."

I felt like his life made a lot more sense than mine did at this point.

"Maybe, I guess. But I think... I haven't really... done anything yet. I haven't made any kind of name for myself, or made anything lasting or remarkable. I don't have any kind of legacy."

He was one of the first people I had befriended in a long time, who didn't have delusions of grandeur and/or a popular internet presence and inflated sense-of-self, padded by reblogs and retweets and a devoted yet ultimately faceless following. He wrote poetry that I had read and enjoyed, but he was as yet untouched by the possibility of internet micro-fame. Internet micro-fame being something I had, for some reason, worked towards and achieved within the last year of my life.

I could tell that he was intrigued though.

"Mmm. It doesn't mean anything though, you know. It doesn't matter if people know you. You're actually living your life instead of trying to present it or perform it or sell it to someone. It feels really refreshing to me. You don't need strangers to validate your work, or your life… You're writing all the time. That's the important thing."

I didn't know if I was giving advice to Jimmy or to myself. Although, either way, I knew that I hadn't really been following it.

"I think it makes a difference though. You probably forgot what it was like before." He told me. "If you hadn't started publishing your magazine and if people didn't know your writing, would you still be happy with your life right now?"

For some reason, I thought of the first lines of the poem, *America* by Allen Ginsberg. I had been thinking about Allen Ginsberg's business sense a lot lately. I was always imagining him going into literary agents' offices, thrusting manuscripts at people and demanding attention.

> *"America I've given you all and now I'm nothing.*
> *America two dollars and twenty-seven cents January 17, 1956."*

"The home of the brave and the land of the free," I thought, unsure if I was being sarcastic or completely sincere with myself. Like Ginsberg, I didn't want to do any of the official stuff properly. I was making everything up as I went along. I didn't know the real answer to his question, but I knew that there was still a lot more work to be done.

I was twenty-five years old, unemployed, homeless, single. I had a small amount of money left in my bank account and no idea of how to get any more without doing a job I didn't want to do. I was drunk and lying down in a Brooklyn park at night with a boy I hardly knew.

I felt more excited than I had done in a long time.

"I just learned that working hard on things makes me less depressed, I think. So, I don't know. It's hard for me to understand the motivation behind anything I do beyond... I don't think I can afford to feel so bad again. I spent too much time already, doing that. It doesn't seem like an option any more. I wouldn't have anything to recover for the next time."

We were silent in the grass for a little while and then he reached over and held my hand in his hand, his so much bigger than mine. We pushed our legs together and I felt the whole of my foot fit into the nook between his ankle and his toes.

"The satisfaction comes in the creating," I said, thinking out loud. "The way people perceive it is their own business. It's terrible to concern ourselves with it, as long as the work remains a compulsion."

Looking up at the night sky, I considered the importance of being patient.

I remembered that moment as we started to walk away from the Robert Burns statue those few weeks later. In comparison to it, we had been so colorful and filled with life. I couldn't think of anything more beautiful than two new people lying together on the grass, in the dark, looking upwards, holding on to each other. And it wasn't for show. We didn't need five thousand people, just our bodies on the ground.

I hoped that there would never be a bronze statue of either one of us, in some far away park, in our dead futures.

"It's funny," Jimmy said, "this statue has been here since 1880. A hundred and seven years before we were even born, all of our lives up until now, and it never moves; it doesn't know anything. It just stays here in this park looking over at the other statues. And we can leave now and we can go to the Whitney gallery, and we can go out tonight, and we can go to the beach tomorrow, but this statue has to just stay here, forever."

I nodded and smiled at him. I thought of a hundred different ways to tell him that it wouldn't help us to worry about legacy. Though I knew it was really me who needed to remember that.

"Jimmy, I want to go and sit on the great lawn," I said. "We can go to the gallery later. We still have lots of time. It's early."

32.

ANDREW
DUNCAN
WORTHINGTON

I AM AN INANIMATE OBJECT

I no longer read magazines in the bathroom. I hardly even take a good novel or textbook in there anymore. Usually it is my laptop that accompanies me to the shitter. We've been together about a little over a year. I hardly go a day without seeing it. We will be announcing our engagement any day. Then I will hold it on my lap, and we will spoon and spoon like we have never spooned before.

I go to the drinking fountain. Salt water comes out. I ask a man why it tastes like that. He says, "They do it for real here." Hmmm. That is an interesting take on water. I fill a bottle full of salt water. I tightly turn the cap closed. I will have to show this to someone. Someone will marvel at this. Perhaps the bank teller will. Yes, I am quite sure the bank will love this.

I go to the bank. The teller tells me to give them money. I say that I didn't bring money and I just want to talk. The teller says there is no time to talk, there's only so much sunlight. The teller gives me a pen to sign my paycheck that I usually bring on Fridays. It is Friday but I didn't pick up my paycheck because I was excited about the salt water.

I go across the street to the grocery store and buy tampons and condoms. As I am waiting in line I also decide to buy a gossip magazine and an eight-pack of store brand peanut butter cups. But I don't have money to pay for the peanut butter cups, so I walk out of the store with the tampons, condoms, gossip magazine, and peanut butter cups. As I leave the store a man says, "Hey." He wants to know where I am going. I tell him I don't know. He says I have to pay for the items. I say I did.

HARRY POTTER AS
A SEX GUIDE

Harry was often brooding throughout the books
he had issues such as mortality and the fate of the universe that
were worrying him but I wonder if his lack of sexual excursion
may have also been a large reason
for his brooding

An asshole killed his mother and left a mark on his forehead immediately thereafter

I read the more romantic sections in *Goblet of Fire* over and over
again
he even had a kind of hot date to the yule ball
but he just broods the whole time about Cho Chang
and then he kind of kills her boyfriend
or at least he feels responsible for his death

He is always too busy to bother

And at the end of the series he kills Voldemort
after coming back from the dead

And then it jumps forward nineteen years
and he must have had sex because he has kids
and he probably has a nice house
and a yard
and he takes care of it
maybe even with muggle landscaping equipment
and Ginny has a garden

and maybe even takes care of it with muggle landscaping equipment but they might just use magic for all of the yard work

FRANK
HINTON

EXCERPT FROM *ETERNAL FREEDOM FROM SOCIAL AND NATURAL PROGRAMMING*

I am nothing.

A girl named Frank stepped out of the shower and began a strange set of jumping jacks. She's showered in the dark and can't see herself. This is the third day she has showered in total darkness. At first it had been terrifying but soon, like any kind of aloneness, a calm, confidence set about her and thus, Frank found it impossible to shower in the presence of light. The darker, the better. She felt the skin on her body rise and fall as she jumped, her small bits of body fat, her breasts, the rump of her ass heaved in the darkness. She made smooth, coordinated arcs; the tips of her fingers pressed outward almost as if beyond the limits of her skin, and as her joints began to soften and extend, she felt herself opening like a kind of flower of the night. The balls of her feet thumped against the floor and she began to sweat. After maybe eighty or ninety jumping jacks she stopped and panting, fumbled for her phone. She wiped the misty condensation from her phone and clicked at it. Two strange lights, one natural, one electric, entered the bathroom and fell across her skin. She processed a small, ephemeral emotion that immediately became translatable into text.

@frankhinton: subtle, unassuming pale light undulating over my fucked body

Frank couldn't remember the time of day. This was a period of minimal responsibility, marked by the ability to sleep and roam at will. Her ultimate goal in the last months had been to achieve a kind of life wherein the cycle of waking by day and sleeping by night was broken down into meaningless, unstructured scenes. This, coupled with her lack of debt, was freedom. She peered through the window and ascertained it was some part of the early afternoon. She opened the bathroom door and paced the hallway on her phone. She scrolled through a series of Facebook photos, semi-consciously judging her friends and their activities, noting and cataloguing each of their physical weaknesses against her own. Every flaw was a necessary compartment in her mental arrangement of the universe. Although she presumed herself to be something of a "good" person, her vast array of judgments about other's physical and mental states (mostly negative) seemed to buoy this air of confidence she held. Her ability to judge others, collect their flaws and arrange them delicately within her world concept had increased a thousand-fold since the inception of her Facebook account.

She clicked "like" on a particularly horse-faced photo of her friend Mallory and noted that the flash had captured an unflattering smear of makeup about her cheeks, the subtle hair upon her philtrum, a slightly canine tooth. Mallory was in general considered beautiful, and had probably slept with more attractive men than Frank, but she was terribly un-photogenic and this, secretly, was what Frank loved most about her/her Facebook feed.

Further along into her scroll, she encountered a series of baby photos, each one containing flickering glints of freakishness: a lobster skinned newborn, a fat little girl, a boy with overly long arms. Each photo was adorned with likes and comments and Frank added her own likes and comments: "CUTE!" or "adorbs..." while simultaneously judging these friends. Somewhere, also vocal in her was a voice, endlessly whispering 'You are inherently good, everyone does this.'

In the living room, Frank sat quietly next to a sleeping male who was curled up semi-fetal and breathing gently. She was unable to discern if this male was one of her friends or one of her sister's friends. She continued to inspect her phone, taking a picture of the sleeping male and uploading it to Instagram with a valencia overlay. She tagged the photo as "shit-kid" and then opened Twitter.

@frankhinton: whenever i close my eyes i see multi-colored cartoon octopi gradually tessellating

Frank placed her phone onto the coffee table and subsumed the living room. There were four other people sleeping gently throughout the space, strewn about the furniture. A kind of creamy brown seemed to pervade the atmosphere. The light, balked by curtains, the absence of electricity, the hum and plosive of human internals in sleep, bottles of different size and shape, drug paraphernalia, strata of dust climbing or descending horizontally within the windless space, coalesced. Frank counted her breaths slowly, inhaling, noting the moment after inhaling, exhaling, noting the moment after exhaling, inhaling and so on. She curled her toes across the floor, each one scraping against the hardwood. Her sweat dried over her body and she noted now, that just a few moments ago her breasts had been bouncing up and down, braless in the full dark of the bathroom. She tried again to capture that slightly excited state, but became suddenly aware of her phone entering power-saving mode and reached out, instinctively, to stop the screen from turning off. She pulled the phone toward her and felt the unknown male's legs extend behind her, forming a kind of pillow for her lower back. He was wearing cheap, shitty Joe Fresh jeans. His socks were mismatched, brown. Often when she came upon sleeping people she liked to imagine them as corpses.

@kenbaumann: a human brain that once dead unravels into a long flat tapeworm of ghost consciousness **retweeted by Frankhinton**

I am everything.

A certain path, seldom walked holds a different Frank, a three hundred forty-seven month old boy between its edges. He walks, in dimming summer light amongst the chamomile, the purpled beach peas, the clusters of unripe crowberries. He's certain he's the only one to walk this path since last summer and can feel familiar stones, grooves and convexities; the muscle memories of some million steps. A dewy sea of wood sorrel spreads on either side of the path now, red veins spreading outward, the pattern seeming to overlay their moist peduncies. Frank can see the sun now cresting, and path soil gives to sand, steps turn crunchy and softer, an instant changes the air, now cool and salty he arrives at the small beach and removes his sneakers, fills the spaces between his toes with red-rich sand, glistening specks of magnesium, seawater that has not yet dried. Great headlands rise up on either side of him, enclosing him in seclusion. The sun pierces the great line at the end of the visible sea and Frank walks forward, steady to meet the water. Feeling heavy, he jumps a few times, extending his arms outward, then stops and looks to see what marks he's made in the sand. The fetch and uprush are strongest here, the drone of wind and wave and shore work to cancel out any conscious thought, instead allowing Frank's mind to flow evenly, like a dead pulse, along a single moment of presence.

This is surely the edge of the world, Frank thinks. Some fog has formed on the horizon when Frank opens his eyes, a salt fish breaks the glass of the ocean, a bird fades beyond sight. The refulgent sun dips into the froth and after ten minutes of this solitude it's closer to night than day.

Shore receded. Frank sits cross-legged and removes a photograph from his pocket. The girl in the picture is sitting next to him on this red sand beach, smiling, bright faced. Frank twins his smile with hers, and perfectly, because she is his twin sister, the love of his life, long dead.

Subtle, pale light creeps imperceptibly across Frank's body. Frank places the photograph back into his pocket and reminds himself this dead and beloved creature is a distraction. There is, Frank thinks, no self beyond the eternal ground of all being. His sister is of this sand, of this light, dust to dust and all that.

Far off the purpled clouds swell and gather, amassing for some storm. Frank watches heavens mix, pokes his finger into the sand, sighs. This is the end of the world.

He stands in fresh twilight and brushes the granules from his shorts. The sea is far off now, and he sits in a hollow scarp riddled with clusters of loose brown algae, seaweed, and clamshells. The magnesium glistens and twinkles with each step and he sighs, turning away from this special place, and walks back into his path, without need of light, into the vague darkness feeling nothing but a distant calm, somewhere outside himself, always slipping away.

SARAH JEAN ALEXANDER

PEOPLE DON'T WANT
PEOPLE ANYMORE

How does a person cope with completing a task
to the absolute highest standard, when everything
goes exactly right. What is left to say when
there is no room for error? Does anyone have fun
anymore? I thought the aurora borealis was
something the internet made up because god
didn't make me as beautiful as the sky.
How do you make a child feel less alone without lying to her?
If nothing happens for no reason anyway,
then I want to be done trying.
Sometimes I think it would be comfortable
to hide under the covers until I pass away and rot,
but I can't shake this diaphanous will to live.
Please continually tell me I am wrong.
You could take an ice cream scooper and
swing it at the sky but you still won't
be able to fly. I want to be more responsible for
the disconsolate ways I make you feel at night.
Nothing will ever taste better than the time
I had a bite of vanilla sundae in my mouth
and Chris Beckmeyer was drinking hot cocoa
and we kissed to see if we could make steam
pour from our mouths.
This is what I mean.
People don't want people anymore. No one tries
hard enough. And those of us that do will be
immediately made small by those of us
that are smaller still.
He is afraid and so is she.

The lines creased into a person's skin when
they wake up in the morning are infallible
and beautiful but I don't think I believe that
they exist anymore. If I need someone to hold my
hand through every door that is shut when I approach it
then I will find someone and grip them tight.
Do you remember how cold I thought my body
felt the first time I became very sick around you?
I write a lot of poems but none of them are true.
Where are we going?
I have learned three mollifying
things since I have been alive:
The northern lights are real.
Children know how to lie.
Magic doesn't happen when two mouths touch,
but we try everyday anyway.

REMEMBER TO

I dreamt about walking around Ikea by myself and buying a lime green ice cube tray. I drive to the post office and pick out a large flat rate shipping box. I put the ice cube tray inside and I see my cat walking in the air in front of me. I grab her before she falls and put her inside the box too. I draw a picture of an onion bagel and on the back of the picture I write "happy birthday" and poke a string through it and tie it around my cat's orange mane. I write a note that says 'we can share this' and tie that note around her mane too. My cat wears two necklaces now. In my dream I pay the postage and the box ships off to you.

To-Do

- make a to-do list and check off at least ten things by midnight
- dress appropriately for the weather and run six miles
- drink a coffee with a splash of milk
- put some money in the bank but not too much
- hide the rest somewhere in my underwear drawer
- put my boots on and then switch them out for a pair without holes on the bottom
- spend some money on groceries
- check "brussels sprouts" and "pickles- big jar" off of my to-buy list

I lie in a bed with dark brown curtains covering the windows but the sun is still lighting up your pale skin and I think, "Wow, I feel like I am a fire next to you." I am the last to fall asleep and the first to wake up when we are with each other. I use this time to study the colors in your beard. I use this time to tell myself, "Don't forget this, don't forget this." I feel mad. I think, "I am a warm body

347

existing next to you." I feel your thighs. I feel safe. I feel alive.

To-Do

- sing along to "*The Vowels, Pt. 2*" while I curl my eyelashes
- draw a picture of a fat puppy and frame it and hang it above my bed
- hug my cat and kiss her on the nose
- put on headphones and listen to rap music while I sit on the corner of my mattress
- start reading the first chapter of *Infinite Jest* and drink a Colt 45
- consider throwing up but brush my teeth instead
- water my wilting plants because I forgot about them for two weeks
- cry loudly and then quietly in the shower

I hand you two teaspoons of Robitussin in a small bottle cap and a glass of orange juice to chase it. I suck on a cough drop and we zip our coats up to our necks and head outside. I hear you sniff. I look up at your face while we walk, your hair and cheekbones framed by a gray morning ceiling. You are touching your nose. I say, "Don't touch your nose" and push your hand away. The skin around your nostrils is raw. You say, "Okay" and we take the L to 8th Avenue and the A downtown to Chambers Street. The sky is even grayer now as we walk out of the train station. You put your left arm across my shoulders and I put my right arm behind your back and clutch onto your jacket. I say "This feels nice" and you agree.

To-Do

- play on the internet for a few hours or all day
- Google "what are these freckles on my cat's mouth she is four years old"

- drink two more cups of coffee with two more splashes of milk
- spend $65 on books using PayPal
- disable PayPal account
- send an email to my sister
- try not to forget my house key
- get locked out for two hours

The pier forks and we stand in between left and right, not making an effort to move from the center of all the wooden planks. I point at a circle across the river and say, "Look at that shitty ferris wheel" and you say, "That's a clock, look at its hands" and I take your hand and ask you, "What time is it?" and you look away from the clock and down at your yellow watch and say, "It's half five, let's eat." I pull my phone out of your coat pocket and Yelp the pizza places nearest to where we are and we choose the only one with five stars. It is raining and we are walking in the rain together. We share a zucchini pizza while wearing wet sweaters and I slip one hand up and inside of your sleeve. As it is happening, I think, "You are something I believe in" and I know this will be a moment that I will remember for a long time and it is a thing you probably do not even notice.

To-Do

- watch a fly try to break through the screen in my bedroom window
- convince myself it really wants to be inside with me
- spend forty five minutes scrolling through Netflix before deciding to watch *King of the Hill*
- spend eight minutes choosing an episode
- eat half a slice of chocolate cake and save the second half for later
- throw away my dead plants
- close my eyes for three hours and stay awake
- look at the sky through my bedroom window

- say "goodbye" to every plane that flies by
- miss you
- be okay

We lie in a bed together. It is late at night or early in the morning and your breath begins to steady. I can tell you are about to fall asleep. I slide closer to you and breathe in and smell the darkness and leftover day on your skin. You wrap your arms around my ribcage and move them up and down slowly. You say, "This is me holding onto you" and we fall asleep.

35.

WILLIS
PLUMMER

ANGLE OF YAWN

You've got a broken faucet and I've got fifteen minutes until class. I dig holes in the dirt in the pots on the windowsill; fill them with seeds, water, and more dirt. Park the driveway in the truck. Flowers will be here soon. My friends are coming to the city from other places to hang out and talk about the lives they lead on the internet. Let the leaves, rustling and quiet, meander across your front yard, searching for the trees they fell from. I look up and the sun is hot and bright in the sky but pouring into my eyes like lemonade. I want only to hold the girl with the B12 deficiency again, but I know that if I could, I would want only a girl with sufficient B vitamins. Jacques Lacan tells us that lack is the rational kernel of love, and we both know my heart is a dirty casserole dish.

The exposed redbrick was not an aesthetic decision; someone designed this building for industrial purposes. I hope it would warm the architect's heart to know the way I live. David, on the roof, climbed the fence, and stood on the ledge. Stoned, I said, "Don't kill yourself" and then, "I'm sorry that was a stupid thing to say." I can't tell you the things I feel I have lost, the girl with the B12 deficiency, for example.

Hold up your hotdog if you're down to party. This is the good part. The poem wants only to point out where it is and where it is not. This is the good part. If you hold a cup to your ear, you can hear the ocean, too. I zip up my trousers and unfold my shirt, iron it, wear it. This is the good part. It's all down hill from here. The meteor and its moon passed by earth and we're all okay. We're just getting better and better. Every day I open my eyes and remember what the world looks like. I fill a mug with hot water and a teabag. Now we're partying. This is the party. Don't forget there will be flowers soon.

I could only describe what we're doing as losing it. My fingers fell through the dark black hair of Texas. I feed the cat and clean out its litter box. This is the good part. Quietly and in a soft voice, David, shortly after being aggressively negative, looked into my eyes and said, "You're better than I thought," and I felt my heart split open, because we're all just kids waiting to get drunk enough. If you're trying not to lose your shit, though, I recommend going to a different room, because this is the good part, and in this room, everybody is losing everything.

ADVENTURE TIME

A giant dog carries me to bed

the ice king wants my princess

I want to save everyone but I cant

my best friend doesn't like the way I play the viola

and the town is full of crying dust clouds

who used to dance with piles of money

I swear I'll get back the money

these values were given to me and I keep them close

the giant dog frightens the dust which returns to raining

I want to hold the dust clouds and purr them to sleep

KEEGAN
CRAWFORD

A CANDLE MELTING ALL THE WAY DOWN UNTIL IT'S NOTHING BUT A WICK

Watch me turn into a bat

and fly into a cave,

I will light candles by my bed

on the ceiling,

to feel no remorse for killing something

feels strange and alien,

my wings are long and I won't know the difference

between having arms and having wings after a while,

I don't want to drink blood but it's necessary for my survival

THOSE PLASTIC HALLOWEEN FANGS

You can't drink blood
while people are watching
because they will distance themselves
from you and push you into the sunlight

"let me kiss you
I will be careful"

everyone dresses up tonight, on halloween
so now I can walk my dog
without being stabbed in the heart

RICHARD
CHIEM

HOW TO SURVIVE A CAR ACCIDENT

Say "yes" when James invites you to L.A. with him for a weekend. Ask what kind of people are going to be there. Walk with your hands in your pockets and realize that you don't know James very well. Feel a warm and mutual respect because you have read his poems in class before and liked the one about the boy who eats a mocking bird. Have conversations about life and death and joke about it. Ask how did that topic come up in the first place. Comment on his black fedora, that you think you like black fedoras.

Meet Jenny in a vacant parking lot, still blue colored from morning light. Look at her in the eyes because she is important to you. Lay on the roof of the car waiting for James in front of his house. Listen to Wu–Tang Clan vibrate the metal of the roof you're laying on. Imagine sitting inside a plane when one flies overhead. You could hear the drug-induced non-anxiety coating James's voice when he wonders where his keys are.

Take the I-5 North towards L.A./San Bernardino. Sit shotgun and get assigned to be DJ. Listen to the calming clicks from your iPod. Take peppermint gum from Jenny. Acknowledge you have never done anything with these two friends before. Jenny appears glowing while driving. James in the backseat sinks into the cushion, closes his eyes.

Open and close windows. Talk about past relationships and laugh in unison during sexual parts. Get distracted with other passengers on the highway. Imagine relationships with those that make eye contact with you. Try, and remember Mary in a positive way and cut wind with your hand through your open window.

Play Bon Iver. Light a cigarette to share around with everyone else in the car. Take unconscious drags of smoke.

Slowly pass a sixteen-wheeler semi truck on your right hand side. Listen to Skinny Love. Notice a car up ahead swerving into your lane. Watch the car swerve back quickly to its own lane. Exhale when Jenny reacts and turns the steering wheel closer towards you. Hold the armrest while your own car swerves out of control. Notice how calm your breath is. Let things happen. Swerve into the semi on your right. Crash with the momentum of the cabin and everything behind you. Close your eyes. Duck somehow. The roof above you caves down and down again. The noise is tremendous. Glass shatters and rains in small bits and pieces and falls on top of yours and your friends' jeans.

Realize the car is stuck underneath the semi. Get dragged underneath while the semi is braking on the the I-5 North.

Lose your glasses. See blurry and near sighted. Leave the car through Jenny's driver's side door and keep walking away. Feel a strange urge to keep walking away. Resolve to baby steps. Jenny is ahead and James is behind you. Ask if everyone is okay with your mouth.

Hear your friends say your name a few times. Watch Jenny cover her own mouth. Experience your blood filming down your cheeks. They say you are the only one injured.

Lay on the hot pavement in front of the truck. Realize you are still chewing your gum, while cars are still passing by. When James starts asking you questions about Bon Iver, notice the softness in his voice and know he is trying to keep you conscious. Chew the stale gum and answer all his questions. Talk about everything you know about Bon Iver. Cover your head with James's white dress shirt. Hear Jenny crying and gasping while she is standing above you with her cell phone. Understand you have a gash. Say something weird, like you are still chewing your gum.

Love your life. Think about fighting.

Say you are conscious when a man appears. Say "thank you" when the man identifies he is a doctor, someone who had pulled over, dressed in civilian clothes. Say your name is "Richard" and call him "Brian." Say you are conscious when there are paramedics. Say you feel no pain in your legs when they ask. Look up at moving clouds when they massage you into a neck brace. Say you are conscious. This is the first time you have been inside an ambulance, so remember everything. Love your life. Feel convinced you have no regrets. Feel the ambulance drive away and the road beneath your back.

Ask how everyone else is doing. Notice how all the paramedics look at you in this way while they apply tubes and pat you down. They all say good. Listen to them discuss how you might be in shock.

Wonder if there is an imaginary clock somewhere inside you ticking. Stare at the ceiling and listen to sirens. Imagine traffic around you opening up and clearing a path. Move your fingers, move your toes inside your shoes.

Arrive safely to the hospital. Know without knowing you are going to be okay. Watch the ceilings change as they guide you down hallways, double doors and elevators. Ask more people how their days are. See smiles and feel touched you have the power to surprise them. Hear more talks that you are in shock. Enter the emergency room become tired under the lights and feel less conscious. Everyone wants you to stay with them. Listen to a disembodied voice, from a doctor walking around with an IV tower, describe your body parts. Your head has a gash. Your stomach is soft and supple. Realize your clothes are being cut with scissors and stay still. Say your name is Richard. Ask where you are. Ask anything you want to say, say anything you want to say.

———

Receive visits from nurses and common doctors. Slowly feel aches and strange pains in broad places in your body. Learn Nurse Renee has been tending to you even when you were unconscious. Feel empty without reason when Nurse Renee tells you everything is going to be okay. Feel alive when she stays there with you for hours on a fold up chair. Your family has been notified. On your head, there are nine staples and dried blood.

Experience bliss in isolating sounds and thoughts and moving your lips slightly. Say you feel good. Ask where your friends are. Leave the emergency room like nothing happened. Feel the sensation of being filmed when hugging James and Jenny and your aunt who arrives from Newport Beach, who all have been waiting for you in the waiting room. Look everyone in the eyes. Notice there are no magazines. Say you are ready to go.

Suddenly turn around and watch Nurse Renee run through some double doors to hand you a slip of paper. She says, "You'll be needing this."

Read a prescription for Vicodin with her name and signature. Watch her shake your hand and wait a moment before she leaves. Eat dinner at a Pho restaurant with your friends and aunt in your hospital gown. Devour hot food and noodles. Talk all night and teach Jenny and James how to say "We almost died" in American Sign Language.

———

Meet Mary in a parking lot, some place random in Santa Monica, and cringe when you notice her new boyfriend. Feel like you should have died when Mary makes a few jokes about Post Traumatic Stress Syndrome and caresses her new boyfriend near his thighs. Listen to The Mountain Goats and remember you authored this mix tape for Mary and watch the highway for hours. Enjoy affinity and human connection watching James sign "We almost died" with his hands in the backseat with you. Listen to Mary joke more.

He says, "We should have called someone else to pick us up from L.A."

Say everything is okay. Find bits of glass everywhere for days.

Get invited to a Halloween party. Go to the Halloween party and shake hands with people you know and people you don't know. Say thank you when someone complements you on your costume, on how how lifelike the wound appears. Say hello. Lip sync some songs you like from the party. Sing the chorus. Rap "Living life without fear. Twenty five carrots in my baby girl's ear." Rap "Birthdays were the worst days. Now we sip champagne when we're thirsty." Say nothing when everyone repeats "party and bullshit," while leaning against a wall.

Laugh only when something is funny. When something is funny, remember to look someone in the eye because you liked what they just said. You want them to know.

38.

TAO
LIN

THREE-DAY CRUISE

After they euthanatize the poodle, they go on the Bahamas cruise. After that, the dad dies of a brain tumor that no one knew about. The mom, then, at Cocoa Beach, teaching herself to swim, drowns; and the son, Paul, too, dies, when he one night sees a car crash happening, is looking, passing by, but then has a dull thought—some sudden vapid mood that almost puts him to sleep—yawns, and swerves, in an abstractly wanting and participatory way, toward the crash. He accelerates, misses, and drives into a pole.

The daughter, Mattie, goes on living. She sometimes shuts her eyes, tight, and then opens them again, placing herself in next week's Sunday. It's a kind of time travel. Something make believe, for kids. Though of course, Mattie knows, she is not a kid. She is in her thirties, in Florida, where she grew up. She has returned. She sometimes feels as if there is a quick-person, five minutes ahead of her, living her life before she gets there. There is one week in all the others when she joins a gym, buys expensive facial creams, and sits sipping broth in the food courts of shopping malls. It is not a bad week. She remembers that week. Then she doesn't remember it. She remembers nothing. All her memories go to noise, go satirical and loud and uncontrollable—they fly like teeth and balloons from her brain to the open bones of her eyes, and clang there, lodge and impact and burst there. The months accumulate like houses in the middle of nowhere. And her sense of irony, finally, her cheap way of paradox, of that self-blanking kind of truth and calm, of easing, sometimes, into the sarcastic haze of living—it goes bad, like an awful, leaden, jam-packed something in her head. Mattie is eating a sandwich. She is scribbling poems on envelopes. She is distracted, she is old. She is dead from something that makes her forget what it is before it kills her.

Mattie is twelve. She feels, today, for the first time, that happiness is something behind her, something mousy and slick and sliding away, into some hole, into some hole of that some hole.

"Do you ever feel sad?" says Mattie. She and Paul are at the supermarket. She is looking at a blow-dryer box, the woman on which has her hair in such a way that she must, Mattie thinks, be flying.

"What's happier," says Paul. He is six. "The most happy rabbit in the world? A man that is normal happy? A cookie? Between one and a hundred how happy is a cookie? A green one." They are at the supermarket for AAA batteries.

"Forty," says Mattie. "Wait. A green one?" She's looking at the blow-dryer box. "I can't see out my right eye," she says. "It's blurry. Oh, now I can."

"Oh," says Paul. He giggles. "What kind of batteries won't rip you off? This one has Michael Jordan on it. Michael Jordan is funny."

"This lady is flying. This is… unacceptable," says Mattie. She's thinking about dirt—dirt on the ground, in hair, dirt in the sky. She had a dream about dirt. "I hate… school."

"Why?" says Paul. He looks stricken for a moment, a little horrified.

"I'm twelve," says Mattie. "I'm twelve years old!"

"Michael Jordan is strange," says Paul.

They buy Energizer batteries. The parking lot gleams from all the cars. They cross the street, into their neighborhood. Some older kids are gliding around on rollerblades, playing street hockey. One little girl has a baseball bat and is chasing a few of the others. It is sunny and October and breezy. "The air tickles," says Paul. He has Michael Jordan in his head, and can't stop giggling. He blocks the wind from his neck with strangling motions and says, "My hands tickle!" In front of their house, he cartwheels onto grass. He runs at Mattie and jump kicks the air in front of her. Mattie pats his head. Paul goes and hops, circuitously, over a red flower plant. He looks at Mattie and then runs into the house, the front door of which is open.

The mom is in the side yard, watering a palmetto with the hose. Her dress is a bit wet, and her hair too. She waves at Mattie. Their toy poodle is sitting very still on top of the mailbox. He is overheated, but has retained good posture. He looks content in a once-wild way.

Mattie waves at her mom and carries the poodle into the living room.

On the sofa, Mattie pets the poodle until it is dark outside. She lies down. She stares sideways through the sliding glass door, at the sky. In third grade she told some classmates that their teacher, Mrs. Beonard, looked like a dolphin, even though Mrs. Beonard looked very much like an owl. She surprised herself then, and liked it.

Mattie sits up, carries the poodle into her room. She arranges it so they lie facing each other on the bed. The poodle is submissive and inaudible. Mattie closes her eyes, and sees her own face. A nerd, she thinks. Someone at school had called her a nerd. She tries not to think about dirt. Her dream about dirt wasn't a good dream. She sneezes. Her head rings—resonates, like a padded bell. The poodle stands. Mattie pets him until he is flat again. She keeps her hand on his body. She sneezes again, hard, the hardest sneeze she has ever sneezed, and this time there's an exquisite, high-pitched squeak from the pappy center of her head, and then she feels perceptually enhanced—honed and lucid as a tiny, soap-washed moon. She closes her eyes. She hears new things. She hears her own shouldery hipbone, low and curving, sounding purly, cello tones. She hears an ant, in the yard, walking up a blade of grass. She falls asleep and wakes up early in the morning, wide-eyed and alert, four hours before school.

The dad goes around one Saturday with a notepad, taking orders for lunch. He goes out, comes back. "Who ordered the toy poodle?" he says. He's holding, in a manhandled way, an apricot-hued poodle, who is a girl. He points at his notepad. "Says here..."

"I ordered that!" says Paul. He is eight. He is taking all the credit for this, in case of future situations. "I knew to order something good like that." He looks around. The world, he feels, is becoming less, is closing in, trying to detain him, clamp him like a bug. He takes the apricot poodle and runs away.

The mom is going around the house, watering her many potted plants.

Mattie comes out from her room, gets the other poodle, goes back to her room.

In bed, the dad says, "It's fair." He's thinking about the poodles. It's a few years later. "One poodle per child. One male, one female."

"Yes," says the mom. "Fair." She has discovered, going through the trash, envelopes postmarked Nevada, from someone named Scarlet Leysen. The dad had taken a business trip there. Two females per male, the mom thinks. "Life isn't fair," she says. "So we should comport extra fair, to compensate." She used to say, "Life isn't fair, but that doesn't mean we can't try to make it fair," but changed it one day while eating a peach, when she was twenty.

"I know," says the dad. "I agree." He goes to pat the mom's shoulder, but pats the bed instead. He moves his hand through the dark and pats it down again, on the mom's face. Her lips and teeth are wet; she has just licked them. "Sorry," says the dad. He gets up, washes his hands, goes out into the rest of the house.

The mom dreams of the dad, dreams that he descends through a trapdoor, into a room that spins. He crouches, leaps, pushes a button on a wall. A rope ladder appears. He catches it, helicopter-style, climbs it, and is back in the bedroom. He lies down. He rolls over, toward her. His head is snoring and fat and looming, and she is afraid. She wakes up and there he is. His head is snoring, but not fat or looming; he is smiling a little.

In the morning, the mom goes looking for the envelopes. She doesn't find any. She sits down with a microwaved waffle, a bowl of dried cranberries, a canister of whipped cream. She plays back the dream in her head. She likes the rope ladder part. She holds the whipped cream vertically down, as it says to on the canister.

Over time, the mom makes herself forget the envelopes, which works, until one day, going through mail, she finds that she has been looking for a very long time at this letter from Nevada with Smurf stickers all over it—Smurfs dressed in pink, Smurfs smooching. She throws a pencil and a wristwatch into the swimming pool. She frowns and paces. She throws a muffin on the floor and doesn't clean it up. This is her little rampage. She locks herself in her bedroom and sits very still on her bed. The world sits beside her, the size and intelligence and badness of a cupcake. In her head, there is a steady, clear-voiced scream, pitched in middle C. It is not unpleasing. She listens to it for some time and then lies down.

The dad is made to sleep on the couch. He buys his own blanket from Kmart, a green one, and a pillow that is supposed to be for dogs. He sleeps with a box of sugar cookies on his chest— something, he knows, that he has always wanted. Instead of toothbrushing, he has mints.

The mom misses the dad. She does not speculate on Scarlet Leysen. She destroys Nevada out of her head, the entire state. She makes it have a lava-y Earthquake. She mostly forgives the dad. Still, though, she knows, the dad should be punished. She begins to make dinner only for herself, Paul, and Mattie. She tries not to look at the dad when they are in the kitchen together. Once, though, she glances and sees that the dad's mouth is moving and that he is lining up three uncut pickles on a piece of bread. They make eye contact and his mouth keeps moving, noiselessly, and then he loudly says, "—and I'm competent." The mom looks away. She grins. She leaves the kitchen. She is a little giddy. Control yourself, she thinks. Each day of punishment is a delay of gratification, an investment towards better, future love.

"Tell your mom to stop being angry at me," says the dad one night to Paul. He is at the fax machine, on a stool, has his head turned around to Paul, who is on the sofa watching TV.

"You," says Paul. He is eleven. He has changed. He is somewhat fat, and his head has grown, he thinks, too big. Some nights, in bed, he spreads his fingers evenly over his skull and pushes inward and counts to one hundred. He has to do something, he knows, contain it—not unlike braces for teeth, which he has. Sometimes he looks in the mirror and imagines a team of dwarves, swarming, smacking at his body. Once, he dreams this. "Hey now," he says in his dream. There is a doorway and the dwarves keep rushing in. "Hey," he says. "Why?"

"She listens to you; not me," says the dad. He moves his face close to Paul's. It is a bewildered, distracted face—the face of someone clearly without secrets, but still somehow untrustable. "She doesn't listen to me," he says. He has just invented a new laser, that afternoon. "You need to tell her. Say to her—"

The fax machine begins to make noises and the dad attends to it.

"You," says Paul. He bites in half his cream-filled Popsicle. He makes a face. His favorite thing to do, now, is to eat something concocted and sludgy—cherry pie-chocolate syrup pudding, marshmallow-maraschino cherry soup—and then, sweet and sticky mouthed, lie down for a nap. He likes to be sleepy, likes the keen apathy and warm coolness of it.

After a few weeks the dad is allowed back in the bedroom.

He is smiling and clear-eyed. "That was terrible," he says. "You were so angry. I tried to impress you by eating healthy." He chuckles. "You were so angry!" He smiles and moves to her and hugs her.

Weekends, the dad puts on swimming trunks, swims two or three laps, then gets distracted and goes, dripping, into the house, to find the poodles. He enforces direction and speed as the poodles are made to swim repeatedly from the deep end to the shallow end. He mock screams at them. The mom has the camcorder. She encourages Paul and Mattie to swim. After the poodles, the dad spends time—too much time, everyone agrees—with the long-handled scrubber, scrubbing at all the fey and faint patches of pool algae.

For dinner the dad is made to eat a bowl of steamed vegetables. He has high cholesterol and is not allowed to eat shrimp or egg yolk. He sometimes complains, but is generally docile and obedient. "Poodles are natural water dogs," he says. "In France, they live in the rivers. Caves of them. Lined up and ready. They ascend one by one. They bob skyward, like penguins. They paddle carefully, heads up, barking at a polite and tactful volume and timbre. People toss them food." The dad chuckles. He has amused himself. "A river crammed with poodles," he says. "Imagine that. Have salmon, then have poodles instead of salmon." He falls asleep on the carpet by the television. He sleeps with his mouth open. His teeth are crooked in a lightly shuffled way and smell of hot summer weeds.

Christmas, the mom has her camcorder. The poodles have their own presents. Neon flea collars, a rubber cheeseburger, a rubber foot! The Christmas tree is plastic and has, mysteriously, over the years, turned from a dark green to a bright and fiery orange. The dad is sheepish and aloof. He has never bought anyone a present. It is just something that he doesn't do; something about his childhood. He doesn't seem to understand. He is an inventor. He leaves the room for a moment. He comes back carrying a big gift-wrapped thing. He sets it on the ground. "Hurry," he says. "Who's it for?" says Paul. "You," says the dad. Paul opens it. It is their two toy poodles. The poodles look around, then move carefully away. The dad almost falls to the carpet. He laughs a kind of laugh that none of them have heard before.

Mattie goes to college in New York City, where she takes too many creative writing courses.

She dislikes enjambment, symbolism, the Best American Poetry series. She writes indignantly, with a kind of whirlpooling impatience. Though sometimes she imagines that her hair is white and fluffy, and then she writes cutely, with many l's, as if to a future granddaughter of hers—some mute and dreamy girl, in a future, enchantless world, without trees or sidewalks.

In Mattie's head, she critiques other people's critiques of her work.

"I have no idea what I'm doing here," she says to classmates. "In college, I mean. Do you?"—here, she likes to lean in close— "Do you know?" One night, she steps off the curb into the street. There is a breeze and her hair sweeps across her face. The street is calm and quiet; there seem to be no other people around. She closes her eyes. A bus that is two buses, swingy and accordioned, comes at her. The bus does not honk. She very slowly opens and closes her eyes, and then crosses the street. She sometimes wonders if she died that night. She remembers the wind, the lightless blacktop, the phantom bus that does not honk.

After college, Mattie stays in New York.

Paul is now in Boston, for his own college education. "I used to walk home to my apartment thinking about crying," he writes in email to Mattie—the mom has encouraged her children to email one another— "three in the morning. Carrying bags of groceries. Finally, I'd cry a little. It was a long walk. I'd put everything into the refrigerator including the plastic bags and go to sleep. In the morning, I'd eat four bowls of Frosted Flakes, go back to sleep. But that gradually stopped. That time of my life. Today, I am changed. Tolerance, life, it moves you to the center of things. How have you been?"

"Then it kills you," writes back Mattie. She likes Paul. They get each other. They do. "It moves you, then it kills you. It says, 'Move here,' then kills you. It puts its hands on your shoulders, moves you, kills you."

Once, they see each other. In Barnes and Noble by Union Square. Mattie sees Paul first, a passing glimpse, the recognition coming a few seconds later. She becomes confused—Paul should be in Boston—and, for a long while after, does not trust herself, feels vaguely that she has suffered some kind of cosmic accident. Is she in Boston? What does that mean? To be in Boston? Later, Paul sees Mattie as she is going down the escalator and he is going up. They seem to look each other in the face. Mattie has an abstract expression, and Paul thinks of screaming her name, but then thinks that that would be a bit ridiculous. Later, he thinks of just saying her name, at a normal volume. Of course, he thinks. They don't ever mention this to each other and, over time, begin to doubt that it happened.

The dad is one day accused by the government of having released false and misleading press releases. It has to do with the company he has founded for his inventions.

In the courtroom, the jury is working-class, weary, and stadium seated—to one side, like one of those multiple missile launchers. The dad's lawyer has not had a good childhood, and now, in adulthood, is often depressed, shy, and nervous—nevertheless the dad trusts him.

The government lawyer is daunting and loud.

In low-security federal prison camp, the dad is productive and healthy. He makes many friends. The inmates are sanguine and witty; ninety-percent are in for drugs. They debate, cook, play poker and ping-pong, watch TV, work out, plan future criminal activity, make criminal connections, study law.

The dad is to be there for seventy months.

The mom visits twice a week. It is a two-hour drive. "Did you feed the dogs?" says the dad. "Dogs are people too."

They talk on the phone. "Don't tattle," says the mom. She has written down a list of things that the dad should not do. "Don't complain, don't spread rumors." She goes to sleep very early now. Her dreams undergo change. They begin to occur nightly—fully formed, with beginnings, middles, and ends. They have subtle plotting and good dialogue.

In the daytime, the mom walks around the house with a new excitement. In emails to her children, she expresses amazement at her own brain. She feels a bit powerful. "I dream every night," she writes, "how about you?" In one dream, the family goes on a Bahamas cruise, has a great time. The mom swims in the dream, though she cannot swim in real life. At dinner in the dream, the mom glances across the hall, notices a girl who has very small teeth, goes over there, asks the girl to open her mouth, and wow! The girl has many layers of teeth—thousands! The mom tells her so, and everyone laughs.

In the morning, the mom looks into and buys four cruise tickets, for when the dad is released from prison.

She and the dogs, walking around the house, sometimes cross paths. They look at one another, make sure not to collide, and continue on to where they are going. Though sometimes the mom blocks the dogs, shunts them into corners—or follows them, at a distance. Mostly, the mom finds, the dogs just walk from one room to another, where they then lie down, sphinx style—a style they have recently taken to for some reason.

Summer nights, when it is black and hot and humid outside, the mom gets a little confused. She gets a panicked feeling that the dad, Mattie, and Paul have all, a long time ago, run off with Scarlet Leysen. She forgets the names of the days of the week. She feels ageless and illusory. She is afraid that she will wake one night and find that her pillow is a dismembered torso, that she has murdered a person! She fears the poodles, that there are two against her one, fears the team of them, the ready conspiracy of them. One night, she hears noises. She turns on all the lights, moves quickly to the sofa, lies on her side, turns the TV to the Weather Channel—the least scary channel, she knows—and thinks hard about Mattie, Paul, and the dad, gets them all talking in her head, then calls softly for the poodles.

In prison, the dad has obtained three patents, published eight papers—through collaboration with the mom—and begun to read Chuang Zhu, other Eastern Philosophers, and books on death. He writes to Mattie and Paul. "I am doing an aerobics class two times a week. I am in charge of a team of people. We dig up grass, plant grass, do things with grass. My daily routine is—" and it says his daily routine.

The mom text messages Mattie, "Just saw a reporter blown away by wind on TV." She emails Paul, "This morning I yelled 'scumbag' and the dogs came running from their rooms with eyes so big, anticipating, they must think scumbag is something delicious."

The apricot poodle is found to have diabetes. The mom is to

inject her with insulin twice daily, which goes okay for a while, until one morning, when the apricot poodle is dead. The mom has been injecting her with air instead of insulin. She buries the dead poodle in the backyard. She carries around the other poodle—who can barely see anymore and sometimes walks into walls—the rest of that day and forgets to feed him.

The prison doctor one day says that the dad's kidney is engorged, but it turns out to be nothing.

For a year, no one hears from Paul. Then they hear from Paul. He claims to have lived in Canada for some time. He has read a book called "Into The Wild," in which a boy graduates college, donates his money to OXFAM, wanders the country alone, hitchhikes into Alaska, writes in his journal that happiness is only real when shared, and, wrapped in a sleeping bag, then, inside an abandoned bus, nearby a frozen river, dies. It's a non-fiction book and Paul recommends it.

The dad is released.

The remaining poodle has begun to twitch. He has cataracts and his gums bleed. He stops eating. Mattie flies home. They broil a pork chop and set it in front of the poodle. The pork chop smells good. It is hot at first but quickly turns cold. The poodle looks at it but does not move.

They all, except Paul, whose plane is delayed, bring the poodle to the pet hospital and have it put to sleep.

Paul arrives in the night, by taxi. He has gained more weight. He looks generally less effective, as a person. He has a friend with him, Christine, who looks worried, and keeps touching her hair.

The cruise is underbooked and overstaffed. It has the casually terminal feel of a nice retirement home—something of zoo-animal complacency and over-the-counter drug proliferation. The railings and walls are clean and shiny, but in an enforced and afflicted way that seems a little sarcastic.

Still, the food is excellent and the passengers are all very happy.

The staff is inspiriting and Filipino.

At dinner, Christine sits alone at a table on the other side of the dining room. She insists on this, says because she isn't part of the family. She eats slowly and carefully—in open view of the family's table—with her face down, and worried. No one seems to know how or when she bought a ticket.

The next day, there is a lunch buffet on the sun deck.

"Let's take five minutes before we eat to think about death," says the dad. They are seated adjacent the pool, which is covered, for now, with a gleaming white tarp. "What it is. How to defeat it. Strategies, options. What are we dealing with? After, we'll share."

The mom likes this about the dad. As a child, she'd always had what she imagined were fascinating thoughts, but didn't ever say them. Once, as a little girl, at recess, she thought that if she ran very fast at a pole and then caught it and swung quickly around, part of her would keep going, and she would become two girls. That same day, sitting on the monkeybars, she also had an idea for a movie—a mystery/horror movie. Someone would wake one morning and find that their pillow had been replaced with a dismembered torso!

"Okay," says the dad. He points at Christine. "You first."

"Death is a toad," Christine says loudly. She makes a defeated face. "A toad... in outer space. It has a cape." She opens her mouth. She seems stunned. "Besides the cape, it's a normal toad."

The dad looks at the mom.

"Death is the end of the dream," says the mom. She blinks. She enunciates carefully. "When you wake up finally, you find that there was nothing real after all." She brings her fruit punch to her mouth, looks down into it, and sips.

"Death is the plural of deaf," says Paul. "It's when everything goes deaf."

"Oh," says Christine. She stands up, sits back down.

"Death is an emotion outside all the other emotions," Mattie says, looking at Christine, who has a worried expression on her face. "A comet, blackblue, fast as ice." She is quoting one of her poems. The next line is a non-sequitur, *the men look two inches into my forehead,* as are the next couple of lines, *i ask for no receipt / but am given a receipt / forced to take it home / unfurl it / like a scroll / staple a wall to it.* There are more lines, a rant on the bronze dirtiness of pennies. It is a long poem. Mattie skips to the end. "Death is a highly polished thought." She feels dazed and shy and occult.

"Is that one of your poems?" says the mom. She smiles.

Mattie nods carefully. There were more lines, actually, she now remembers, *life is the sarcastic joke of death / and death is the sarcastic mouth that eats the ironic food / the organic water / the life that fills with teeth / the pecans you like, the nuts / the hardened brains of smaller animals.* It just kept going, that poem.

"Death is the end of the fear of death," says the dad. "To avoid it we must not stop fearing it and so life is fear. Death is time because time allows us to move toward death which we fear at all times when alive. We move around and that is fear. Movement through space requires time. Without death there is no movement through space and no life and no fear. To be aware of death is to be alive is to fear is to move around in space and time toward death."

They arrive at port in the Bahamas. There are five other gigantic cruise ships. There is the sun-toned city of Nassau, with its conch divers, horse-drawn carriages, cool-black men and women—all in view, yards away— but the tourists are funneled onto a ferry and taken to some other island, where there is a buffet, a pavilion, a long, pragmatic beach, and an inner-tube hut.

They sit facing the ocean. Christine sits straightbacked on the edge of a lounge chair. Mattie lies on an adjacent lounge chair. Paul and the dad are on the pier—there is a low, kid-sized pier—observing some fish. The mom is standing back, on a grassy area, drinking a tropical drink. She is thinking about in her dream, when she was swimming. It was here. Was it here?

"Why are you worried?" Mattie asks Christine. "You seem worried, I mean."

"I'm..." Christine touches the back of her hand. "The sky... it begins immediately off of our skin. It goes forever, past the stars. Anything beyond can reach down, grab us, pull us off the planet."

"You're just improvising, aren't you?" says Mattie. "When you talk. Each moment, you're just making up stuff. I mean, that's what we all do, I guess. I'm not critiquing." She looks at Christine. A lot of time seems to pass. "It's okay, It's good, I like what you say; the toad thing. I'm not attacking. No; not at all."

Christine stands abruptly up. Her chair makes a noise. She falls to the sand and stands back up. "I'm..." she says. She points wanly in some direction, then goes there, touching her hair and pointing.

That night, they are taken to a hotel that is also a casino and a fish aquarium. There is one wall that is a fish tank of only piranhas. They are the color of mangoes and have flat, koala noses. They all face in one direction, and are all very still, except for a few up top that tremble and look a bit anxious.

"Where's Christine?" asks the mom. Paul shrugs. No one seems to know. They don't dwell on it. They play roulette. Paul later says, "Christine told me, she said, 'I'm not sure, but I might be disappearing into the islands of the Bahamas.' If anyone's wondering about that."

They sleep on their backs. The ship leaves the Bahamas in the night.

The third day is a day at sea.

At dinner, the dad and the mom sit facing Mattie and Paul.

The mom looks over at Christine's table. A different woman is there. Older, with chandelier earrings, a lot of make-up. Her glass of water is empty and on the edge of her table.

Mattie reads the menu in her head, "...a bed of carrots, broccoli, and four other green," then out loud, "red, healthy, steamed vegetables." She looks up.

"You're the sarcastic one," says the dad. He's looking at Mattie. He brings his hand up from under the table. He points at Paul. "You. What are you? You're sarcastic too, aren't you?"

"I'm the outwardly depressed, inwardly content one," says

Paul.

"He's the sarcastic-sarcastic one," says Mattie. "Two sarcastics." She flips her menu over, looks at the back of it.

"I'm the outwardly depressed, inwardly content one," says Paul.

The soup is green and good. The salad is crunchy, with water droplets all over and in it. Mattie has ordered the steamed vegetables. She eats most of it. She crushes a carrot by pressing down hard with her spoon, which then squeals against the plate. I'm the stupid one, she thinks. She grins a little. She reaches for the sugar, changes her mind, moves her hand to her water, changes her mind, brings her hand to her head, scratches behind her ear.

"I saw that," says the dad. "I saw starting with the childlike behavior with the carrot." He looks at Mattie, at Paul. I made you two, he thinks. He stands and reaches across the table and pats Mattie on the head. He pats Paul, too, on the head. He sits back down. He pats the mom on the head. The mom pats the dad on the head. She smiles. She turns and looks quickly over at Christine's table again.

"Sorry," she says. "I don't know why I keep looking."

That night, after the farewell show in the Moonbeam lounge— a dancing, singing, juggling thing— there is the midnight buffet. It has three ice sculptures. A swan, a bear, a dolphin. The foods are also sculpted. There are owly apples, starfishy cheeses, cookies shaped esoterically like ocean sunfish. People take photos of their plates. They eat cautiously at first, then, having realized something, violently, biting off heads and fins and limbs, grinning. The mom runs down to their room and comes back with the camcorder.

After the buffet, they go up to the top deck. The air is cool, and the ocean, all around, is black and smooth. The stars are rich and streaky, as if behind water. They go down one deck, into a glass-enclosed area. It is late and there are just a few other people here.

There is a ping-pong table. The dad challenges Mattie and

Paul. The mom starts up her camcorder, which is digital. "If I lose," says the dad, "I'll buy you both cars." The mom zooms wildly in on the dad's face. She pans back and steps in closer. Paul's body is languid and cascaded, chin to chest to stomach, but his arms are speedy and graceful. The dad stands rigidly, up close to the table. He does not bend his back or twist his hips. He tosses his paddle from hand to hand. "Ambidextrous," he says. He is winning. From his time in prison, he has become an expert at ping-pong. He flips over his paddle and serves with the handle end—a slow, high lob to Paul. Mattie chops the ball down massively, tennis-style, and, while doing that, knocks Paul to the floor. The ball bounces hard and loud and high. The dad leaps and tosses his paddle into the air. The paddle does not connect with the ball. The dad catches his paddle. "Mattie," he says. "Mattie!" The mom's hand is shaking a little. She tries to keep the camcorder steady with both hands. She hears Mattie laughing and Paul saying, "What the hell was that? What was that!" She tries to zoom in on Mattie laughing. She pans back and sees Paul on the floor still. His face is startled and young. He has taken off a shoe. He throws it at Mattie. Mattie whacks the shoe at the dad, who pivots and whacks the shoe behind him, where it goes spinning over the railing into the dark. The mom pushes the camcorder at Mattie's chest. Mattie is laughing and she looks and takes the camcorder. The mom runs off, into the fore of the ship—a dark, open area with lounge chairs, railing, the sky, the ocean. Mattie sets the camcorder down on the ping-pong table. She runs and follows her mom. There is a cool breeze and it is very calm and quiet. The floor is wood. The mom is at the railing. Her form is small and vague.

Mattie goes closer, hears that her mom is weeping, and hesitates. She stops smiling and feels that her cheeks are tired. She glances away, turning her ear flat to the sandpapery roar of the wind, then looks back, quiet again. The mom has turned a little. Mattie has a sudden bad thought and is about to say, "Mom, wait," but the mom now turns fully around. She is crying loud and wet. She steps slowly toward Mattie. She cries with her arms at her sides. "Mattie," she says. She flings a fist up to her shoulder, pushes it back down to her side. There's a contrary draft of wind and the mom's hair sweeps, diagonal, across her face. The ocean behind her is pooling and dark and quietly moving. The sky is black and close. "Oh, Mattie," she says. Her voice is loud and clear. "I'm so happy."

39.

MIRA
GONZALEZ

LOVE LETTER

I spend a lot of time alone. Most of my time is spent transporting myself from one destination to another. In the mornings I wake up at 7:00a.m. and press snooze on my alarm. The alarm goes off again fifteen minutes later, which allows me exactly fifteen minutes to put on clothes and get out the door by 7:30a.m. I pry myself out of bed. This is the most difficult part of my day. Getting out of bed feels like actual torture. I have always been this way. Even as a child I had a hard time waking up in the morning. The cold air outside my comforter feels piercing and hellish, despite living in Los Angeles where the temperature almost never goes below sixty degrees. Every day when I wake up I swear that I would pay any amount of money to sleep for just one more hour.

I make coffee, pour it into a glass jar and take it in my car with me. I have gone exactly three days without coffee since age thirteen and they were some of the worst days of my life. I drive a black Ford Expedition and the air conditioning only works sometimes. I drink my coffee while driving down the 10 freeway, eastbound. I listen to pop radio, or sometimes I listen to Sam Cooke songs from a CD that has been in my car for three years. Driving by myself has recently become one of my favorite activities.

I have grown to appreciate being alone. I used to hate it but now I need it. My desire to be by myself at least eighty percent of the time is the downfall of most of my relationships. It's not for any specific reason except that I am hyper aware of how other people might perceive me in any given social situation and I am free to do whatever I want when nobody is watching.

I am productive when I'm alone. Not when I'm lonely, of course, but when I'm alone and content with being alone. That is, when I'm not craving or pursuing any kind of relationship, I can write whole novels or clean my entire house. To be content with being alone involves a kind of fear. I have to be afraid of letting someone know me. Which means that these periods of productive aloneness usually come after having recently been wronged by someone who I felt close to. My contentment with being alone stems from a temporary distrust in humanity and a vague but omnipresent feeling that everyone is out to hurt me.

So, after I get off the freeway, I am usually almost finished with my jar of coffee. By the time I arrive and park my car, I'm completely finished, and if I'm not then I drink the remaining (now lukewarm) coffee as fast as I can, because I was supposed to be there at 8:00a.m., and by the time I park my car it is 8:05a.m. Luckily, I work for my dad, so I can always use 'years of neglectful parenting resulting in lingering emotional trauma' as an excuse for being five minutes late.

I put my key in the door and I am immediately handed a crying infant. My dad leaves for work and the infant's mother (my dad's wife) leaves for yoga class and errands. The infant continues crying for the next fifteen minutes. Sometimes less, never more. I hold her against my chest, with her tiny head over my shoulder. I bounce her up and down. I cradle her in my arms and walk around the massive empty house until she calms down. Then I give her a pacifier and put her in her crib. She vomits on herself and falls asleep. I will clean the vomit when she wakes up. I go downstairs and make coffee.

By the time I arrive home at noon Daniel has already gone on his morning run. Or at least, I assume he has, because he is in the shower and his running shoes are on my bedroom floor. While he showers I make the bed. Making the bed isn't something I normally do but I would like him to think I'm the sort of person who makes her bed regularly. I am only trying to not let him see me at my worst.

Daniel makes me happy, which is something I can't say about most people. I have been infatuated, sure. Definitely codependent. I have even been deeply, painfully in love. I've experienced heartbreak and trauma and boredom. It's important to me that I experience extremely negative emotions as well as extremely positive ones and everything in between. True happiness caused by the company of another human though, is rare. The kind of happiness I'm talking about is uncomplicated. It comes easily and feels comfortable. It's the kind of happiness that stems from a mutual understanding that all people are separate entities who will never cross any distance, conceptual or otherwise, to be closer than they are at the moment when their bodies are pressed together. It comes from accepting that you will only know the thoughts of another person at their whim when they decide to express something to you, imperfectly, using language.

My relationship before I met Daniel was with a person who was loyal to me during a time when I desperately wanted to feel desirable. He hit me the first time we had sex and gave me a bloody nose, then wouldn't let me wash my face. This was a period in my life when I had begun wanting things like that. I felt as if, not only would he accept me at my bloody-faced worst, but he *wanted* me that way. Which ended up working out well because I wanted me that way too. I didn't want to try anymore. I didn't want good sex or good friends. Drugs weren't even appealing. I was ready to give up entirely, and if I was going to give up, it's only fair that the person I'm dating should want someone who has given up. I became comfortable with letting him see me at my worst.

I asked him to stop having sex with me after giving me the bloody nose and he did. I fell asleep in his arms that night and most nights after. I never washed my face and he never apologized for hitting me because he knew he didn't have to.

Daniel never hits me during sex. Not being injured during sex might be normal for most people but I have spent a large portion of my life requesting violent sex from people who are unsatisfied with themselves and with me. It's not so much about the violence itself as it is about the power dynamic. I am the object; you are the objectifier. Not with Daniel though. He interacts with me in a way that says 'This body has value,' rather than 'This body belongs to me and I will do what I want with it.'

What I never understood until recently is that, unfortunately, your body belongs to you and nobody else. You can give other people permission to touch your body or insert themselves into it. You can put food and drugs in your body. You can mutilate your body or ask others to mutilate it for you. You can be overly cautious with your body. You can feel, temporarily, as if your body has become an inanimate object that exists solely for the pleasure of another person. For someone who hates their own body, any one of those things can feel freeing, but you will never fully unload the burden of having a body onto another person. You can never say 'Here, I don't like this body very much and you seem to like it a lot, so take it away from me.'

I have tried to do that anyways though. I tried so hard. I thought, maybe, if I no longer had control over what was being done to my body, then I could somehow no longer feel responsible for it. That was a short-term solution.

My body doesn't belong to Daniel. No part of me belongs to him and no part of him belongs to me. We are two people who are each wholly responsible for maintaining our own, separate lives. We enjoy the company of one another, and are inclined to spend time together for that reason, but I know that I can never unload the burden of owning my own body onto him so I will never try to.

When Daniel gets out of the shower, he walks into my room wearing only a towel. I ask him about his run while he gets dressed and he tells me a story about a homeless person approaching him when he had taken a break from running to catch his breath. The homeless person offered to teach him witchcraft for $5. He politely declined and now Daniel may never know witchcraft.

That night, Daniel and I decide to take all the drugs we have; two pills of Morphine, four pills of Valium, one pill of Xanax. I have been repeatedly advised against mixing benzodiazepines and opiates but anything feels okay in small doses. At least, that's what we tell ourselves.

This is his last night in Los Angeles. We planned our drug binge so that he would be hungover on a plane and I would be hungover in my house. After this he will go to another city to finish some things he has been working on, and I will stay in Los Angeles to finish some things I've been working on, then we will meet in New York the following month to show each other the things we have been working on.

In basing our well being on goals and ideas instead of relationships, we are able to maintain something that has room to grow. We spend time apart, then make plans to meet in a city where nobody knows us and focus on loving each other. We slowly, almost imperceptibly, learn to be productive in the company of one another, then fully integrate ourselves into each other's lives. We grow affectionate, as individuals who recognize one another as independent entities with our own perspectives on the world.

Most importantly though, when I wake up next to him, I am able to get out of bed without pushing snooze on my alarm.

SCOTT
MCCLANAHAN

KIDNEY STONES

I just wanted to be changed. I wanted to be changed more than anything in this world. That morning I was down at Rite Aid with my uncle Terry copying some of my grandma's old pictures when I felt this pain in my back. Of course, I didn't pay it any mind and just kept copying the picture of this old black and white shot of my grandfather from the late 30s.

It was one where he got in a fight with a police officer and they put him in jail.

It was a mugshot picture.

There was another picture of him somebody took a couple of years later, after he got religion.

He was sitting on the hood of a car, holding a Bible in his lap.

I stood and stared at the pictures and the pictures stared back. I thought about my grandfather who was a moonshiner once and then gave it all up to follow the Lord. I thought about Saul of Tarsus on the road to Damascus and being struck by a blinding light. He heard a voice and changed his name to Paul. That's how easy it was—you just had to change your name to Paul.

My uncle Terry put the picture of my grandfather Elgie holding the Bible on the picture scanner.

I giggled again because it was so stupid—the way it all sounded.

It all sounded so ridiculous really, how all of these visions were always about good and evil, God and the Devil.

We copied the Bible picture down and I started feeling this pain even more. I leaned over the counter hoping it would go away.

Go away. Go away.

But it didn't.

My uncle asked me in his strange hillbilly/New York/New Jersey/San Francisco accent, "You all right boy?"

So I smiled and said, "No I'm fine. I'm fine."

At first it came in waves, but then I was in pain.

"You need to go to the doctor boy?" he said again.

I shook my head no.

And so we finished up the pictures and I tried pretending I was fine.

I'm fine.

I'm fine.

Besides that I had to go to work that evening. I'd just luckily found a job a couple of weeks before and I couldn't lose it now.

But when I got home I could barely walk I was in so much pain.

I thought, "Oh shit, I think I'm having kidney stones."

So I sat around for another hour or so and took a whole handful of ibuprofen, hoping that would take care of it. But I needed to get going. I couldn't lose this job now. Things had been going so bad lately. I got into my car and started driving the hour it took to get to work and the pain was still surging in my back.

On the way there I thought about my grandfather and the road to Damascus.

"You're fine. You're fine."

But about halfway into the drive, I couldn't take it anymore.

I pulled over to this nasty little gas station and I went inside. My kidney stones were hurting me so much by this point, I had to bend over and start looking for a bathroom.

Picture this: A grown man bent over and searching desperately for a bathroom.

There was a pot-bellied woman working behind the counter who'd just finished checking in some deer this guy had killed, and there was an old man in there too spitting his Skoal spit into his Skoal cup and saying, "That Summer's County Bobcat defense sure is awesome this year. Might even take them to the playoffs."

He was smoking a cigarette too and holding it between his middle and ring fingers.

Spit. Smoke. Spit. Smoke.

I asked, "Where is your bathroom?" all out of breath and about ready to fall over. The old woman looked at me like I was some kind of meth-taking crazy man and pointed at the door towards the back.

"You got the shit pains don't you boy?" she said.

I smiled and shook my head like everything was okay and went into the bathroom all bent over and shut the door behind me. There wasn't a lock. There was a hole in the floor someone had stuffed a bunch of trash inside: cigarette packages, used tampons, candy wrappers, old newspapers.

"You're fine. You're fine," I kept saying to myself, and I could hear them talking outside.

I put my hand against the wall and I felt something stabbing me in the back. I breathed deep and the whole world went black.

I passed out.

The floor was cold and I dreamed my kidney stone dreams. I dreamed about the mugshot picture of my grandfather. I dreamed about my grandfather on the front of a car with a Bible on his lap, and a blinding light.

I dreamed about how he was a moonshiner once, and then he was a moonshiner no more.

And then I woke up.

I heard a voice outside the door saying, "Are you okay in there?"

I was still just sprawled on the floor. "Are you okay in there?" she said, trying to get the door open, but because I was passed out in front of it, the door wouldn't budge.

I cleared my throat and tried being as normal as possible. "Oh yeah I'm fine. Just give me a second. I think I'm just getting ready to pass a kidney stone."

Then the old woman said, "Well sonny, we don't allow people to pass kidney stones at the One Stop."

I didn't listen to her though.

I got up and unbuckled my pants and felt glass moving inside of me. Then I felt it moving through me and I passed it.

I SAW SOMETHING I COULDN'T BELIEVE.

I watched the kidney stone float in the toilet water and then sink.

THEN I HEARD SOMETHING I COULDN'T BELIEVE. IT WAS A LOUD VOICE SHOUTING FROM HIGH ABOVE.

I COULDN'T EVEN TALK ABOUT IT.

The old woman said, "Do I need to call the law? I'll call the law if I have to."

"No I'm fine. I'm fine," I said, standing over the toilet. "Just give me a second."

I washed my face and walked outside.

They were all standing there and looking at me strange. It was like somebody didn't come in and pass out in the gas station bathroom every day.

I walked outside and I felt like everything was different now.

I felt like the old life was behind me.

I drove off to work and wondered if it really happened. I wondered if I saw what I saw and heard what I heard. And when I got to work I sat in the car for a few minutes before I went inside and asked myself, "Did that really happen? Did that…really…happen?"

When I went inside work I didn't tell anybody about the pain from the kidney stones on the way there. I didn't tell them about what had gone down.

And they didn't tell me about their pain either.

They didn't tell me about how their dads drank.

And the woman in the corner didn't tell me about how her husband cheated on her and she thought about killing herself.

The man in the front didn't tell me his mother died when he was eleven years old, and every day when he came home, he watched her die. He watched her die every day beside the television cartoons.

The other girl in the back didn't tell about how she was raped one night by this older guy when she was thirteen.

I didn't tell them about my pain either.

I didn't tell them about how Saul saw a blinding light on the road to Damascus and changed his name to Paul.

I didn't tell them about how everything changes in this world. How could I?

How could I tell them about what happened to me in the bathroom on the way there?

How could I tell them about the blinding light, and how I passed a kidney stone shaped like a crucifix? How could I tell them about hearing a loud voice, shouting from on high, "Surely this is the TRUE Son of God in whom I'm well pleased. Arise now and awake the new prophet of the Lord."

And how can I tell you now what I know for sure?

How can I tell you now that my kingdom is at hand?

GO FORTH AND PREACH THIS GOSPEL CHILDREN.

POETRY AND THE IMAGE MACRO

BY

MICHAEL
HESSEL-MIEL

This essay is indebted to my conversations with Jamey Strathman, with whom I have done some longer, collaborative writing on the art of the image macro. It is dedicated to him.

If "image macro" is an unfamiliar term, don't worry. You've seen one before. People call them "memes" sometimes—but the proper term is *image macro*, a pairing of image and caption. Image macro is the name of the format that serves to transmit the bulk of meme culture, which, in the last few years, has come into its own as a subgenre of poetry. I'm not certain everybody identified with alt lit feels strongly about macros but for me they are one of my favorites. Everybody I know has made at least one, whether as a standalone work, a piece of self-promotion, a playful experiment, or just as a post on a friend's Facebook wall. There's something about them that feels easy to do, opening up a space of low-stakes play that also expands our horizons of what poetry can be. The question is often how we can consider image macros to be poetry. Just like other kinds of word-image pairings throughout history (emblematic poems, graphic design/advertising, concrete poetry), it seems to be neither literature nor visual art. What makes macros amazing is the same as what makes poetry so powerful.

I've spent maybe three years thinking about, and making image macros (maybe five or six hundred total), for the last two in particular considering image macros to be my primary genre of poetry. To some degree it's an obsession. I like thinking about different ways of putting images together, putting words over them. Sometimes, it's just that I want to include a picture of something that I think is funny or meaningful. Other times, I have a line that I want to give voice to, and I find the right combination of images to capture it. I want to cut images out with in Microsoft Paint, index finger on the trackpad, or carefully adjust the spacing and line breaks of the words to play against my image's negative space. That physical component makes me feel connected.

One of the first people that I saw using the image macro as poetry was Steve Roggenbuck. His early flarf work juxtaposed images and put non-sequitur bits of found language into poetry. The
works were absurd and something poetic seemed to come out of
that. I want to compare it to haiku, in that there is brevity, a
sudden contrast of a very small amount of elements alongside a
sense of humor. Not all macros are funny (my series, *mspaint and
heartbreak* was meant to show the kind of emotion they're capable
of) but a lot of the power lies there.

I was not alone in picking up techniques from Steve. But now I've
gone from that first collage I made at a coffee shop, cutting out a
picture of Riker to paste on a pyramid, looking over my shoulder
and feeling a nervous, guilty pleasure, to basically letting macros
be my primary art form. And others have as well—along with
the works that people submit to *Internet Poetry* and informally
circulate on Facebook (especially the "People Who Aumm…"
group) a lot of artists are taking up macros, each with a personally
developed voice. Steve Roggenbuck, myself, Dave Shaw, Penny
Goring, James Ganas, Jamey Strathman—none of us has the same
approach to the image macro. Different possibilities keep opening
up providing the image macro countless directions it can go in.
The works posted on *Internet Poetry* in 2012 are radically different
than those from 2013, and likewise, year by year. It will evolve.

The image macro plays a strange role in alt lit, because it draws
upon features of a broader internet meme culture that, frankly, I
think some might feel to be irrelevant to literature. But those were
the first macros I saw, becoming acquainted with them through
gamer friends, back when things like lolcats were still edgy and
largely unexplored territory. Much of it was coming from 4chan's
notorious "/b" messageboard. I wasn't "in on it" enough to get
the references but I loved the way familiar images took on new
meanings, the new sorts of expressions that were coming from the
words. Looking back, we can see that the pairing of word and im-

age produces a novel effect, one we can see in parallel with rhyme, or metaphor—a base unit for a broad range of poetry in practice.

Communicating with word-image pairings isn't strange; it's a vast portion of how we interact. 4chan's memes almost always paired word and image in some way down to the board's structure in the first place—a sequence of image posts with an added comment or caption. With a simple constraint, you see conventions for memes emerging, approaches to language and the use of images, the kinds of statements that can be made. It's poetry because it's based in communication. Snapchat, in the pairing of image and word, is effectively a communications medium based around the image macro; its power as a medium of communication comes with the simplicity of that same pairing, drawing on the same impulse that makes image macros work.

I am hesitant to define poetry, but I want to at least say that poetry is tied up in the ways that we communicate. It's simultaneously made of the stuff of our everyday forms of communication, while also being a special, experimental, or heightened form of it. But that's what's amazing about it. When we see forms of digital communication becoming common, we see poetic forms that reflect our connectivity The image macro is one piece of a wide range of possible poetic futures; it seems to have a long, bright future ahead of it.

I'm going to roll with it :)

AFTERWORD

BY

CHRISTOPHER HIGGS

"Those who are creating the modern composition authentically are naturally only of importance when they are dead because by that time the modern composition having become past is classified and the description of it is classical."

— Gertrude Stein,
"Composition as Explanation"

At the behest of British poet and critic Dame Edith Sitwell, Gertrude Stein wrote her now famous essay, "Composition as Explanation," in the winter of 1925–26 and delivered it as a lecture to the Cambridge Literary Club and at Oxford University that summer. Later that year, Leonard and Virginia Woolf's Hogarth Press saw fit to publish it. Nearly one hundred years later, it stands as one of the greatest and most enduring works of critical creative writing in the English language, and perhaps more importantly for our present purposes I believe it offers an extraordinary insight into how we might frame our understanding of Alt Lit.

Stein's essay opens with a two-sentence paragraph, which speaks directly to her central concern. I would argue it likewise speaks to the central concern of Alt Lit:

> *There is singularly nothing that makes a difference a difference in beginning and in the middle and in ending except that each generation has something different at which they are all looking. By this I mean so simply that anybody knows it that composition is the difference which makes each and all of them then different from other generations and this is what makes everything different otherwise they are all alike and everybody knows it because everybody says it.*

In other words, while content remains forever the same (love, death, redemption, betrayal, etc.) the narrative element which changes from generation to generation is form: not *what* is being said but *how* it is being said. Each generation has something different at which they are all looking, and for the current generation that thing is the internet.

Critics, therefore, who ignore the form of Alt Lit in favor of the content miss the defining characteristic. Seth Abramson, for example, writing recently for *The Huffington Post*, claimed that the term "Alt Lit" has "gradually devolved into meaninglessness ... [however, in practice] the "alt-lit" designation merely signifies that something is really good, yet underappreciated; or delightfully quirky, but with few financial resources behind it; or obscure, but with no desire to become any less so; or edgy, but not unlovable; or some combination of these qualities." To my way of thinking, Abramson's misguided attempt at a definition does little to help readers distinguish Alt Lit from more common categories such as cult or underground. However well-meaning, Abramson seems to completely miss the central defining characteristic of Alt Lit.

Kenneth Goldsmith, on the other hand, writing recently for *The New York Times* blog, gets much closer to identifying the crux of what makes Alt Lit a discrete literary categorization by focusing on the primacy of the internet. Likewise, in a 2012 interview with Josh Spilker at *Vol. 1 Brooklyn*, Frank Hinton described Alt Lit as "a population of people that are connected with one another through their interest in the online publishing world." Following Goldsmith and Hinton, I would venture to define Alt Lit as exemplified in the works presented in this anthology as an emergent form of contemporary literature produced primarily by writers under the age of forty, centered on and drawing from the internet, online culture, and social media. What they are writing about is no different from what all writers have always written about: loneliness, exuberance, alienation, jubilation, connection, anger, humor, sorrow, love, and so on. The difference they illustrate comes from their engagement with current technologies.

A dangerous game, to be sure, given the contentiousness between those who see the internet as a negative force and those who see its positive potential. As battles continue to rage in academia over the legitimacy of online publishing, Stein's words ring truer than ever, "If every one were not so indolent they would realise that beauty is beauty even when it is irritating and stimulating not only when it is accepted and classic." If only the old guard would realize the beauty of the internet as passionately as these young avant-garde writers have done, we wouldn't have to wait a hundred years for an institutional seal of approval. Sadly, many in the old guard staunchly hold their nose in the air, clutching their traditional paper-based publication model, while the new guard actively seeks to explore alternative digital-based publication models. Many in the old guard cling to their traditional system because it reinforces their gatekeeping status, whereas the new guard encourages the excessive proliferation of publication that undermines the role of the gatekeeper. That said, the present anthology you are reading at this moment is a paper-based object, and by virtue of selection it serves as a kind of gatekeeping artifact. While the writers collected in this anthology represent many of the pioneers in the field, many other contemporary Alt-Lit writers have been excluded from these pages, which could suggest a perceived division between minor and major figures. Since such hierarchical division seems antithetical to the ethos of Alt Lit, we find ourselves at a seemingly irresolvable impasse. On the one hand, Alt Lit democratizes the field of literature by utilizing the conditions created by the internet to allow more people more access to publication and consumption. On the other hand, demonstrating the current literary landscape requires a selection process. To encourage those suspicious members of the old guard to begin taking Alt Lit seriously, an anthology such as this one is necessary as a way to reach across the aisle and speak their language.

One hundred years from now everyone in this anthology will be dead. According to Stein that means Alt Lit will finally be considered "classic." Therefore, we can assume it will be taught in secondary and post-secondary schools as representative of the 21st Century Lost Generation. (Remember, it was Gertrude Stein who coined the phrase the first time around in reference to Hemingway and his contemporaries.) Students will be quizzed on the defining characteristics of Alt Lit, required to write essays on the work of Steve Roggenbuck, Gabby Bess, Tao Lin and others. Academic conferences will hold special panels examining Alt Lit in its historical context, mapping out the aesthetic affinities it shares with antecedents such as Walt Whitman, the Imagists, Dadaists, Surrealists, Flarifists, Confessionalists, New Narrativists, Beats, New York School poets, L=A=N=G=U=A=G=E poets, and conceptual artists such as John Baldessari, Jenny Holzer, and Ed Ruscha, as well as Fluxus works from artists such as Yoko Ono and John Cage. Scrutiny will be applied to the diversity of voices, the inclusivity of Alt Lit in terms of race, gender, and class. Someone will no doubt write a paper about the use of pseudonyms by many Alt Lit writers. A scholar will likely write a paper about the international nature of Alt Lit, citing Luna Miguel (Spain), Crispin Best (England), Jackson Nieuwland (Australia), and Guillaume Morissette (Canada) among others. Probably that paper will utilize theorists who elaborate on the deterritorializing aspect of the internet. Too bad none of us will be around to see this coming appreciation. It sounds like a very promising future.

ACKNOWLEDGMENTS

Special thanks goes out to all the editors that originally published the following pieces:

An excerpt from the novel, *Person* (Lazy Fascist). © 2010 by Sam Pink. Reprinted with permission of the publisher.

An excerpt from the novel, *Even Though I Don't Miss You* (Short Flight/Long Drive). © 2013 by Chelsea Martin. Reprinted with permission of the author.

"Little Rock" by Megan Boyle first published in *Pop Serial #2.* © 2012 by Megan Boyle. Reprinted with permission of the author.

"Hey You" by Beach Sloth first published in *I Want to YouTube Down the Rivers of America.* © 2013 by Beach Sloth. Reprinted with permission of the author.

"Holy Shit I Have Been So Lonely," "I Am a Reformed Movie Monster and I Love You So Much," and "When We're Old in a Cave and Lighting Fires" by Diana Salier first published in *Letters from Robots* (Night Bomb Press) and *Thunderclap Press* respectively. © 2012 by Diana Salier. Reprinted with permission of the author.

"Karpman Drama Triangle" by Guillaume Morissette first published in *I Am My Own Betrayal* (Maison Kasini). © 2012 by Guillaume Morissette. Reprinted with permission of the author.

"The Apartment" by Jordan Castro first published by *Unreality House.* © 2013 by Jordan Castro. Reprinted with permission of the author.

"Post-Swallow" by Gabby Bess first published by *Wonder.* "Post-Swallow," "Post-Body," and "Post-Labor" by Gabby Bess will be published in *Post-Pussy* (Coconut Books). © 2015 by Gabby Bess. Reprinted with permission of the author.

"A New Person" by Alexander J Allison first published in *PANK.* © 2012 by Alexander J Allison. Reprinted with permission of the author.

RECOMMENDED READING

Alone with Other People
by Gabby Bess
Civil Coping Mechanisms
ISBN: 978-1937865177

selected unpublished blog posts of a mexican panda express employee
by Megan Boyle
Muumuu House
ISBN: 978-0982206720

Grow Up
by Ben Brooks
Penguin
ISBN: 978-0143121091

Scorch Atlas
by Blake Butler
Featherproof Books
ISBN: 978-0977199280

what purpose did i serve in your life
by Marie Calloway
Tyrant Books
ISBN: 978-0985023584

Baby Babe
by Ana Carrete
Civil Coping Mechanisms
ISBN: 978-1937865108

Young Americans
by Jordan Castro
Civil Coping Mechanisms
ISBN: 978-1937865047

You Private Person
by Richard Chiem
Scrambler Books
ISBN: 978-0578098920

The Collected Works of Noah Cicero Vol. I
by Noah Cicero
Lazy Fascist Press
ISBN: 978-1621050919

Action, Figure
by Frank Hinton
Tiny Hardcore Press
ISBN: 978-0983562566

Fast Machine
by Elizabeth Ellen
Short Flight/Long Drive
ISBN: 978-0982530177

Black Cloud
by Juliet Escoria
Civil Coping Mechanisms
ISBN: 978-1937865245

Go To Work and Do Your Job. Care for Your Children. Pay Your Bills. Obey the Law. Buy Products.
by Noah Cicero
Lazy Fascist Press
ISBN: 978-1621051282

i will never be beautiful enough to make us beautiful together
by Mira Gonzalez
Sorry House
ISBN: 978-0988839403

During My Nervous Breakdown I Want to Have a Biographer Present
by Brandon Scott Gorrell
Muumuu House
ISBN: 978-0982206713

Bed
by Tao Lin
Melville House
ISBN: 978-1933633268

Taipei
by Tao Lin
Vintage Contemporaries
ISBN: 978-0307950178

I Am Ready to Die a Violent Death
by Heiko Julien
Civil Coping Mechanisms
ISBN: 978-1937865214

Horse Girl
by Kalliopi Mathios
Plain Wrap Press
ISBN: 978-0985597641

Sometimes My Heart Pushes My Ribs
by Ellen Kennedy
Muumuu House
ISBN: 978-0982206706

I Will Always Be Your Whore:
Love Songs for Billy Corgan
by Alexandra Naughton
Punk Hostage Press
ISBN: 978-1940213910

The Collected Works of
Scott McClanahan Vol. I
by Scott McClanahan
Lazy Fascist Press
ISBN: 978-1621050339

Shoplifting from American Apparel
by Tao Lin
Melville House
ISBN: 978-1933633787

Even Though I Don't Miss You
by Chelsea Martin
Short Flight/Long Drive
ISBN: 978-0989695008

Everything Was Fine Until Whatever
by Chelsea Martin
Future Tense Books
ISBN: 978-1892061355

Crapalachia: A Biography of Place
by Scott McClanahan
Two Dollar Radio
ISBN: 978-1937512033

Hill William
by Scott McClanahan
Tyrant Books
ISBN: 978-0985023553

Bluebird and Other Tattoos
by Luna Miguel
Scrambler Books
ISBN: 978-0578098906

New Tab
by Guillaume Morissette
Vehicule Press
ISBN: 978-1550653724

Rontel
by Sam Pink
Lazy Fascist Press
ISBN: 978-1621050797

Witch Piss
by Sam Pink
Lazy Fascist Press
ISBN: 978-1621051343

The Collected Suicide Notes
of Sam Pink
by Sam Pink
Lazy Fascist Press
ISBN: 978-1621051060

Letters from Robots
by Diana Salier
Night Bomb Press
ISBN: 978-0984084227

Orange Juice and Other Stories
by Timothy Willis Sanders
Publishing Genius
ISBN: 978-0983170693

You Can Make Anything Sad
by Spencer Madsen
Publishing Genius
ISBN: 978-0988750364

Animals
by Janey Smith
Plain Wrap Press
ISBN: 978-0615525952

Walls
by Andrew Duncan Worthington
Civil Coping Mechanisms
ISBN: 978-1937865283

Scarecrone
by Melissa Broder
Publishing Genius
ISBN: 978-0988750371

Normally Special
by xTx
Tiny Hardcore Press
ISBN: 978-0982469767

Matt Meets Vik
by Timothy Willis Sanders
Civil Coping Mechanisms
ISBN: 978-1937865290

The Drunk Sonnets
by Daniel Bailey
Magic Helicopter Press
ISBN: 978-0984140602

CRUNK JUICE
by Steve Roggenbuck
Boost House
Creative Commons License

Alt Lit Gossip
http://www.altlitgossip.com/

The Yolo Pages
http://www.boost-house.com/store/the-
yolo-pages

Cityscapes
http://altlitcityscapes.tumblr.com/

HTML Giant
http://htmlgiant.com/

Illuminati Girl Gang
http://illuminatigirlgang.com/

Lazy Fascist Review
http://lazyfascistpress.com/

Metazen
http://www.metazen.ca/

New Wave Vomit
http://newwavevomit.com/newwavevom-
it.com/n_w_v.html

Pop Serial
http://www.popserial.net/

Shabby Doll House
http://shabbydollhouse.com/

http://copingmechanisms.net/coping

.

CPSIA information can be obtained
at www.ICGtesting.com
Printed in the USA
FFOW03n1242170315
11799FF